# Divas Inc.

# DONNA HILL

ST. MARTIN'S GRIFFIN

*New York*

www.stmartins.com

Book design by Amanda Dewey

Library of Congress Cataloging-in-Publication Data

Hill, Donna (Donna O.)
    Divas, Inc. / Donna Hill.—1st ed.
        p. cm.
    ISBN 0-312-31651-8
    EAN 978-0312-31651-8
    1. African American women—Fiction. 2. Female friendship—Fiction. 3. Apartment houses—Fiction. 4. New York (N.Y.)—Fiction. 5. Single women—Fiction. 6. House sitting—Fiction. I. Title: Divas, Incorporated. II. Title.

PS3558.I3864D588 2004
813'.54—dc22

                                                    2004045055

4  6  8  10  9  7  5

Divas, Inc. *is lovingly dedicated to all the true divas out there.*
*You know who you are.*
*All you have to do is look in the mirror!*

"You know when a diva walks into a room...
and you know when she leaves."
—DIVAS, INCORPORATED SOCIETY

# Acknowledgments

Many thanks go out to all the incredible, unstoppable, unflap-pable, Sisterfriends who have shared my life. Those who have in-fluenced me and compelled me to reach for higher ground: Gwynne Forster, for all her class and wit; Leslie Esdaile Banks, who is always willing to send out a big Philly hug; Pittershawn Palmer, whose amazing grace and energy astound me; Monique Greenwood—what can I say, I want to be like you when I grow up; Lolita Files, a fun-loving *soulsustuh* with the biggest heart; Jacque-line Thomas, who epitomizes the word "lady;" Christine Battle-Ellington, my left-coast sister in spirit; LaToya Mclean, who continues to bring sunshine into my days with a simple phone call; Francis Ray, who trusted me enough to go along for the ride; Monica Jackson, who has a lock on diva-ness by her willingness to give; and Tina McCray, for the inner strength she is only beginning to realize she possesses. There are so many more women who have graced my life in myriad ways—please know that you are in my heart and spirit.

And most of all, to the true divas in my life: God for making woman; my mom, Dorothy, and my sister, Lisa, for their love and support, and their uncompromising style and attitude. And of course, to my darling divas in training—my daughters, Nichole and Dawne, ya'll gonna put a hurting on the world!


Visit all the divas at http://divasincsociety.org


Peace

# Delicious Diva Tips

1. Always wear sexy underwear even if you are just cleaning the house—you never know who may drop by.
2. A true diva's purse always has a comb, her favorite perfume, lipstick, mirror, and mad money!
3. Your hair is your crowning glory. If you can't get to the salon, invest in hats, scarves, and hair accessories.
4. A great place to stay in shape and meet men is in the gym . . . or the Laundromat (you can always tell if they live alone).
5. Read every day. There is always something in the news that can be used to strike up a conversation.
6. Bone up on sports and key players even if you hate them. They're great icebreakers.
7. If you really want to get ahead at your job, do the work, come

early, stay late, but never take on more than you can really handle.

8. Never be afraid to ask for suggestions, even if you know all the answers.

9. Find the designer outlets in your area and keep track of when they have their sales.

10. Walk with attitude. If people think you know where you are going, they will be sure to follow your lead.

11. Sprinkle a little of your favorite perfume, cologne, or oil on his sheets. He's bound to think of you in his dreams even when you are gone.

12. First impressions are lasting, so give them your best smile, but check your teeth first!

13. When in doubt just do it anyway. What's life without adventure?

14. Find that one person who can help you get to where you want to go and is not threatened by your ambition—because they've already made it.

15. Most of all, have fun and take charge of your life. Surround yourself with people of like minds and determination. There's nothing worse than getting to the top and having no one to share it with.

# Too Complicated
# for Words

*L*et me just say this: I've gotten myself into one helluva jam, and if Tiffany and Chantel find out what I've done—well, I don't even want to think about it. At the moment, I'm in between boyfriends—literally—Tiffany's and Chantel's, to be more specific. I never actually meant for it to happen. It just did.

You see, this all started when they went out of town and sort of left me in charge. It was the opportunity of a lifetime, the moment I'd been waiting for since we were all lined up in our bassinets waiting to be christened: Tiffany in her white satin-and-pearl dress with matching bloomers, Chantel in eggshell silk and silk tights, and me . . . plain white cotton, a bargain disposable diaper that was chafing around my thighs, and white ribbed socks—you know, the kind that come six in a pack. Do I sound bitter, bitchy?

Wait, I'm sorry. Let me begin at the beginning and at least introduce myself before you starting thinking the worst.

My name is Margaret Drew. Yeah, I know, real plain and ordinary. That's how most people think of me. To be truthful, it fits. At least it did, then it didn't, then it did again. Basically, that's how I got into this mess in the first place. But I'm getting ahead of myself again.

As I was saying, my name is Margaret, but for the purposes of this drama, you can call me Maggie. And believe me, this is drama, à la daytime-soap action. I'm a thirty-something, solid-size ten . . . well, twelve on a good day. And that depends on *before* or *after* PMS, eight hours of dedicated, no-kind-of-sex-at-all sleep, and a manageable hairdo. I buy all my *good* clothes on sale. I *am* the find-a-damned-good-sale Princess of Harlem. I can squeeze my feet into a size nine for three solid hours before breaking into a cold sweat, which is just about long enough to have a decent meal, catch a cab, and get home before my dogs swell. In an average month, I have about fifty dollars in my checking account, and my savings account hovers around the ten-dollar mark with careful financial planning. I've lived in the same one-bedroom apartment on 127th Street and St. Nicholas Avenue since my second year in college—you do the math—and I refuse to fall into the stereotype of "single woman found living with her cat(s)." Besides, cats make me sneeze. I opted for goldfish instead.

Wait! Ssssh. I think I just heard a car pull up. Ouch! Darn couch. I've been living here long enough to know my way around in the dark. Oh, did I forget to mention that I'm sitting here in the dark? Why? you ask. Well, I'm hiding, if you must know, until I figure out what to do about Calvin and James—those are Tiffany's and Chantel's boyfriends. Both of whom I've been alternately dating for the past six weeks—hence, my dilemma, among a host of other catastrophes.

You see this all started that night in the restaurant—well, actually, back in grade school. . . .

It was the first day of school. The weather was perfect for September: not too hot, not too cold. I was six—actually, I was five. My mother doctored my birth certificate so that I wouldn't have to wait another year to get into school, and she drilled it into my head so I wouldn't forget how old I was supposed to be. I guess I learned even back then to pretend to be something that I wasn't.

Anyway, I was all excited about going to first grade, especially because I would be going to school with Tiffany and Chantel. Even in kindergarten, they were the most popular girls in class— in some circles. All the girls, except me, hated them. To be truthful, Tiffany and Chantel were the kind of little girls that you loved to hate, but pretended you didn't. Everything about them was perfect; they knew it and had no qualms about flaunting it. They even had this way of moving their hips like metronomes in their frilly dresses that had the other little girls rolling their eyes. "Who do those hussies think they are?" the girls would whisper behind their backs. Well—maybe they didn't use the word *hussy,* but you get the picture. But the teachers thought they were "so adorable" with their designer toddler outfits and Shirley Temple curls, and they had all the little boys waiting on them hand and foot.

"Oh, Stevie," Tiffany would say in her tiny, sweet voice, "won't you share your crayons with me? Mine are all old and broken." She'd smile, flashing dimples and perfect little teeth, and Stevie would all but pour his whole box of Crayolas in her lap.

"Billie," Chantel would coo—everyone had an *ie* at the end of his name—"is one plus one really two?"

Billie would scoot over on the red rug, grab her hand, and hold up her pudgy fingers then count all the way to five, much to Chantel's delight—and his. It never dawned on poor Billie that Chantel, even at the tender age of five, could count to a hundred, subtract two boys from three, and still wind up with four.

"Hey, Willie," I remember saying one day at the lunch table, testing out my own feminine wiles. "Would you like to share some of my sandwich?" I grinned and suddenly wondered if it mattered that my two front teeth were missing. He screwed up his face and tossed his Twinkie at me. That was the last time I had anything to say to Willie with the *ie*.

But things were going to be different, I decided as I peeked out my window that September morning on the dawn of first grade. I was going to be different. I was going to work as hard as I could to be just like Tiffany and Chantel. The teachers and all the boys were going to just love me.

Ha!

Is it possible for a five-year-old, pretending to be six, to have acne? Well, I did. Each week without fail, I broke out—on my forehead, my nose, my chin—you name it. My mother made my embarrassing condition worse by always lathering my face in Vaseline.

"I don't want my child going out in the street ashy," she said each and every morning as she smeared the goo on my face, and if there was any left over, she would put a dab on the toe of each patent leather shoe and shine them with a tissue. I pledged each morning as I marched off to school that when I grew up, I would never allow a jar of Vaseline within one hundred yards of my home!

But for some reason that escapes all logic, Tiffany and Chantel let me hang around with them—at the lunch table, on the playground, at the movies, slumber parties, you name it. It wasn't until years later that I really understood why.

# Growing Up Third

*I* suppose it would help a little if I told you a bit about how and where I grew up. It wasn't a bad place. At that time, the brownstones that have now become the rage could be bought for a song. The neighborhood I grew up in (or "the hood" as it's called in some circles) was tagged Bedford-Stuyvesant in the heart of Brooklyn, New York. Most of the families that lived in the hood owned their own homes. So I guess you could call it a middle-class hood. Tiffany lived two houses down, and Chantel lived across the street. Tiffany and Chantel were like sisters. They walked alike, they talked alike—they were so close, they began to look alike. I, on the other hand, was more or less like a tagalong stepsister and didn't look anything like them, a fact that was duly noted by everyone who saw us together.

Most Friday nights, our moms would get together at Tiffany's house to play cards, and me and the girls would hang out in Tiffany's room and talk about who we were going to be when we grew up.

Tiffany's room was something right out of a commercial for upset stomachs. Brilliant white curtains hung in the windows, framing her four-poster canopy bed. The entire room was painted a Pepto-Bismol pink, with flower accents: pillows, quilts, shams, and dust ruffles. Tiffany was the first person our age that had her own television and record player in her room. So if you could get your stomach to stop twirling from the profusion of flowers and make it believe that it didn't have to swallow "the pink stuff," it was actually a pretty cool place to hang out.

"I know one thing," twelve-year-old Tiffany announced as she posed in front of the full-length mirror. "I'm going to be rich and fabulous when I grow up." She smiled at her reflection and turned her profile from left to right. "Don't you think so, Chantie?"

Chantel giggled, as she was prone to do at anything and everything Tiffany said. "Me, too," she said, bobbing her head, swinging her shoulder-length pigtails merrily.

"What about you, Maggie?" Tiffany asked, not taking her eyes off her reflection.

"I'm going to be a writer," I said.

They turned to me simultaneously, their perfect adolescent faces twisting in confusion.

"A writer?" they harmonized.

Tiffany scowled. "What kind of career is that?"

"What kind of career is that?" Chantel echoed.

"I . . . would write stories like Zora Neale Hurston."

There was a moment of silence, and then they both broke out into gut-busting laughter.

"You are too funny, Maggie," Tiffany said, returning to admire her image in the mirror.

"You sure are," said Chantel.

"Writers are poor . . . and live in *apartments,*" Tiffany said with disdain. "And they wear secondhand clothes." That notion seemed to disturb her the most. She gave a little shiver.

My smile was weak and forced. "Just kidding. Geez, can't you guys take a joke?" They almost looked relieved, and from that moment on, I promised myself that I would keep my mouth shut and just watch.

Tiffany finally tore herself away from the mirror and sashayed over to her dresser, where she went through an incredible assortment of nail polish. It was the dreaded manicure time. I quickly took a look at my chewed-off nails and summarily hid them under my thighs.

"I'll do yours, Chantie, if you do mine," Tiffany offered magnanimously.

"Pink!"

I felt my stomach roll.

Tiffany plucked the bottle of pink polish off the dresser and took a seat on the pink carpeted floor. (Oh, yeah, the carpet was pink, too.) She held her right hand out to Chantel.

"And don't smear it," Tiffany instructed.

While they were engaged in a heavy discussion of nail polish etiquette, I stretched out on the floor with my ragged nails tucked beneath my chin and gazed out the window.

One day my life would be different, I thought. I would be a rich and famous author, traveling the world while my fans tossed roses at my feet and shouted my name from their windows as I passed.

Wherever I went, my entourage would be close at hand, ready to do my bidding.

"Is there anything I can get for you, Madam Drew?" my manservant would inquire in his most groveling voice.

"No, thank you, Willie." (Yes, Twinkie Willie.) "But do bring the car around. I should be ready for my shopping spree in about two hours."

"Yes, madam," he would humbly murmur, bowing his way out the door.

"Oh, Willie, please tell Tiffie and Chantie that I will see them now."

"Yes, Madam Drew."

Moments later, there is a light tapping on the oak wood door of my massive study.

"Come in." My voice rings out like music.

"You rang for us?" they chorus as they tiptoe into my sanctuary, keeping their eyes lowered.

"Yes, girls. I want you to take some dictation, Tiffie, while Chantie does my nails."

They quickly take their places. Tiffany at the desk with her notebook at the ready and Chantel at my side with polish in hand. While she meticulously paints and repaints my three-inch-long nails, I dictate my latest masterpiece: "Once upon a time there was a beautiful little girl who had two wicked, ugly stepsisters."


Maggie! Maggie! Wake up."

My eyes flew open, and I looked around. Where was I? This wasn't my beautiful mansion with humble servants. It was the stomach-commercial room with the wicked stepsisters. I rubbed my eyes and sat up. "Guess I dozed off."

"Well, at least sit up. You're getting Vaseline all over my rug," Tiffany complained.

I rubbed my chin, which now, on top of my latest pimple outbreak, had a thin coating of pink fibers attached to it.

"Sorry."

"Did you do your take-home math test?" Tiffany asked. I knew that tone. "I finished it during study hall." I yawned and pulled myself up, careful to keep my nails out of view, lest they descend upon me with nail polish and emery boards.

"Can you help me with mine?"

"Me, too."

"You're so good at math."

"And English."

I knew, even at twelve years old (really eleven), that all the praise was pure bull, but I loved it nonetheless because it was true. I may not have been the cutest, but I was one of the smartest kids in class. I picked the pink lint from my chin and silently cursed my mother and her Vaseline.

"Want me to do yours for you?"

"Would you?" Tiffany asked, already knowing that I would, since she was handing me her rexo.

Chantel pretended to plead. "Mine, too?"

"Sure."

Faster than you could say, "Beam me up, Scottie," I was immersed in math homework while Chantel and Tiffany busied themselves with their nails. Their homework assignments and I were summarily forgotten. I suppose it was a good thing, since I didn't have any nails to busy myself with. But it would have been nice if they at least looked my way every now and then.

I guess you must be wondering why I bothered to hang around with those two. I asked myself the same question and still do. The only answer that I can come up with is that even at an early age, I had masochistic tendencies. Or in simple terms, as my grandmother would say, "If you look for trouble, you'll get kicked in the ass." Grandma always improvised on old sayings. However, hanging out with Tiffany and Chantel did have its advantages. There weren't a lot, but there were a few. You see, for some strange reason, as long as I was around, Mrs. Lane and Mrs. Hollis would let

Tiffany and Chantel go wherever they wanted. Even then, I was the mascot/chaperon, a distinctive honor I've carried with me to this day.

"Can we go roller-skating?" Tiffany would ask her mother.

"Sure, if Margaret is going."

"There's a new movie playing downtown," Chantel would say to her mom. "Can we go?"

"Sure, if Margaret is going."

And with the laundry list of activities that Tiffany and Chantel were regularly involved in over the years, I always had plenty to do. In addition to the fact that none of the girls in the entire borough of Brooklyn could stand them, I was their only other friend—of sorts. They were hated with the vengeance that females could feel for one another, but they were always invited to every party and event—because if Tiffany and Chantel were in the vicinity, the boys were sure to follow.

Although their powers were pretty strong even as toddlers, they were magnified a hundred-fold by the time we reached our teens.

I remember one time in particular that almost made me bow down at their feet. We (or rather they) had been invited to Melody Grimes's sweet-sixteen party. We were all getting ready at Tiffany's house because she had the most mirrors. Go figure.

I sat on the edge of Tiffany's bed, fighting to hold my dinner down as they spun and twirled in front of the mirror, and I tried to keep from getting buried beneath the discarded outfits they tossed in my direction for nearly an hour.

"Red is definitely your color," Tiffany said, tossing her shoulder-length hair over her shoulder as Chantel posed in a fire-engine-red miniskirt and bloodred halter top.

"You think so?" Chantel arched a thin brow beneath her perfectly cut bangs.

Her sandy-brown skin and long, dancer's legs were fully exposed, leaving little to the imagination. She posed in several angles in the mirror, reminding me of a photo shoot without the photographer.

"Would I lie to you?" Tiffany crossed the room and adjusted the spaghetti strap on Chantel's shoulder. "You should put your hair up—it accentuates your neck."

*Accentuates?* I chewed off a ragged nail.

"What do you think, Maggie?" Tiffany asked, spinning Chantel to face me.

My first thought was that she looked like a spoiled tomato, but I knew that wouldn't go off well. If there was one thing I learned about being around those two, it was agree, agree, agree.

"I think it looks . . . really red." They both frowned. Their expressions were so identical, it was almost comical. But I didn't laugh. That was a no-no, too. "But red is great . . . especially on you."

They smiled in unison.

Tiffany put her hand on her hip and cocked her head to the right. "Is that what you're wearing?" she asked me.

*Gulp.* "Yeah. Why?" I stood up and looked in the full-length mirror. My white blouse had seen better days, but it was clean and starched with the precision that only Grandma could achieve. I'd decided on black slacks to hide the bandage on my knee—a little accident while walking.

The Doublemint twins turned to each other and shrugged. I wasn't certain what that meant, but I got the distinct impression that my attire was being dissed and dismissed. And it's not as if they couldn't have offered me an outfit, if what I had on was so distasteful. Between the two of them, they had enough designer clothes to outfit the *Essence* fashion show for two seasons. But I was used to making do. Unlike Tiffany and Chantel, who had two parents and fathers who made good money, my mom was a single mother, taking care of me and Grandma on a post-office salary and trying not to "go postal" while keeping a roof over our heads and food in our bellies. The fact that we even lived on the same block was only because my dad's insurance money paid off the mortgage for the house when he passed away.

I looked at myself in the mirror again. No, maybe my outfit didn't measure up to theirs, but I still looked "nice."

"Just because you're doing bad doesn't mean you have to let everyone know," my grandmother would remind me—constantly. "You can make people believe anything you want them to believe if you dress the part." As I mentioned earlier, Grandma was full of questionable sayings. So, with those words of suspect wisdom tucked neatly away in my psyche, I went out every day in my designer knockoffs and faced the world. But deep in my heart, I knew that one day I, too, would be the real thing.

The doorbell chimed (it didn't ring) downstairs, and Tiffany gave herself one last look in the mirror. She was quite stunning. After several hours of wardrobe changes, she'd finally decided on a jersey wrap dress in a hot pink (of course) with a daring dip down the middle. Tiffany had the kind of complexion that females would pay a pretty penny for: smooth as butter with a perfect caramel tone. Even as a teen, she had one of those knockout bodies that are only "as seen on TV."

"That's Rickie," she said, and proceeded to take a seat on the bed.

"Isn't that our ride?" I asked. "Shouldn't we go down?"

Tiffany raised her chin and examined her nails. "Rule number one: Make them wait. They will appreciate you more when you finally show up."

"Oh," I murmured, and wondered where she got her information.

"You're so funny, Maggie," Chantel took a seat next to Tiffany.

I grinned, not sure what I'd done that was so amusing.

"Tiffany!" her mother called from the bottom of the stairs.

"Yes, Mother."

"Rickie is here, honey."

"I'll be down." She continued to examine her nails. "Do you think this is the right color for this outfit?" she asked no one in particular.

"Perfect," Chantel said.

I nodded in agreement and plopped down in the overstuffed chair by the window.

After a twenty-minute discussion of clothes, hairstyles, and every male on the high school basketball team, Tiffany was ready to go.

We piled into Rickie's dad's blue Oldsmobile and headed out to pick up Chantel's date, Paulie. I was squeezed in the backseat with Chantel and Paul. By the time we arrived at Melody's party, it was in full swing. We were a fashionable hour late. And the instant we walked in, Tiffany and Chantel became the center of attention. The hours spent in front of the mirror paid off. No one in the room could compare to either of them. The other girls tripped over themselves, trying to ask them about their hair, their outfits. And the boys simply drooled, waiting their turn to get a little time with them. And for some bizarre reason, Paul and Rick didn't seem to mind. Quite the opposite—they seemed to take some sort of pride in the fact that their dates were so hot, and they stood around, preening like proud peacocks.

As I was wandering around the party, pretty much unnoticed, I heard the term for the very first time.

"Those two need to go into business," a girl named Sandra said to her friend, referring to Tiffany and Chantel.

"As what?"

"Divas," she sneered.

Her friend laughed. "Yeah. They could call themselves Divas, Incorporated."

Somehow the moniker traveled like a speeding train and stuck like glue. From that night until right now, Tiffany and Chantel were known as Divas, Incorporated.

But instead of being offended, they proudly draped the title around themselves and flaunted it. Their motto became, "Don't you wanna be me?" A motto that ultimately brought me to my present fiasco.

# Let's Just Flash
# Forward, Okay

For the sake of brevity, I'm not going to bend your ear about my entire adolescence and teen years. Suffice it to say, it was nothing spectacular. I didn't date much, and for the most part, I was either the third or fifth wheel. I didn't mind really. It gave me the opportunity to see a bunch of free movies, hitch rides and get a meal or two out of Chantel and Tiffany to keep my mouth shut. Both their parents seemed to be under the misconception that if I tagged along, their precious daughters would be in good hands. If their mothers only knew!

We all made it out of high school at the top of our class, virginity in tact (at least mine was), and no brushes with the law or drugs. I was valedictorian, and Tiffany and Chantel shared the salutatorian spotlight. The truth was, they were both smarter than I, but they'd decided years earlier that being too smart could be a handicap with men. They used their intelligence to their advantage at advantageous times.

In any event, we all wound up at Columbia University. I was on scholarship. Tiffany and Chantel were on American Express, Platinum MasterCard, and stock dividends care of Daddy. They wouldn't dream of going to school on a scholarship. In their minds, a scholarship was the equivalent of being poor, no matter how smart you had to be to get one. Well, Chantel sailed through corporate marketing, Tiffany studied telecommunications, and I . . . English.

Right out of school, Tiffany landed a job with NBC as a producer. Chantel got a gig as a marketing director for Donna Karan, and I . . . senior editor at University Press. My job wasn't bad. Actually, I enjoyed it. I was responsible for reading and green-lighting all incoming manuscripts by these high brow types whose books wound up as curriculum in the colleges. I still had my secret desire to be a great writer one day, but even now kept it to myself.

With our new careers, and living in different neighborhoods, we didn't see each other as much as we once did, but we made it a point to get together once per month on Friday night at the Soul Café on Forty-second Street in Manhattan.

It was on a Friday night that my life changed for good. We met at seven, our usual time and place, and as usual, the conversation was about their great jobs, their incredible love lives, and how they were going to continue to scale the corporate ladder.

"There's a promotion coming up for senior producer," Tiffany said as she took a sip of her white wine.

"Are you going to go for it?" I asked.

"It means more money and more clout. So what do you think?" She arched a brow and adjusted her Versace jacket around her waist.

Chantel laughed. "You should know Tiffie by now, Maggie. She will never let an opportunity get past her even if she doesn't really want it."

"That's part of the fun," Tiffany said with her own tinkling laugh. "But to be truthful, I'm exhausted. I've worked nonstop for two years without a vacation."

"You were only trying to solidify your place at the network and let them know you were serious about the job," Chantel offered, patting Tiffany's hand.

"I know. But all work and no play makes Tiffany a dull girl. I've really been thinking about getting away. I have more vacation time than I know what to do with."

"So do I," Chantel complained. "At least six weeks." She took a mouthful of her salad and checked her reflection in the mirror mounted on the wall opposite us.

"Calvin has been bugging me to go away with him for forever, and I keep coming up with excuses," Tiffany said.

"So why don't you go?" I asked.

She frowned. "Haven't you learned anything, Maggie? You don't take vacations with your boyfriend. That takes all the fun out of it."

That was a new one on me. I thought the whole point of going away with your boyfriend *was* to have fun. Go figure.

"Maggie, you are still so funny," Chantel said over a mouth of mixed greens.

I half smiled.

"I've been dying to go to Europe," Chantel said a bit wistfully. "I've been watching the prices for flights, and there are some really good deals out there. Not that money is an issue," she quickly qualified, looking at both of us.

Tiffany leaned eagerly across the table, her size 36Cs dipping precariously close to the bowl of ranch dressing. I watched, enthralled as they delicately skirted disaster.

She took Chantel's hands in hers. "Then why not?" she stated more than asked.

Chantel tipped her head to the side, a sly smile moving across her mouth. "What are you thinking?"

"Europe, what else? We can certainly afford it. The weather is supposed to be perfect now, and we have the time. We've been dying to go. Paris in spring. Need I say more?"

Chantel clapped her hands in delight, and her face lit up as if she'd been told she'd won an all-expense-paid visit to Elizabeth Arden. "Then let's do it! And none of that two-week stuff."

"No, if we do Europe, it definitely needs to be at least a month."

"Six weeks," I tossed in with enthusiasm, and they both turned and looked at me as if I'd just arrived.

"Six weeks it is," Tiffany said, grinning like she'd discovered the secret of youth everlasting.

Wow, six weeks in Europe, I thought. I'd never been any farther than Florida. How exciting. But what would I wear? And to be truthful, I certainly didn't have enough money for an extended vacation, but with good planning, I just might be able to pull it off. I could already see myself walking along the Seine, or tooling around Paris with a black tam cocked to the side while I ordered croissants from an outdoor café.

Will there be anything else, mademoiselle?" Willie (who is now a French waiter) asks.

"*Oui,* Willie," I murmur. "You!" At that point, I would tear my tam from my head, throw Willie down onto the linen-topped table, and have my way with him.

Of course, there would be a roving photographer passing by who would snap pictures and sell them to the *National Enquirer.* FAMOUS AMERICAN AUTHOR OVERCOME BY YEARS OF UNRE-

QUITED LUST, JUMPS BONES OF WAITER. I'd wind up on all the talk shows and become a household name. My book sales would shoot through the roof, and my publisher would offer me a million-dollar contract for my next book.

So how about it, Maggie?" Tiffany asked, interrupting the signing of the contract.

I blinked. "Sure. I think it's a great idea," I muttered, and had the icky sensation that there was trouble afoot.

"You're such a peach, Maggie," Chantel cooed. "What would we do without you?"

"We'll be sure to leave you with plenty of instructions about the apartments, mail, messages, and the days the housekeeper has off," Tiffany assured me.

"Huh?" I was totally confused. What did all of this have to do with going to Europe? What had I agreed to?

"I was just saying that while Chantel and I are in Europe, we'll be sure to leave you all the instructions for taking care of our apartments. We wouldn't leave you in the lurch like that," Tiffany said, smiling brightly.

My stomach started to turn, and heat spread through my body like wildfire. Taking care of their apartments . . . leaving me instructions . . . Panic ran through my veins. They were going without me! They hadn't even asked if I wanted to come along. They wanted me to house-sit while they gallivanted all over Europe for six weeks—*without me!* I could feel tears burning behind my eyes. But I refused to break down and cry. Not in front of them. Never! How could they do this to me after all these years? I looked from one to the other, at their fancy designer suits, perfect weaves, caps, and colored contacts, and it took all of my home training not to jump up and strangle them. They had everything, and what they didn't have, they took. They even had someone to take over their lives for them when they didn't feel like being bothered. Wait . . . what had I just thought? Someone to take over their lives. Of course! Break out the band, Margaret Drew's day has finally arrived.

A happy bubble formed in the pit of my stomach and almost slipped out of my mouth in a gush of laughter. This was better than any trip to Europe. This was the day I'd been living for, and I hadn't even known it until that moment. I was finally going to be what I'd always wanted to be—a diva!

# This Better
# Be Fun

*I*t would be at least two weeks before Tiffany and Chantel took off for Europe. In the meantime, I tried to stay focused on my job and the mundane tasks of my everyday life, which consisted of arriving at my desk at eight, having lunch with Larry Pickett from the mailroom at noon, and riding home in his ten-year-old Toyota to my mom and grandma by seven.

"Morning, Margaret," Larry greeted as he sorted through the mail and piled the daily delivery of manuscripts on my desk. "How was your weekend?"

"Not bad." I shrugged. "It was the same as usual. Stayed home and did some reading." (I was itching to tell Larry about my windfall, but as Grandma would say, "Don't count your change before you check the price," which was the equivalent to "Don't count your chickens, blah, blah, blah.") "What about you? Do anything interesting?"

"Actually, I went upstate with some friends to a cabin and hung out in the woods."

I smiled. "Sounds itchy. Me and the great outdoors don't get along very well—too much trees and grass."

Larry laughed. He had the greatest laugh. "A city girl to the bone. But you would've enjoyed it. The cabin has all the comforts of home."

"Hmmm, well, when I think woods, I think wolves and raccoons. I prefer more manageable animals sniffing around the door."

"Margaret, you are one funny woman." He shook his head in amusement. "Are we still on for lunch?"

"Sure, I'll meet you in the cafeteria at noon."

"Great. See you later." He started to walk away, stopped, and turned. "Hope you find a gem in that pile."

"Thanks." I waved good-bye, and he strolled down the corridor, pushing his mail cart. I don't know what prompted me, but I started staring at his buns and the way they moved beneath the khaki slacks. Oh, did I mention that I have a real thing for buns?

Anyway, on a scale of one to ten, I would have to rate his buns a nine and a half. Not too big, not too small, and tight enough to squeeze. Overall, Larry Pickett was a good-looking man. He was probably a little over six feet, around 190 pounds, no noticeable gut, clean-shaved with a birch-brown complexion, late thirties, and from what I could tell, very single. Everyone liked Larry, especially Beverly Woods, the secretary on the second floor. She obviously had the hots for Larry, but he didn't seem to pay her much more attention than he paid me.

I'm not sure how we fell into the habit of eating lunch together every day, but we'd been doing it for about two years, and I could feel Beverly longing to be in my shoes whenever she would see us together.

"Why don't you ever ask Beverly to lunch?" I asked Larry as he chewed his ham-and-cheese hero.

He shrugged. "Not really my type."

That was the last thing I expected him to say. "What do you mean she's not your type?" Mind you, Beverly was a looker—tall, shapely, dynamite smile, a great dresser—and she seemed to get along with everyone. I was truly stumped by his response.

He leaned forward and lowered his voice. "There's a certain kind of woman that you only fantasize about."

My eyebrows rose in expectation of his answer. "What kind of woman is that?"

"Women like Beverly. She's what you call high maintenance." He chuckled lightly. "Nothing like you at all."

I reared back in my seat. "What is that supposed to mean?"

"Just that you're uncomplicated, easygoing . . . good company."

He might as well have slapped me upside the head. "Thanks," I muttered into my bowl of chicken noodle soup. In other words, plain and ordinary. Humph. But not for long. "Tiffany and Chantel are going to Europe for six weeks," I said, and waited for his reaction.

"Good riddance," he grumbled, and tore off another chunk of his sandwich.

I flinched. I should have expected his response. There was no love between them from the moment they met. I would like to think of it as a simple case of mistaken identity. That's just my take. And I say that because for some strange reason Tiffany and Chantel thought that Larry was one of the owners of the company.

Hee hee. Go figure. All right, all right, I might have had a little something to do with that by the way I talked about him. But I never actually *said* he owned the company, just that without him University Press wouldn't be able to function. And it's true. Can I help it if they took that the wrong way?

I guess I got tired of them always talking about the "incredible" men they meet at their jobs. Television stars, corporate executives, actors—you name 'em, they met 'em. So, one Friday night during our monthly soiree, I "accidentally" threw Larry's name into the mix, and you would think I said I'd been trapped naked in an elevator with Denzel Washington, the way their eyes lit up.

"Oh, really?" Tiffany said in a hushed whisper. Her mouth curved into that smile that bordered on sinister. "What does he look like?"

"Tell, tell," Chantel urged.

That was my moment to shine, so I let them have it. By the time I finished regaling them with all Larry's charms and virtues, I could see the wheels turning in Tiffany's mind, and Chantel was practically salivating.

"You will have to introduce us," Tiffany said, pulling out her compact and powdering her nose. "It's always great to network— if you know what I mean."

"How is it that you have such close contact with one of the bigwigs, anyway? I thought you just read manuscripts," said Chantel.

Did she smell a rat? "Exactly, and my opinion . . . is necessary in the decision-making process. He, uh, relies on me."

They both stared at me for what felt like forever.

"You are dependable. I have to give you that," Tiffany finally admitted.

"Always have been," Chantel said.

I didn't even want to think if that was a compliment or not; besides, they'd never meet Larry Pickett anyway.

Wrong! No less than a week later, just as I was leaving for the day, who steps off the elevator but the dynamic duo, dressed to kill. I almost had a conniption right there at my desk.

Every head in the department, male and female, turned as my friends slunk down the corridor. I said *slunk* because that's exactly how they walk, like cats on a runway. I remember them practicing that walk for hours in Tiffany's backyard. Whenever I would try, I would trip over my feet. I finally gave up. They didn't. Now they had it down to an art form.

Tiffany stopped at my desk. "Hi, Margaret." She had on a midnight blue Donna Karan suit, 1950s style, complete with padded shoulders, cinched waist, and narrow skirt à la Joan Crawford. She rested her hip against my desk.

"Surprise," Chantel chimed, equally decked out in a black wrap dress with a wide patent leather belt that drew her waist to within inches of cutting off all air to her brain and pushed her dynamic breasts to "reach out and squeeze me" proportions.

"W-what are you two doing here?" My eyes darted nervously around the office. I prayed that Larry would have somehow forgotten that we ride home together every single, solitary day—and that he'd just go without me.

"Well, well, good afternoon, ladies."

A bolt of lightning would have gone a long way at that moment.

Being the man-hunters that they were, they instinctively turned toward the sound of a masculine voice, the same way a lion sniffs out dinner.

"Well, hello," they chorused.

I wondered if they heard my knees knocking. I sat down behind my desk just to be sure and prayed for morning.

"You must be Tiffany and Chantel," Larry said, sticking his hand out to one and then the other.

"So Margaret has told you all about us," Tiffany said, stepping closer to her prey.

"A little," he said with caution, taking a step backwards.

"And your name is?"

"Larry. Larry Pickett."

"Well, finally we meet the man himself," Chantel said, taking her position next to Tiffany in a flanking maneuver.

Larry looked from one to the other, totally confused, but sensing "Danger, Will Robinson." He scratched his head. "The man himself? What has Margaret been telling you ladies?"

Maybe if I faked a convulsion, I could put a quick halt to it all, I thought as misery and humiliation engulfed me.

Tiffany's tinkling laughter filled the air. "All about how important you are and that this whole operation would cease to function without you."

Larry laughed out loud. "I never knew pushing a mail cart was that important, but I suppose so."

The duo leaped back as if they'd seen a snake in the grass. "Mail cart!" they cried, turning the heads of everyone in earshot.

Larry's voice took on an edge and tone I'd never heard before. "You got a problem with that?" His shoulders hunched, and he looked them up and down as if something in the fridge had suddenly gone ripe. "I should have known the minute I set eyes on you two." He shook his head in disgust and walked away.

It took me months to repair the damage in my relationship with Larry. We would still eat lunch together and drive home together, but conversation was forced. He couldn't understand why a nice girl like me would be caught dead in the company of women like them. "Tiffany and Chantel give women across America a bad rap," he said after I'd apologized for the zillionth time.

As for Tiffany and Chantel, they never brought it up again but were always quick to remind me that my taste in men was all in my mouth. Humph.

So anyway, as I said, I can understand Larry's indifference about them leaving town.

"I'm going to be house-sitting for them while they're gone," I said, breaking the long run of silence between us. The mention of Tiffany and Chantel usually did that.

Larry looked up from his sandwich. "You've got to be kidding. Why in the world would you do something like that?"

"Because . . . they asked me, and I wanted to."

"Of course they asked you—or what is more likely, they told you in that way of theirs that sounds like a question but really isn't."

Now I was pissed. "Do you think that I'm so thick-headed I wouldn't know the difference between a question and a statement?"

"Those two aren't worth your time."

"They're my friends."

"If you say so. But with friends like them, who needs enemies? Hey, look—I don't want to fight with you. You're a grown woman and perfectly capable of making your own decisions."

I sniffed. "Thanks for the vote of confidence."

"They're not your type. I don't know why you hang around with them anyway."

"My type? What does that mean?"

He took a long swallow of his soda and put the can down hard on the table. "They are totally out of your league, Margaret. Listen, I gotta run." He stood and took up his tray. "Pick you up at five?" he stated more than asked.

I looked up at him and all of a sudden he wasn't Larry Pickett, the mailman. He was Twinkie Willie who'd just made me feel small and insignificant. I added his name to my list.

By the time I was done, no one would ever call me plain, ordinary Margaret "Maggie" Drew again. I felt like rubbing my palms together. Tiffany and Chantel couldn't leave fast enough.

# Countdown!

*Y*ou've been acting like a mouse in search of cheese all afternoon," Grandma complained. "Running around here like good sense done left you all by your lonesome." She reared back in her rocking chair as it screamed against her weight and stared me down. "What's wrong with ya?"

"Nothing," I lied smooth as a silk scarf and continued dusting the mantel for the third time with alternate peeks at the clock. I was due to meet up with Tiffany and Chantel to pick up their keys and get my marching orders. They were leaving! Yippee!

"Nothing! Don't you lie to me."

Well, maybe not quite as smooth as silk. "What do you mean, Grandma?" I asked innocently.

"What did I tell you about answering a question with a question? Only a fool does that, and I ain't raised no fools." She pursed her lips, and her eyes bulged the way people do when they've accidentally eaten a sour candy instead of a sweet one. It never dawned on Grandma that she'd just done what she told me not to. But that was Grandma.

"Nothing's wrong. Honest." I gave her my best good-granddaughter look.

"Humph." She rocked for a few minutes and then stopped. "Where's my pocketbook?"

"Right there by your feet, where you always keep it."

"Are you sassing me? Is that what you're doing?"

"No, ma'am."

"Humph, I didn't think so. I didn't raise no fools, and you'd be a fool to sass me, which would mean that we ain't related and you would have no business up in my house." She snapped her head for emphasis.

Do you see what I have to endure?

"Pass me my purse."

I put down my dust rag, walked over to her, and handed her the trusty pocketbook. What I'm going to tell you is probably more information than you need to know, but my grandmother, in a word, is nuts.

My grandmother, whom everyone—including my mother—calls Grandma (I don't even remember her real name), is at least one hundred and seventy-five years old if she's a day. I say that because if you give her half a New York minute, she will tell you, in detail, how she survived during the Civil War. Now if I remember correctly, the Civil War was a helluva long time ago. And don't get her started on the weather, either. She has survived every storm and natural disaster known to mankind—barefoot and hungry.

Anyway, although I had my own place in Harlem, I came back to the old homestead every day after work to have dinner with

Grandma and my mother, a ritual that I'd somehow gotten tricked into years earlier. It was my job to "watch" Grandma until my mother came in from her job at the post office. Saturday was generally my day off—which was today. However, my mother somehow hypnotized me into believing that she really needed to work on a Saturday, and would I please forgo my life and "watch" Grandma until she came home. So I did what I usually did on a weekday—prepare dinner and listen to Grandma's stories about her childhood, which shifted from one decade to the next depending on what she'd seen on television. She loved the History Channel.

Grandma dug in her purse for her wallet and pulled out a crisp one-hundred-dollar bill and handed it to me.

"I need one roll of toilet paper," she said, and snapped her wallet shut.

"A roll of toilet paper?"

"Yes, chile. Are you deaf?"

"No, ma'am."

"Then go on so you can get back before I need to use it."

"Yes, ma'am."

I took my jacket from the hook by the door and headed out. Mind you, my grandmother hasn't had a job in more than thirty years. She wasn't working when I met her, but she always had a brand-new one-hundred-dollar bill in her purse. And she would always send me to the corner store to buy one item with a price tag of less than a dollar.

Old Man Joe, who owned the corner store, which had been there in Grandma's words "since the year of the flood," would just shake his head when he saw me coming.

"What'll it be today, Margaret?"

"Toilet paper, Joe. Can you make change?"

Joe looked at me for a minute and kinda grinned. He shuffled five steps to the left and reached beneath the counter for the tin box, which he kept out of my view. Then he shuffled five steps to the right and retrieved the tiny silver key.

"Let me check," he said, just as he'd been saying every time I came in with a hundred-dollar bill. He stuck the key in the lock, and the cover snapped open. He glanced up at me over the top of his glasses to ensure that I couldn't see inside the box and started counting. "How much is one hundred dollars take away fifty-two cents?" he asked.

"Ninety-nine dollars and forty-eight cents."

He slapped his thigh and grinned like he'd just won lotto. "I got it!"

"Thanks." I put my hundred-dollar bill on the counter, and he meticulously counted out one hundred dollars—in singles.

It was probably a gene from my father's side of the family that kept me from going totally insane.

"Here ya go." He handed me the money, turned to the counter behind him, and took down a roll of Scott toilet tissue in—what else? Pepto-Bismol pink. "That will be fifty-two cents."

I handed him a dollar from the stack.

He hit a button on his rickety cash register, and the drawer creaked open, spewing particles of dust in the air. He grunted and pursed his lips. "Don't you have anything smaller?"

I felt my fingers stiffen and my arms begin to rise as my hands went for his scraggly throat. The morning headline would read, LOCAL GIRL GONE BAD, KILLS BELOVED NEIGHBORHOOD SHOP-KEEPER OVER TOILET PAPER DISPUTE.

I shook my head to clear the vision of Old Man Joe in a heap on the floor while flashbulbs popped frantically, capturing the moment.

"Uh, yes," I mumbled, and dug in my pocket. Thankfully, I always dumped change in my coat pockets and the bottom of my purse. I slid the exact change across the scarred wooden counter, while he wrapped my purchase in a brown paper bag— the only store in the English-speaking world that still had brown paper bags.

"Thanks, Joe." I stuffed the one hundred singles in my pocket.

"Say hello to Grandma for me, will ya?" He gave me a wink.

"I sure will," I said through my teeth.

As I walked back down the long block to the house, I was still mulling over the whole hundred-dollar-bill issue and wondering how Grandma managed to keep a hundred dollars when I could barely keep ten and I had a job. I walked past a card table that had recently been set up in front of Mrs. Washington's house, and three wannabe thugs were gathered around as a card dealer called out the three-card monte.

Now everyone with a grain of sense knew that the only way you won is if the dealer wanted you to win and that at least one of the men standing around (who'd been slated to win) was in cahoots with the dealer. I shook my head and thought to myself, *Suckers*. It was the old bait and switch.

Suddenly I stopped dead in my tracks. I watched over my shoulder as the dealer rapidly moved the cards on the table, blinding onlookers to which card was the ace of spades, then I glanced back down the block to Grandma's house. Grandma's face seemed to merge with that of the man in the wide-brimmed hat, dark shades, and fake diamond ring shuffling the cards. A beam of bright white light appeared before me, and through the blinding light a voice said, *Fool, all this time Grandma would give you the hundred-dollar bill, Joe would make change, but you would always pay for everything. So Grandma would get back exactly what she sent you with—one hundred dollars. Hm-mmm.* The light slowly dissolved, and the street appeared before me once again. What a scam! My grandma had milked me for a small fortune. I stormed off toward the house, ready to finally face down the enemy.

By the time I flew through the door, Grandma was fast asleep in her rocking chair. I could hear my mother cussing in the kitchen to no one in particular about the rotten day she'd had at the post office. I breezed by Grandma (lucky for her) and pushed through the swinging door into the kitchen.

"Hi, Mom."

She turned from stirring the pot of rice. "Hey, sweetie," she said, as calm as if she hadn't just called everyone who'd ever worked for the United States Postal Service every name but a child of God. "Grandma send you to the store again?"

"Umm-hmm." I couldn't keep the disgusted tone out of my voice.

She chuckled and recovered the pot. "Those two are something else. How was your day?"

"Same as usual." I put the brown paper bag on the table and pulled the change from my pocket.

"Just leave her hundred dollars on the sideboard. I'll take it down to Joe's on my way to church tomorrow."

Reality struck. "You knew what she'd been doing all this time?"

"Of course. She did the same thing to me for years until I figured it out. Took you a little longer than I thought, though. Don't get bent out of shape—it's just two old people having some fun."

I stood there for a few minutes with my mouth open. It was true—my mother and grandmother were both certifiable. What chance did I have?

"Staying for dinner?" she asked, as if she hadn't said anything of previous importance.

"No. I have to meet Tiffany and Chantel. They're leaving today. Remember?"

"Oh, right. And you're house-sitting."

"Yes, six weeks."

"You should have gone with them. Sounds like fun."

I wouldn't know, I thought, seeing that they never asked me. But I had plans of my own. "I'd better be going."

"See you Monday?"

"I'll try. If I have time."

"Grandma will be very disappointed."

That was my mother's way of saying that I'd never hear the end of it and neither would she.

I sighed. "Okay, okay. I'll work it out." I walked over to her and gave her a light peck on the cheek. "The chicken should be done," I mumbled, and hurried out—but stopped at the threshold. "Mom what is Grandma's real name?"

My mother turned toward me with a frown on her face, and for several moments I could see the list of possible names scroll across her forehead. "You know something, sweetheart . . . it really doesn't matter."

I shook my head and walked out.


By the time I arrived at Tiffany's town house on Central Park West, I had ten minutes to spare. I darted up the stone steps and rang the buzzer. Several moments later, Tiffany appeared, looking snooty as always.

"I was getting worried. Come in. Come in." She whirled away and swished down the corridor that led to the only sunken living room I'd ever seen. There were enough Gucci suitcases to open a showroom, and I immediately wondered what was left in her closet.

"The car should be here any minute, so let me go over a few things."

Car! She needed a minibus, but I didn't say anything.

"First the plants get watered three times per week. No more, no less. That's very important." She wagged a finger at me for emphasis then pranced over to her indoor forest that lined the windowsill from one wall to the next. Then she began talking to the flora and fauna as if they were small children.

I gritted my teeth and made a vow that folks would be ice-skating down below before I started chatting with plants. Sorry. No dice.

"Virginia needs to be walked by seven a.m. and again at ten."

Virginia was her French poodle. (What else?)

"Sybil comes in on Saturdays to clean and do laundry, but I don't like leaving her alone. So be sure to be here when she arrives. She usually works for about three to four hours."

Three to four hours every Saturday for six weeks! She had to be kidding. I'd figure something else out. "Sure. No problem."

"Are you writing any of this down?" she suddenly asked, spinning toward me like a top.

"I have it all up here," I said with a bright smile, tapping my temple with my index finger.

She gave me a suspicious look for a moment. "Well, you always were the smartest one in class," she said, as if that fact was one she still grappled with. She arched a brow and murmured something I couldn't quite make out; then she crossed the gleaming parquet floors, her heels sounding like gunshots in the hood: *pop, pop, pop.* She reached the antique desk and opened the drawer.

"This is the combination to the alarm." She held up a piece of paper that was no bigger than a thumbnail. "Make sure you deactivate it within thirty seconds of coming in or the police will show up. And please don't forget to reset it even when you're in the house. And here is the key to the mailbox." She handed me a tiny silver key along with the tiny slip of paper. She looked around. "I think that's it." She beamed at me. "Any questions?"

"I don't think so."

"Good. I'll call and check in from time to time. And as soon as we get settled, I'll give you the number to the hotel in case of any emergency. And for heaven's sake, do not under any circumstances give the number to Calvin." She frowned. "We're through, at least until I get back," she added with a huff and jut of her chin. "He said he would stop by and pick up his things one day next week. Just watch his every move. They are in a box marked X in my bedroom closet. Give them to him and let him be on his way." She waved her hand as if to dismiss me and the entire topic of Calvin.

Mind you, in any woman's book, Calvin was a tasty morsel, and I always thought that Tiffany treated him like last week's lunch— but that was just my opinion.

"Maybe being away from me for a few weeks will show him how much he really loves me."

I shrugged, not really knowing what to say, and Tiffany didn't seem to care anyway. The doorbell chimed.

"That's the driver," she sang, and practically skipped to the front door to buzz him in.

As I walked behind her to the front door, I hoped that the driver brought along his team of weight lifters. Instead, it was my grandfather or somebody's grandfather. The man was as old as dirt and stooped almost in half.

Ultimately it took me and grandpa a half hour to get all Tiffany's bags out of her apartment and into the limo, while she supervised the move. Ha, go figure. And there were still Chantel's bags to load. Sigh . . . They couldn't leave fast enough.

# And Away
# They Go

Tiffany and Chantel were gone. At that very moment, barring a natural disaster or a hijacking, they should have been zooming across the Atlantic en route to Europe. Can you see me grinning?

Mind you, the average third wheel may have been offended by the Doublemint Twins' lack of concern about not letting her accompany them on their trip. Not this third wheel. I looked at it as a new lease on life, a golden opportunity, the light at the end of the tunnel. Strangely, it was as if I were free from all the things that were cluttering my life.

As the cab I'd hopped into after leaving Chantel's apartment whizzed—well not exactly *whizzed,* more like crept and crawled—through Manhattan traffic, heading toward my abode in Harlem, I was truly in the throes of ecstasy.

I patted the breast pocket of my Kmart blouse, feeling the metallic bulge, ensuring myself that the keys to the castles were in place. The uncomfortable, tattered vinyl seating beckoned me, and I leaned back, resigning myself to the fact that the twenty-minute ride would instead be more like an hour. With this in mind, I surrendered to the hum of the motor, the rolling motion of the tires on the street, and allowed my mind to wander, to slip away from reality.

Soon, visions of gorgeous men-in-waiting surrounded me—all muscle—willing to answer my every beck and call. I was in demand. I was in heaven.

Would you care for a massage?" a man—whom for the purposes of this vignette I will call Adonis—asked me in a deep, seductive Barry White voice. "I've dreamed about running my hands over your body."

I rolled onto my very flat stomach and tucked my hands beneath my chin.

"You may begin," I said in a suddenly acquired British accent. I closed my eyes as his steely fingers (that's what they're called in romance novels) kneaded my shoulders, spine, moving slowly and expertly down to . . .

Ten dollar!" the cabbie barked in a very distinct foreign accent, successfully chasing away Adonis. Reluctantly, I opened my eyes.

I sat up, peeling my back away from the now-damp vinyl seat. I peeked out the window, and my third-floor walk-up peeked right back at me. Sighing, I reached for my purse. It wasn't there. A moment of panic gripped me until I realized it must have fallen on the floor during my massage. I bent down as best I could in the

tight quarters and searched the sticky and dim confines of the cab.
Nothing! Uh-oh. Now long-term panic set in. Everything of value
was in my purse: wallet, checkbook, combs, brushes, toothpicks,
Band-Aids, aspirin, makeup, a change of underwear, and a pack of
condoms (just in case). I wasn't the kind of woman who "changed
purses." No. I had one everyday purse that I used *every day*. This
was one of those every days, and I didn't have my purse. My mind
raced through the possibilities. Then it hit me. I could see it as
clear as day sitting on Tiffany's antique table, wailing at me for
leaving it. I'd put it down so that I would be better able to haul
her bags, and I'd never retrieved it. *Oh, please forgive me, baby.
Mommy's going to get you back.*

"Ten dollar!" he barked again, fiercer this time.

"I . . . I don't have my purse," I stammered, snapping to and
praying that he would have mercy on me. What woman travels
without her purse? He had to know that it must have been some
horrific incident to separate a woman from her purse.

"I call police! Ten dollar!" He turned toward me, emitting a
cloud of garlic and cigar breath.

His bushy, mustache-like eyebrows knitted together into an
ominous black line, and I suddenly saw myself behind bars, fighting off the advances of once-upon-a-time women who now preferred to be called Joe.

Obviously, purses were not a necessity of life where he came from.

"Uh, just a minute." I dug in my coat pockets and the jacket
pocket of my suit, thankful for my quirky habit of hoarding
change and single dollars, and after about five minutes of lining
up quarters and dimes, I handed him five dollars in silver, a fifty-
cent piece, four crumpled singles, and fifty pennies. (I needed to
get rid of those anyway.) He cussed me viciously in his native
tongue, a dialect that I couldn't decipher, but you know when you

are being cussed out, no matter the language. The instant I opened the door, he started to speed off. I leaped to the curb to avoid becoming a hood ornament on his cab, but not before being coated in a plume of car exhaust. My fifteen-dollar Payless shoes were splattered with street water.

Worse for wear, but not defeated, I headed for my building—only to realize that I couldn't get in. I didn't have any keys. My keys, like everything else of value in my life, were in my purse!

"Damnit!" What was I going to do now? I looked up and down the block, hoping to see my knight in shining armor heading my way or at the very least a hero in an SUV. Of course, that was a waste of brain cells. This on-the-rise-one-day-soon neighborhood was quiet as a cemetery, and the few stragglers who lurked on the corner were the sort that I wouldn't ask for any kind of assistance.

At a loss and out of immediate options, I sat down on the cold stone steps to mull over my predicament. I mulled for a good ten minutes until the obvious finally got tired of waiting for me to figure it out and hit me in the head.

I may not have had *my* keys but I had *Tiffany's* keys. And that's where my purse was. Normalcy could be restored. Standing, I dug into my pocket again and scrounged up two dollars in a meager collection of nickels and dimes. A quick train ride uptown, pop into Tiffany's place, grab my purse, and I could head back home. A snap.

I arrived at Tiffany's town house nearly an hour later. The street was lined from end to end with BMWs, Mercedes, Jaguars, and Lexuses. This was the kind of neighborhood where you could actually hear the upper crust crunch. Did Tiffany really make that much money as a TV producer to afford this place? I wondered as I approached her building.

I pulled her keys out of the breast pocket of my blouse, stuck it in the lock, and stepped into the darkened foyer. Before I could reach for the light, I was set upon by a snarling, man-eating beast. All fur, fangs, and menace. When the hell did Tiffany get a badass Doberman?

Dazed, I shook my head to clear it and glanced at the flashing red light of the alarm on the wall. *"You have thirty seconds to deactivate the system or the police will be dispatched to this location,"* the alarm warned. A talking alarm—figures.

The beast dug its teeth into the sleeve of my jacket, and I knew my throat was next. But I'd rather battle the blood-crazed beast than a trigger-happy New York City cop.

With strength born of terror, I flung the animal off my arm, hurling it down the spit-shine corridor, and hurried over to the panel. Its yelps echoed down the hallway. But I had no time to waste. Trying to clear my mind, I hit the light switch and pulled the tiny slip of paper from my pocket. My fingers trembled. I could hear my thundering heartbeat pound in my ears. I punched in the numbers and prayed that my dizziness from the animal assault did not hamper my vision.

Five seconds . . . The last two numbers blurred. Three seconds . . . Focus, concentrate, think. Was it a seven or a nine? I squeezed my eyes hard to clear them. Two seconds . . . *Red wire or blue, Maggie?* I hit the nine, still wondering if the sequence was correct, and silently prayed not to be blown to kingdom come.

*Beep.*

I waited for sirens, flashing red lights, and pounding on the door. Silence. The only sound to be heard was whimpering coming from the beast, which had somehow morphed back into Virginia, the French poodle. She lay curled in a ball, licking her paws. Uh-oh.

I inched over to the injured pooch with the intention of offering some comfort, and it bared its teeth at me, then growled low in its throat. I backed away and, using the wall for support, inched down the hallway and into the living room, keeping a wary eye on my assailant. My purse, sitting forlorn on the antique table, called out to me, begging me to take it home. Quickly, before Virginia fully recovered, I darted across the room and snatched up my purse, holding it close to my breasts, just as the doorbell rang.

I froze.

The bell pealed again. I tiptoed over to the window and peeked out, certain that a cavalcade of squad cars had encircled the building. But all I saw was a FedEx truck. Hmmm.

I crept down the hall, mindful of Virginia, and pressed the intercom. "Yes?"

"Package for Tiffany Lane."

Virginia stood. Her fluffy ears perked up at the sound of her mistress's name.

I bent down and gave the mutt an "oh no you don't" look. She quickly backed away, scurrying into a corner.

I pressed the buzzer and opened the front door.

"Sign here," the FedEx guy said.

He handed me one of those Etch A Sketch boards and a fake pen to scratch my signature. I scribbled something unintelligible and handed it back in return for a box, which I tucked under my arm.

"Margaret?"

I glanced up into the eyes of the delivery man. My brow arched in question, and then an overwhelming sensation of seasickness swept through my stomach.

"Willie!"

He grinned, flashing a set of reasonably white teeth with a little chip in the front.

"Wow," he said, looking over my shoulder and into the apartment. "You've come a long way. Who would have thought that Diva Tiffany would share an apartment with you?"

At that moment, I fully understood the phrase, "She bristled."

"For your information . . . this . . . is my apartment." I swallowed. "Tiffany is only staying here temporarily." Where had that come from?

His eyes widened in surprise, crinkling a healing zit on his forehead. "Really?" The corner of his mouth curved. "So, huh, since I know where you live, maybe we can get together—for old times' sake."

I put my hand on my hip. "I don't think my fiancé would appreciate that."

"Fiancé. So you're engaged?" he asked, even more perplexed by that announcement.

"Yes." I jutted my chin for effect and casually tucked my ringless hand behind my back.

He shook his head in amazement. "Go figure," he murmured. "Well, this is my regular route now, so maybe I'll see you sometime . . . and your fiancé."

I forced a fake smile. "Maybe."

"You take care. And tell Tiffany that Willie said hello." He turned to leave, then stopped. "What ever happened to the other one, Chantel?"

"She's with Tiffany at the moment." At least that much was true. "I'll tell her you said hello, as well."

"Do that. Well, take it easy, Maggie."

"Hmmm." I shut the door and peered through the peephole. Willie was standing out front, looking up at the building. Finally he returned to his truck and drove away.

Breathing a sigh of relief, I walked back down the hall, with the intention of depositing the box in Tiffany's room and getting the heck out of Dodge.

I stepped into the inner sanctum and was immediately transported to Tiffany's childhood bedroom of years earlier. Pink abounded. I felt my stomach rise in revolt. Taking a deep breath, I stepped onto the hot-pink carpet and over to her dresser, where I intended to deposit the box. But something stopped me. Call it . . . *nosiness?*

Lifting the box to my ears, I gently shook it. I'd seen many television characters do that when a box was received. I checked the return address and couldn't make it out. I turned it over. Shook it again. Hmmm. It could be anything. Perhaps the enclosed items were something that Tiffany needed to know about as soon as possible, I convinced myself as I sat on the side of her bed, placing the box next to me.

I stared at the box. My purse, hanging on my shoulder, advised me to just go home. Decisions, decisions.

There was whimpering and the sound of nails tapping against the floor. The noise drew closer. Virginia appeared in the doorway, staring at me, daring me, it seemed, to invade the recesses of her mistress's package. That was all the challenge I needed.

Staring Virginia down, I lifted the box onto my lap. The beast's ears rose; its back arched. I gave it a menacing look and tore open the box. Adrenaline rushed through my veins as I peeled away the paper only to find . . .

# Surprise, Surprise

*B*ooks! I couldn't believe it. What a letdown. Three of them filled the interior of the box. I didn't even know that Tiffany read books. Go figure. I took out the top book and read the title. *Men Who Love Women Who Hate Them.* (Raised brows.) *How to Succeed in the World on Looks Alone.* I laughed. *Why Other Women Want to Be You: The Truth Behind the Myth.* Hmmm, perhaps this was more interesting than I thought.

Briefly, I flipped through the pages; then I noticed a note at the bottom of the box.

Dear Sister Diva,

As promised, enclosed are the latest additions to our training collection. We are sure that you will find them in-

formative as well as entertaining. No Diva worth her manicure would be without them.

We hope that you will be joining us for our annual soiree. It
is certain to be a spectacular affair. All the information is available on our Web site, divalicious.com. Of course, you must be
a registered member with a password to access the site.

As you know, this is recruitment month, and we will be
considering new applicants based on member recommenda-
tions. The perfect opportunity to give them a taste of what
Divas, Inc., can afford them is to have them join us at the
soiree. Do let us know if you will be bringing a guest.

On that note, remember the Diva motto: *Me first!*

Yours in sisterhood,

*The Grand Diva*

I read the letter three more times. *Divas, Inc.?* There actually
*was* such a thing? But where? Who were these women? Was it some
secret Masons society, but for girls? Did they meet in grandiose
mansions as in the movie *Eyes Wide Shut* with Tom Cruise and
Nicole Kidman, with their true identities hidden behind masks?

Questions ran rampant in my fertile mind, the endless scenarios
blooming like roses in a well-tended garden. The big question now
was; How will Margaret Drew get invited to the soiree? Information and a plan were necessary. I stared at the books. Some of the answers to my questions, I was certain, lay tucked between the pages.

As a first reader and assistant editor for the University Press, my
days were filled with reading everything from the mundane to the
mundane-er in a matter of days and writing full reports on the
lifeless tomes. This would be a breeze. I felt giddy with delight.

Dropping the books back into the box, I planned to bring them home, give them a thorough perusal, and take copious notes. For years I'd stayed in the shadows, content to tag along, be graced by their sunshine and only imagine what life would be like to be a true diva. Now, all that eluded me for decades had been dropped into my lap by none other than Twinkie Willie. Oh, the irony of it all! In my hot little hands rested the secrets that only a chosen few ever shared. I would absorb every word, emulate every move, and attain every attribute. On these pages were life lessons. Lessons that I was determined to master, rising like a phoenix from the ashes. I would finally remake Margaret Drew into the image that had only lived in my mind. And as Grandma always said, "If you don't be yourself, somebody else will be you." Which made absolutely no sense, but it seemed like the perfect Grandma-ism for the moment.

I tossed my head back and laughed. Laughed loud and long, drawing Virginia timidly into the room. I flashed her a stop-dead stare and pointed an ominous finger in her direction. "Be careful, before a house falls on you, too, my pretty!" Her animal instincts shifted into gear, and she jetted from the room as I jumped atop the bed with the books high above my head and announced, "There's a new sheriff in town."

I got down from the bed. Catching my reflection in the full-length mirror, I noted a sense of purpose etched into the curve of my brow. I was no longer ordinary Margaret Drew. The woman who stood before me was svelte, with perfect nails and hair, donned true designer clothes, rode in a fancy sports car with hordes of men trailing behind her. Instead of disappearing into a crowd, this new and improved Margaret drew (no pun intended) the throngs like a magnet. She would appear powerful and helpless at the same time. Able to pretend to have a conversation on any topic, and her every word would be received with awe and admiration.

I blinked, and the image before me morphed into the person I faced every day. An ordinary thirty-something woman who wore glasses, was a bit overweight, and bit her nails down to the quick. She was a nice enough person whom no one really took seriously. One who wore secondhand clothes and lived in a tiny one-bedroom apartment in a questionable (if up-and-coming) neighborhood. She didn't have a fancy job or fancy friends, unless you really wanted to count Tiffany and Chantel. But what she did have were the keys to the castle, the secrets of the divas, and she was certain there were more where they came from. It was simply a matter of uncovering them.

I looked around the bedroom. Where to begin? I walked across the pink carpet to the wall-to-wall closet and slid open the doors. Before me, lined up by color and design, was every kind of outfit from casual to "meet the Queen of England." How could Tiffany possibly have so many outfits with the number of suitcases she took with her? I wondered in awe.

Gingerly I ran my hand across the exquisite fabric and immediately nicked a red wool jersey dress with a broken nail. Terrified of the damage I'd caused, I pulled my hand away, only to find that the thread of the dress came right along with me! In no time, I'd unraveled a fingertip-size hole in the front of the dress. Disengaging the thread from my torn nail, I removed the dress from the hanger and stuffed it in the bottom of the closet until I could figure out what to do. House-sitting was going to be more difficult than I'd thought.

Shutting the closet door, I turned to find Virginia staring at me in what seemed like disapproval.

"What are you looking at?"

"Woof."

I squeezed my eyes into tiny slits. "Remember what I told you about that house falling on you," I said in my most threatening voice.

Virginia whirled around and hightailed it down the hallway once again. At least we seemed to be reaching an understanding.

Deciding it was best, at least for the moment, to abandon the search of the closet, I turned my attention back to the task at hand: examining the books. But we all know that good reading must be accompanied by good food, and I was starving.

To the kitchen.

Much to my dismay, the cupboards were bare and the refrigerator wasn't doing much better. There was an echo in the cupboards, and if my eyes weren't playing tricks on me, I'd swear I saw cobwebs. The refrigerator contained a bottle of seltzer water, two apples, a yellowed head of broccoli, half a stick of margarine, a wilted carrot, and a tube of Cheez Whiz. Cheez Whiz?

There was nothing in there that I could put together to make anything. Maybe all those suitcases and trunks were filled with food and not clothes. That was the only logical conclusion that I could come to.

I turned and damn near tripped over Virginia, whose expression had turned to pleading. She raised herself up on her hind legs, her front paws held in that begging position dogs practice for TV pet tricks.

"You hungry, too, huh? What does Tiffany do for food around here, anyway?"

Virginia scampered over to the other side of the kitchen and stood up near a row of drawers.

"Forks, spoons, knives?" I asked. "Big deal." I walked over to the drawers and pulled one open.

There had to be at least one hundred menus from what appeared to be every restaurant in Manhattan. French, Chinese,

Spanish, Indonesian, Indian, African, Italian, Kosher, Jamaican—
you name it—there was a menu for it.

"Wow."

Taking a handful of menus I took a seat at the table, and darn it
if Virginia didn't hop up in the chair next to me.

"So what will it be?" I asked, and immediately wondered when
I'd started talking to dogs. Were the plants next?

She pushed the menus around with the tip of her nose. The Italian menu struck my fancy, and I plucked it from the pile.

Glancing through the menu, I made my selection, but I'd be
darned if I was going to ask Virginia what she wanted. I went to
the phone and called the restaurant.

The moment the call connected a cheery Italian hostess greeted
me by name—well not exactly by *my* name.

"Good evening, Ms. Lane. And how are you tonight?"

"Uh . . . fine," I stammered, once it registered that this faceless
stranger knew who I was. Or wasn't. Big Brother has caller ID.

"What will you have tonight, your usual?"

"Oh, geez, I'm so tired tonight I can't remember what my usual
is." I laughed lightly, looked down at Virginia, and winked.

"A mixed green salad with house dressing, vegetable lasagna,
and a bottle of white wine," the voice said.

"Hmmm. I feel like something different tonight." I covered my
mouth and chuckled. "How about veal parmesan, with angel hair
pasta and mushroom sauce?"

"Wonderful choice."

"How much will that be?"

"Excuse me, Ms. Lane?"

"The cost . . . How much will it be?"

"Don't you want to put it on your account?"

"Account?" I looked down at Virginia, and she shrugged.

"Sure . . . why not? Put it on the account." I covered my mouth and giggled again.

"Very well. Your food should arrive within thirty minutes."

"Thank you." I hung up the phone and turned to Virginia. "That was easy."

"Woof, woof."

After stuffing the menus back in the drawer, I returned to the bedroom with Virginia close on my heels. I laid the books out on the bed and started to read.

# Well, I'll Be . . .
# A Diva

Being a pretty good speed-reader, I quickly deduced that this divalicious business was more than just a notion. There was real work involved: from how high you held your nose to the pitch of climactic yells during a fake orgasm. There was an entire chapter dedicated to that subject, titled, "Best Actress for Oscar-Worthy Orgasms," complete with black-and-white graphics—which I studied diligently.

Just to try out the technique, I lay supine on the bed and attempted to put "the look" on my face (half-closed eyes and pouty mouth). I thrashed my head back and forth as it said to do on page 125, and I began to moan, my cries rising in intensity at ten-second intervals until Virginia, not able to stand it any longer, ran to the window and began howling in earnest, snapping me back to reality.

I sat up and looked at her. "How did I do?"

She shook her head as vigorously as if she had fleas. I got the picture. I needed practice.

Book after book, the pages were loaded with the secrets and necessary devices needed to create *the* Diva, from clothes, to lifestyle, to perfecting "the attitude," to dictating who was an acceptable man.

I read for hours while Virginia and I devoured our Italian dinner, and before I drifted off to a sleep filled with terrifying images of being hauled to the big house for pretending to be someone I wasn't, I realized that it was going to take my every waking hour to get ready in time for the soiree. But first I had to get myself invited and find the handbook—the real key to divadom that was mentioned in all the books.

When I opened my eyes the following morning, I was certain I'd died and was now a resident of my own personal hell, where everything for all time would exist in shades of pink. I squeezed my eyes shut and slowly opened them. It was worse. It was hell on earth—Tiffany's bedroom.

Slowly I sat up and looked around, only to find Virginia standing at the foot of the bed with her leash in her mouth.

"You've got to be kidding me." I took a glance at the bedside clock. It was 6:45. "Do you know what time it is? What day it is?" I turned the clock so that Virginia could see for herself.

She barked in response.

"All right, all right." I pushed up from the bed and stood; then I trudged off to the master bathroom, which was equipped not only with a tub and stall shower, but also a Jacuzzi. I would definitely have to check that out. I opened the linen closet and selected a matching pink face cloth and towel.

Fortunately it was Sunday, and I didn't have to worry about rushing home to change clothes for work. And after walking the dog, I could get back to the task at hand—snooping. Plus I still had Chantel's apartment to tackle.

Turning on the water in the sink, I looked into the vanity mirror, assessing the image before me. A lesson from one of the books popped into my head, and slowly I tilted my chin upward—just so—until my somewhat pudgy nose was on par with a nose that had smelled something unpleasant. I attempted to arch my brow for effect, but I didn't quite have the hang of it, and so I appeared as if I had some sort of facial paralysis. I'd have to work on that one.

After my bathroom constitutional, I smoothed out my wrinkled clothes, hooked Virginia's leash to her collar, and headed out. Virginia obviously knew which way she wanted to go, so I let her walk me down the street as I took in the neighborhood on a Sunday morning, allowing my thoughts to wander.

All through the night, interspersed between dreams of prison and receiving my Academy Award, I was haunted by the words that repeatedly appeared on the pages I read: *The handbook. Refer to the handbook. It is your Bible. When in doubt, read your handbook.*

What was it? Where was it, and how could I get my hands on one? I mused. Surely Tiffany had it somewhere in her apartment. That would be my mission for the day. Pumped with excitement, I couldn't wait to get back.

"Well, hello, Virginia."

Virginia came to a stop and happily ran up and down the leg of the man who'd suddenly appeared in front of us. He was at least six feet, kind of preppy-looking in a pair of beige khakis, brown loafers, and some kind of polo shirt that I was certain had an emblem on it beneath his chocolate brown leather bomber jacket.

He laughed deep in his throat and then looked at me from behind wire-rimmed glasses. "You're definitely not Tiffany," he said, as if that were some sort of a greeting.

I tried the nose thing again. "Apparently not." I quickly raised my chin to a 180-degree angle, allowing me to see only across the top of his head from beneath my glasses.

"Are you all right? Did you hurt yourself?"

He ran behind me so quickly, I didn't have time to react.

"What the h—?"

He slid his arms beneath my pits, locked his hands behind my head, put his knee in my back, lifted me off the ground, and pulled.

My eyes and mouth rounded to the size of a Spalding handball, when every bone in my back cracked and snapped. Holy shit!

Slowly, he lowered me to my feet and released me. "You should be fine now."

I shook my head to clear it, momentarily dazed while the madman stood in front of me with the biggest grin on his face.

"Are you out of your mind?" I yelled. "You . . . you don't even know me. . . . You . . . you could have killed me! You . . . you—"

"I doubt it. I'm a chiropractor. I see cases like yours every day."

"Cases like mine. What case? I don't have a case!" I couldn't believe I was having this conversation with a man who'd assaulted me in the middle of a ritzy neighborhood on a Sunday morning. I looked around for help, but everyone was moseying along the street oblivious of my plight.

"SSS, better known as sudden spinal spasm."

"What!" My voice could have shattered glass.

"You see," he began in that pain-in-the-neck tone that somebody who knows something you don't takes when they start explaining things. "Your spinal column and the surrounding muscles went into a sudden spasm, causing your chin to jut skyward and freeze there, holding your entire body immobile." He smiled.

I blinked rapidly and shook my head, trying to make sense of what he'd said and then . . . it did. The nose thing.

Suddenly mortified, I mumbled, "Uh . . . thank you." I tried to walk past him, pulling Virginia along with me.

"You never answered my question," he said, catching up to me.

I snapped my head in his direction and prayed that he didn't think that that too, was another symptom of SSS. "I didn't know you asked one."

"I suppose you could say it was more of a statement."

I sighed. "And what was that?"

"You're not Tiffany."

I stopped dead in my tracks, jerking Virginia to a stop. Placing my hand on my hip, I gave him Grandma's evil eye—the one with your left eye closed and your right one squinting. "If I remember correctly, we already agreed on that."

"Well, if you're not Tiffany, then what are you doing with Virginia? Tiffie never lets anyone walk Ginnie."

"*Tiffie* is away, and I'm looking after her place."

"Really? She didn't mention she was leaving."

"I'm sure she had her reasons," I said, my voice dripping sarcasm. "Does she tell you everything?"

"Does a woman ever tell a man everything?"

The corner of his mouth turned up, and for the first time I realized he was kind of cute in a geeky way. I would never have thought that Tiffany would even hold a conversation with anyone who remotely resembled a geek—especially of the male species. Must be some information I missed in one of those manuals.

"Who are you, anyway?"

"Wayne Hathaway."

I nodded. "Well, nice meeting you, Wayne. And, uh, thanks again for the, uh, whatever it was you did to me back there." I continued down the street. He trailed a few steps behind me. I picked up my pace.

"Oh, sure, anytime," he said, sounding a bit winded.

"I don't think so," I mumbled.

"You never said when Tiffany would be back."

"It will be a while," I tossed over my shoulder as I'd seen women do in the movies, so only your profile was exposed.

"Then maybe I'll see you again," he called out as I hurried up the steps.

I turned once, gave him a whisper of a smile, and disappeared into the corridor. *What an exit,* I thought as I shut the door behind me. I'd seen it done a million times and had lived for the opportunity to try it.

Safely behind closed doors, I unhooked Virginia, who went straight for her empty bowl of food. She turned and gave me an accusing look.

"Hey, you see what we had to eat last night," I said in my defense. "There's nothing in this place other than clothes, shoes, and furniture." I plopped down into a floral-printed kitchen chair.

Virginia whimpered, and I momentarily felt sorry for her when my own stomach began to ask, "Where's the food?" If I was to do a proper search for one handbook, I was going to need sustenance. I glanced toward the menu drawer, and Virginia immediately began to wag her tail.

We were in sync.

I located a menu for a local Spanish restaurant that delivered breakfast and maintained an ongoing account for Señorita Lane. I ordered breakfast *and* lunch—just to be sure.

While we waited for the delivery, I decided to investigate the bedroom.

# Sherlock and
# Virginia

*I* stood in the center of the bedroom, looking for clues, for a hint to where the real secrets were hidden, where the most delicious info could be found. My eyes or my instincts kept going back to the closet. I know I'd tried it before, but my gut told me I'd missed something. I walked toward the closet, but my swift partner, getting the hint, darted past me and began scratching at the floor.

"All right, all right—take it easy. I have everything under control." I opened the sliding doors and stood in front of the great wall of clothing. The small red heap of fabric on the floor reminded me of my last foray into chic designer wonderland. Perhaps I needed rubber gloves this time. I retreated to the kitchen and found a pair beneath the sink. Donning the gloves, I returned to the bedroom, but didn't venture farther than the middle of the room. This had all the makings of a badly written Hardy Boys mystery.

Virginia, sensing my hesitation, woofed loudly as if hot on the scent of something worthwhile. She darted between my legs, heading deep into the recesses of the closet, knocking over several boxes in the process.

"What is it, girl?" I asked, echoing an episode of *Lassie*.

I got down on my hands and knees (suddenly thankful for the earlier spinal adjustment) and crawled beneath the overgrowth, my every move hampered by a landmine of low and high heels, stilettos, boots, sneakers, and shoe trees. By this time, Virginia was in the back of the closet, playing around as if she were in the park. Pushing aside a pink ball gown, I frowned in confusion when Virginia jumped up and down in delight.

"It's just a wall," I said, disappointed once again.

I started to turn around and go back the way I'd come, when Virginia grabbed my shirt between her teeth.

"Hey! What's with you? No more games. Let's go." I snatched my arm away, and I came back sleeveless.

She sat there, staring at me with half my shirt in her mouth.

Outraged, I dived for her. She did a fancy shake-and-bake basketball move on me, and I went down face first while I simultaneously became entangled in one of the gowns, pulling down the entire rack of clothes on top of both of us. My glasses went flying, and everything became one big blur.

Virginia yelped frantically, trying to tear and claw through the debris. I struggled for air, certain that I would be buried alive, to be found weeks later, mummified, a look of mortification on my face, entombed beneath an avalanche of ball gowns and shoe boxes.

Suddenly, daylight peeked through as I dug out from beneath

the last dress. I tossed it to the side, gulped in huge lungfuls of air, and struggled to sit up. With my vision impaired, I noticed that the back wall of the closet was no longer there. At first, I thought I was seeing things then panic set in. I'd knocked out Tiffany's wall! I rubbed the knot on my forehead inflicted by the falling rack.

Virginia scampered over my head and darted into the now open space.

"Virginia. Come back here," I hissed. She ignored me. What choice did I have but to follow her?

The moment I crossed the threshold on my hands and knees, the phone rang. On reflex I tried to get to it, but somehow, just like in those old black-and-white haunted house movies, the door slid shut, locking me and Virginia inside the secret closet.

"I'm sorry I can't speak with you right now, but if you think you are important, please leave me a message," Tiffany's recorded voice rang out.

"Tiffany, this is Calvin. Tiffany, pick up the phone. I know you're home. We need to talk, Tiffie. I'm coming over."

"Coming over!" I turned to Virginia in a panic. I swear the dog shrugged. "We have to get out of here."

I turned around in a circle, looking for an exit, but at the same time taking in the contents of the closet. I blinked several times to be sure I wasn't seeing things.

Then the doorbell rang.

Calvin! No, that wasn't possible—unless he'd actually called from in front of the house. A stalker! Did he have a key? What if he walked right in? I started to sweat.

The bell rang again.

Virginia looked up at me with what looked like real fear in her eyes and whimpered.

I pressed the door, the wall, the floor. Nothing happened.

The bell rang again, this time more insistent. Our delivery! My stomach cried out. Help and food were a mere room or two away.

"Help! Help us. We're trapped," I shouted, envisioning myself immured forever in a closet. I banged on the wall. "Help."

Then as suddenly as it shut, the closet door opened with a loud bang.

"Well, I'll be . . . Come on, girl, let's get out of here."

We tramped over the pile of fallen clothing and made it to safety. I hurried to the front door, so happy to be free that I was oblivious of how I must have looked when I pulled open the door and found not our food delivery but Wayne Hathaway, the street chiropractor.

I leaped back on the off chance he thought I needed another spontaneous alignment. But in my haste to get away, I tumbled backwards over Virginia and landed with a thump on the floor.

"Wayne . . . what are you doing here?" I asked, looking up.

"Are you all right?" He reached for me and pulled me to my feet.

"I'm . . . fine." I forced a smile, tried to smooth my hair and clothing and focus on the blurry image in front of me. I tried to peek around him to see if there was any sign of Calvin.

"Expecting someone?"

"Yes. No. What is it?"

"You have a knot on your head."

I gingerly touched the sore spot. "Little accident," I murmured. "What are you doing here?" I asked again. "I told you that Tiffany was out of town."

"I know. But I thought I would check on you. Sometimes those spasms come back without warning."

"I'm sure that won't be a problem," I assured him.

"Why do you have on rubber gloves?"

I quickly snatched them off and balled them in my fist. "Cleaning," I muttered.

The delivery man walked up behind him. Great, a diversion.

"Delivery for Señorita Lane," he said in a heavy Spanish accent.

"Oh, you must be mistaken," Wayne offered, always helpful. "Ms. Lane is out of town."

"Thank you," I interjected, stepping around Wayne and taking the package. I cut Wayne a harsh Grandma look. "I placed the order."

The delivery man stood there for several moments, looking from me to Wayne.

"Can you give him a tip, please?" I asked under my breath.

"Sure." Wayne dug in his pants pocket, took out his wallet, and handed the delivery man a five-dollar bill.

"*Gracias, gracias,*" he said, beaming as if he'd hit the lotto, and scurried down the stairs.

Was that the going rate in this part of town, or was Wayne Hathaway trying to impress me?

"Smells good," Wayne said, inching farther inside.

I held the bag close to my chest. "There's only enough for one."

Virginia yelped in dissent.

"I think it's time for you to go now, Wayne. Thanks for dropping by—and for the tip and for anything else you may have on your mind to do." Calvin could turn up at any minute, I realized, my blood pressure rising. Tiffany's bedroom was a shambles. I looked like a car-wreck survivor, and I needed to get back in that closet. Wayne had to go.

Virginia started running circles around Wayne's legs.

He laughed and scooped her up. "She always does that when she wants me to come in."

I arched a skeptical brow, mindful not to raise my chin to a suspicious level. I stared at Virginia, wondering how she could betray me like that.

"Listen, Wayne, I appreciate your concern, but I really have a lot to do. And I'm sure you do, as well." I made the words sound as dismissive as possible.

"Maybe I could help. You should let me take a look at that knot on your head."

"No thanks." I reached for Virginia, but she snuggled deeper into his arms.

"What happened to your shirt?" he asked, trying to buy time.

"Fashion statement. Good-bye, Wayne." At this point, he could *take* Virginia—as long as he left before Calvin arrived.

"You know, there have been a few break-ins lately." He tried to look past me and into the apartment. "Maybe I should take a look around."

Suddenly we heard sirens. They were loud and coming fast. In a wink, two squad cars pulled to a screeching halt in front of Tiffany's town house. Three officers jumped from the cars like in a SWAT operation, running like a platoon of combat troops under fire, with guns drawn. It was indeed an unnerving sight.

"Put your hands where I can see them!" one cop shouted.

Wayne threw up his hands, tossing Virginia into the air in the process. She landed on Wayne's head, jumped off his shoulder, and took off down the street, her legs windmilling underneath her.

Oh, shit! Virginia!

The officer came up the stairs, took one look at me, and handcuffed Wayne.

"My dog!" I did a great imitation of an alarmed Macaulay Culkin in *Home Alone*.

"Are you the owner of this apartment, ma'am?" he asked, ignoring my concern.

I had to think fast. "Uh . . . uh. Yes."

"Your neighbors reported someone yelling for help, a possible robbery, and then your alarm went off. Your security company notified the precinct."

"Is this the man who broke in and assaulted you?" the second officer asked, directing a glare at Wayne.

I thought about the morning assault on the street, Wayne's wanting to ease his way into the apartment. All the pieces fit if I really wanted to be mean. I glanced at Wayne. *I bet you're sorry you stopped by now.*

"Uh, no, officer. This is all really a big mistake. I forgot to reset the alarm when I opened the door for Wayne. He's a good friend of mine."

"How'd you get that knot on your head, and why is your shirt ripped?" He looked at me suspiciously and then at Wayne, who wore a disbelieving frown.

"Oh, this is just an old shirt. I was doing some, uh, cleaning and bumped my head." I hiccupped. "Clumsy me."

"I'd better take a look inside." He brushed by me and went in.

The second officer took a shouting, struggling Wayne and put him in the patrol car. This was getting worse by the minute, and Virginia was nowhere in sight. All that had to happen now was for Calvin to pull up.

And he did.

# Could Things Get
# Any Worse?

*W*hat's going on here?" Calvin demanded as he tried to push past the officers.

"Keep back, sir. We have everything under control."

"Everything like what? This is my girlfriend's apartment. Tiffany! Tiffany!" he called out, bobbing and weaving his head between the hulking bodies of the officers to get a better look. "Are you all right?"

By this time, a small crowd had gathered, the hum of their collective whispers growing by the minute. Others peeked from doorways and windows. Cars with Sunday-morning churchgoers slowed to rubberneck and take in the scene, and any minute I fully expected the news vans to pull up, unloading hordes of overzealous reporters and camera crews. How would I ever explain this to Grandma when she saw my face all over the eleven o'clock news?

"You know the woman who lives here?" one of the officers asked Calvin.

"Yes," he said, tugging on the lapels of his jacket.

"Lemme see some ID, fella."

Calvin threw the officer a male version of the nose thing—not quite 180 degrees, more like 90—before whipping out his identification. CALVIN RUSSELL, ESQ.

The officer looked closely at the ID, back at Calvin, and then at the ID. "Come with me." He steered Calvin with a hand to his back up the steps.

"Mag—," Calvin blurted out.

My goose was cooked if I didn't think fast. I ran toward him, arms extended. "Calvin . . . darling," I cried with as much drama as I could muster, throwing myself lovingly into his arms. "Oh, Calvin. It's just so awful."

"What the—?"

"Just play along. I swear I'll explain everything," I whispered in his ear.

He stepped back, his expression teetering between fury and absolute bafflement. *Is this woman crazy?* was written all over his face. He held me at arm's length like you would a deranged cat clawing the air, and I was sure he'd give me up to save himself and it would be off to the big house for me. Convict number: 3478594. Cell block: 8.

"This is . . . Tiffany Lane. My, uh, girlfriend. She, uh, lives here." He didn't sound too convincing, but I hoped it would suffice.

The officer looked at me, then at Calvin. "What about the guy in the squad car?" he asked, hitching a thumb over his shoulder in the direction of Wayne. "Do you know him?"

Calvin stooped down a bit and looked through the car window. Wayne had his face pressed to the glass, like a confused puppy in a pet shop.

"That's the Hathaway fellow. He lives down the street. Harmless."

"Cut him loose, Joe," the cop called out to his partner in the car.

The officer uncuffed Wayne, who immediately leaped from the car, muttering a string of obscenities and something about his civil rights being violated.

The first officer, who'd been searching the premises, reappeared at the door. "No one else here," he reported. "The place is clean."

"Sorry for the confusion, ma'am."

They all mumbled their apologies with a warning that they would have to file a report of the "incident" and reminded me about the alarm. It was a necessary formality.

The crowd slowly began to disperse, disappointed that there had been no real action or gunfire, the cops pulled off, and by degrees my world returned to seminormal.

"Do you want to tell me what the hell is going on around here, Maggie? Why are you pretending to be Tiffany? Where is she?"

"She's away," Wayne offered, rubbing his sore wrists. "They cuffed me," he moaned. "They actually cuffed me."

"Away? Away where? How is it that you know Tiffany is away and I don't?" he demanded of Wayne.

"Do you always ask more than one question at a time?" I said, stomping off toward the kitchen. By this time, my head was throbbing. I wanted to be alone, to have time to sort things out. Everything seemed to be moving much too fast.

Both men trailed behind me, a longtime fantasy now turned nightmarishly true.

"What about Virginia?" Wayne asked. "Doesn't anyone care that she's out there all alone?"

"If you hadn't thrown her up in the air, she'd be here right now," I quickly reminded him.

"You threw her up in the air?" Calvin asked incredulously.

"When was the last time you looked down the barrel of a loaded gun?" Wayne tossed back in his own defense. "I had no intention of being a statistic."

Calvin pursed his lips and then turned to me. "Where is Tiffany?"

"She's out of town. I'm watching the house until she gets back."

"Well, you're doing one helluva job! Cops, gunplay, a missing dog."

"Listen." I pointed my finger at him. "I've had a really rough day. *A really rough day,*" I repeated, enunciating every word. "You have no idea." I whirled toward Wayne. "Starting with you. So both of you, back off!" I growled from between my teeth.

They jumped back and looked at me with something close to fear dancing in their eyes. I can only imagine what thoughts were running through their minds. I probably looked wild, manic, and capable of anything. There was a steely squint to my eyes. (That's the only way I could keep everything in focus until I retrieved my glasses). My hair was standing on top of my head, my shirt was torn, and I was still sporting a knot as if I'd been in a brutal battle. The thing was, whatever I'd had to face down over the past few hours, I'd survived. And they knew it. (So what if it had been only a rack of clothes and a temperamental dog?) I'd come out victorious, and they sensed my power.

"Have a seat," I instructed them. I walked into the bedroom and retrieved the box marked *X* and brought it to Calvin. "Tiffany said to give you this."

He looked at the box and then at me. "Did she say anything else?" he asked hopefully.

"No. Sorry," I added, feeling bad for him. Tiffany always did treat Calvin shabbily, although he seemed like a nice enough guy.

He pressed his lips together, stood, and tucked the box beneath his arm.

"I guess I'll be going, then," he said, resigned to the fact that his love was nowhere in sight. He still seemed stunned that she'd left town without telling him. Most men don't like being kept in the dark about things like that. For reasons of masculinity and control, they needed to keep tabs on their women. (Page 162 Training Manual.)

I walked him to the door.

"How long will you be staying here?" he asked suspiciously.

One of those tricky lawyer questions. He'd never get me to confess. "Until Tiffany gets back."

"But if there was an emergency, you would know how to reach her, wouldn't you?" He flashed me an engaging smile. Phony but slightly effective.

"Good-bye, Calvin."

He cinched his eyes together. "Why were you pretending to be Tiffany?"

I arched a brow and folded my hands beneath my bosom. "What would you have done under the circumstances?"

"Hmmm. You're pretty tough," he said. "I never noticed that before about you."

*I don't think you notice me at all.* "Thanks and good-bye. I really have a lot to do today, and I still have to find Virginia."

"I could—"

I closed the door in his face, locked it, and returned to the kitchen—where Wayne was still lamenting his false detainment.

"I think I have a case against them," he said the moment I entered the room. "Did you see how they handled me, as if I was some common criminal? You'd testify on my behalf, wouldn't you? You were a witness to the entire ordeal. I was assaulted, manhandled. Nobody treats me like that. Nobody!"

He was getting more worked up by the minute. What he needed to do was to redirect his energy, pull himself together, and get out of the apartment.

A passage in the workbook, the section on "Men in General" popped into my head. I smiled.

"Wayne, hon," I said, sweet as sugar. "I know this morning has been tough on you. It's been tough on all of us." I batted my eyes like Mae West would do in her old movies. "But what's really important is finding Virginia and getting her home safely." I stroked his arm. "I could use your help now. She adores you. You said so yourself."

Wayne peered at me. "Do you have something in your eye?"

"No! Now are you going to look for Virginia or not? You were the one who threw her up in the air in the first place."

He stood. "Fine. Blame it all on me." He walked sadly toward the door. "I'll be back."

Sigh. "I'm sure you will." I shut the door behind him.

# Collecting Evidence

*N*ow that I'd finally disposed of everyone, I possessed only one thought. I hurried back into the bedroom. Without Virginia's help, I was virtually on my own, but I knew I could do it. I had a brief moment imagining poor, helpless Virginia now in the clutches of some dastardly villain who steals well-trained poodles and puts them into service to fetch for liver-spotted old ladies. Oh, well. I shrugged. She was a savvy dog and would probably find her way back before Wayne did. With that in mind, I plowed forward, stepping into the wilderness, fighting through an arsenal of frills, frocks, deadly hangers, and falling hatboxes until I finally made it to the "door."

I gave the blank wall a withering stare, willing it to open. When that failed to work, I resorted to stomping, dancing, speaking in tongues, and belting out Luther Vandross ballads, when suddenly the door mysteriously opened with a sinister creak. In a flash one of Grandma's sayings popped into my head: *Once a fool, second time a fool twice.* With those words of wisdom dancing in my head, I quickly propped a shoe box in the doorway, ensuring my speedy escape.

My eyes darted like Ping-Pong balls around the dimly lit interior. I expected at any moment to be tapped on the shoulder with a cold, crooked finger and whisked away by the ghosts of Christmas past, my soul forever lost and tormented, doomed to wander the halls of Tiffany's town house for all time. They would write stories about my disappearance. I would become a legend. Mothers would tell the sad story to their daughters, and fathers would warn their sons. Sad, so very sad. But anyway, back to the search.

Humanlike silhouettes filled the room, casting long, spooky shadows on the floor. A chill ran up my leg. Where was Virginia when I needed her? I tiptoed farther into the room. The floor squeaked beneath my nimble steps—well, not exactly nimble. What I needed was some light. I peered into the darkness and noticed a stack of pocketbooks. There was always something of value to be found in a pocketbook. After rifling through three, I finally hit pay dirt—a mangled book of matches.

Through the flicking flame of my match unbelievable images materialized in front of me. I must be hallucinating, I thought, the events of the day finally taking their toll.

I stepped even farther into the room, and a scream more terrifying than any Stephen King movie rose from my throat when I bumped into something almost human. I went crashing to the ground, my fall cushioned by the body of something hard and plastic. It gave me a shiver, but what was more chilling—*perplexing* was a better word—was the bizarre treasure trove of ghetto-fabulous paraphernalia that filled the room from end to end. Slowly I stood and lit another match, holding it aloft.

Afro puffs, blond and platinum wigs, fake Nubian locks and cornrow wigs were perched on bodiless heads on a long table against the wall. Mega hoop earrings, hot pants, leather mini-skirts, fake gold bracelets, tube tops, and hooker heels adorned at least a dozen lifelike mannequins.

"What the—?"

Easing between the bodies, I took a closer look. What did it all mean? Why did Tiffany have these things and have them hidden away in a secret closet? Everything in the room represented all that she abhorred, turned her nose up at, shunned in public, and yet . . .

I was sure there was an explanation. I just didn't know what it was. And that's when I noticed a boom box. A boom box? Cautiously I pressed the PLAY button, expecting smooth jazz to filter through the speakers. Instead the booming, raucous beat of rapper DMX blasted into the room, startling me so soundly that I stumbled backward, knocking down a mannequin, which set off a chain reaction—in some circles, called the domino effect. In a wink, the mannequins were on the floor in various degrees of disassembly. Body parts were everywhere.

I needed to get the hell out of there before something else happened. Scrambling to my feet, I noticed what appeared to be a rack of videotapes. Videotapes! Ah-ha! I inched over to get a better look. They were three deep and ten across. They all said the same thing: DIVAS, INC. TRAINING VIDEO.

I knew deep in my soul that these tapes held the answers that I'd been seeking. I took three, turned off the CD player, and was about to make my escape when—

Smoke!

I smelled smoke. Frantically I looked around the room, uncertain if I should run for my life or find out what was burning and put it out—and quick. I could already imagine me trying to explain to Tiffany why her town house was nothing but a shell when she returned.

Crawling around between plastic hands and legs, sniffing the air like a well-trained hunting dog, I finally found the culprit, a smoldering platinum wig, which now sported black tips. I stomped it like a bug until all traces of smoke and what it once was had been obliterated beneath my feet. Breathing hard from exertion and mental duress, I gingerly picked up what was left of the wig, tucked the videos under my arm, and beat a hasty retreat.

Emerging from the darkness of the closet and into the hot pink of the bedroom gave me an instant migraine. I stumbled across the room and collapsed on the bed, facedown, and began laughing hysterically. What kind of double life did Tiffany live?

Slowly I rolled over, catching my breath, and clutched my possessions close to my chest. I still couldn't shake the weird images in the closet. My only conclusion was that the room was some sort of *intervention* room, a place where divas who have somehow fallen from grace were sent to give them a taste of what life could be like for them if they couldn't live up to expectations. Or maybe it was to divas what a bottle of booze was to an ex-alcoholic—a reminder to stay away from it. My head spun with possibilities. And I still hadn't found the handbook.

The doorbell rang.

Groaning, I pulled myself up and went to the door. This time I remembered to disconnect the alarm. One police incident per day was enough for me. I peeked through the peephole, and two big, black beady eyes stared back at me.

"Virginia!" I squealed, pulling open the door.

She leaped into my arms, as happy to see me as I was peculiarly happy to see her.

Wayne stepped in. "What about me? Don't I even get a hello, a 'Thank you, Wayne, for finding Virginia'?"

"Thanks," I gritted through my teeth.

"What happened to you? And is something burning? I smell smoke."

I rolled my eyes. "Nothing happened to me, and nothing's burning." *At least not anymore.* "Maybe it's the neighbor's burning lunch or something."

Wayne frowned. "Are you going to let me come in or what?"

"Why?"

"Because it would be the nice thing to do. Do you have any idea how many blocks I walked in the heat looking for Virginia? Can't you even offer me a glass of water?"

"How long have we known each other, Wayne?"

He shrugged and pursed his lips. "Since this morning."

"Do you know what eternity feels like, Wayne?"

"No, I don't."

"I do." I heaved a sigh and stepped aside. "Come in. I'll get you something to drink. And then we're leaving."

With Wayne settled in the living room, I returned to the bedroom to collect the evidence. I'd taken a shopping bag from the broom closet in the kitchen and filled it with the burned wig, the videotapes, the tattered red dress, and the books. I looked around—the bedroom was a mess. Shoe prints dotted the rug, the clothes were falling out of the closet, and the room did have the distinct smell of smoke. I opened a window, kicked the clothes in the closet, and shut the door. I'd have to come back and hunt for the handbook later along with the password so I could confirm my reservation for the soiree.

So much to do, so little time. Next stop, Chantel's place.

# Fancy Footwork

What's in the shopping bag?" Wayne asked, suspicion lacing every syllable.

"Things," I replied, holding the bag tighter. I double-stepped down the street with Wayne and Virginia hot on my heels. A raindrop popped me on the nose.

"Where are you going?"

I stopped dead in my tracks in the middle of the street and whirled toward him. "Don't you have someplace to go, something to do?"

"No."

I heaved a sigh. "Well, I do, and I'd prefer to do it without you."

Have you ever heard the expression, "His face dropped"? Well, that's exactly what happened to Wayne's face, and for a hot New York minute, I was almost sorry for being so hard on him. Almost. After all, he had found Virginia. "Look, Wayne, I have errands to run."

"Maybe I could help."

"Why, for heaven's sake?"

He shrugged slightly. "You interest me. I think you're quite fascinating."

Me? Fascinating? "Nice try, Wayne." I continued toward the corner and stuck my arm out to hail a cab. Several slowed, took one look at my disheveled appearance, and whizzed by.

Then it started to rain. I mean *really* rain. Of course. Why not?

"Do you have an umbrella in that bag of yours?"

"No, I don't," I murmured, looking upward at the darkening skies. And just when you thought things can't get any worse, they did just that. The skies opened up, and what was only moments ago a sprinkle turned into a monsoon.

"We need to get out of this," Wayne shouted over a blast of thunder.

I held my ground, determined to finish what I'd set out to do. I hadn't let the police, Calvin the irate boyfriend, the damned closet, or nearly losing Virginia beat me. I certainly could beat old Mother Nature. Geez, she'd been around since the beginning of time. What could she whip out that I couldn't handle?

The skies suddenly lit up like the Fourth of July as lightning streaked across the heavens followed by a blast of thunder that set off all the car alarms on the block.

Virginia yelped as if she'd been stabbed and started running around in circles, tying my legs together with her leash. I spun around in the opposite direction to disengage myself from the leash.

"Why have the gods forsaken me?" I screamed to the skies, only to be slapped across the face with a horizontal gush of rain.

Without a word, Wayne grabbed my hand and jogged with me, Virginia, and my shopping bag down the street to safety.

I resigned myself to whatever new calamity would befall me next. This was just the first day, I thought. I had five weeks and six days to go. How would I ever survive?

Upon reaching Wayne's place, I found a spot on the sofa, covered my face with my hands, and closed my eyes, wishing the horrific morning to disappear. When I opened my eyes, Wayne was staring at me from a footstool at the end of the couch. He handed me a thick, navy blue towel.

"Thanks." I wiped my face and hair.

"You should get out of those wet clothes before you catch a cold. I'm sure I have something you can put on until your things dry."

Take off my clothes? Yeah, right. Did I look like I was born yesterday? "I'm fine, thanks." I looked around. "Where's Virginia?"

"In the kitchen. I gave her something to eat."

My stomach growled.

"I can fix you something, too, if you like."

"Why are you being so nice to me?"

He smiled. "You've had a bad day."

"You think so?" I asked, sarcasm dripping from my lips.

"It's definitely at the top of the bad-day list," he said.

"Bad day! Ha! I laugh in the face of days far worse than this," I stated, exuding confidence. Although I couldn't think of one day in my entire lifetime that was worse than this one. Then I sneezed.

"You really should get out of those clothes," he suggested again.

"I'm fine, and I need to go." I stood. I sneezed again before I picked up my shopping bag and started for the door.

Wayne looked at me with a raised brow. "I couldn't help but notice the wig and the tapes in your bag," Wayne said, his ominous words halting me at the door.

Slowly I turned, and suddenly Wayne was no longer the nosy

do-good neighbor—he was Lieutenant Columbo, with wrinkled raincoat, squinty eye, and a ragged cigar hanging from the corner of his mouth.

I narrowed my eyes. "Do you always look in women's bags?" I asked as I looked him up and down.

"Sometimes," he said, throwing me off guard. "Especially bags like yours."

Hmmm. Well, he had me there. Think fast. I put my hand on my hip and circled him slowly. "Is that right? And so you took it upon yourself to investigate my belongings," I said, turning the tables on him.

"Forget it. I was just curious about the training videos and the wig. I thought maybe you were auditioning for something. That's all."

I looked at him in surprise. I hadn't thought of that one. "Well, actually I *am*."

His expression brightened. "Wow, that's exciting. Television, movies, or Broadway?"

I smiled. "All three."

He frowned. "How did you manage that?"

I was less sure now. "I have a wonderful agent."

"Oh." He looked confused for a moment. "Well, good luck."

"Thanks. Look, I really have to go."

"Sure."

He walked me to the door. "Here's an umbrella. It's still raining."

"I'll bring it back tomorrow."

"Don't worry about it. I have plenty."

Plenty? Who had plenty of umbrellas? Wayne was certainly a strange fellow.

"See you tomorrow," he called out as I trotted down the steps with Virginia in tow.

By some miracle, a cab finally stopped, and if there was any justice in the world, I would arrive at Chantel's without further incident.

But of course, in Margaretville, there is no justice. My ten-minute cab ride turned into a forty-minute trip through hell. Apparently there was a dragnet out for a convict who'd escaped from custody at the local precinct. The police had streets blocked off and were stopping cars at every intersection. Helicopters buzzed overhead with searchlights beaming down on the street.

Finally we arrived in front of Chantel's condo on Ninety-sixth Street. I practically crawled into her apartment. I was exhausted, damp, and sporting a major migraine. I took Virginia with me into the bedroom and collapsed across the bed. What a day.

I guess I must have dozed off—or fainted again. But when I woke up, it was nearly midnight. Groaning, I sat up and rubbed my eyes. I'd blown the entire evening, but I was too tired to go home and too tired to do any searching.

Tramping off toward the bathroom, I decided to take a long, hot bath and call it a night. I knew that Chantel was a fiend for lotions, creams, and bath paraphernalia, so I was certain I'd find something good-smelling and soothing in the bathroom.

I checked the cabinet beneath the sink and found an array of body wash, sea salts, bubble bath, and . . . a diary!

Now we were cooking with gas.

# You Won't
# Believe This

Gingerly, I lifted the copper-colored leather-bound book emblazoned with the letters, CHANTEL HOLLIS: MY DIARY. I held it in my hot little hands with glee. Darting back to the bedroom, bath forgotten, I was suddenly full of renewed energy.

"Look what I found, Virginia." I held up the book for her to see, sure that she would share my enthusiasm. She took one look, closed her eyes, and went back to sleep.

"Fine," I huffed.

I plopped down on the bed, and as you may have already guessed, this was not as easy as it appeared. The sucker had a lock on it the size of the Hope diamond. So I spent the next hour searching for the key in the jewelry box, the nightstand drawer, even in the ice trays in the freezer. (I remember seeing that one on a Court TV episode.) Nothing. But not to be daunted by something as minor as a lock without a key, I went to the kitchen in search of tools.

I checked the kitchen drawers beneath the sink, on top of the fridge, broom closet, coat closet—and nothing. Not a screwdriver, nail, hammer, a roll of Scotch tape, or even a spare lightbulb. It was painfully obvious that Chantel didn't lift a finger to do any more than get a manicure.

Momentarily baffled, I shook my head. How did she function from day to day? Returning to the bedroom, I sat down next to Virginia, who'd made herself at home between two overstuffed pillows on Chantel's canopy bed, and contemplated my next move. But I had to finally admit that exhaustion got the best of me. Tomorrow was another day. I hoped.

Resigned that my quest had come to a screeching halt, I opted for that long overdue bath. Hopefully an hour in the steamy, fragrant filled tub would relieve some of the bumps, bruises, and stiff limbs from my day of endless accidents.

By the time I emerged from the water, the bubbles had dissipated to a thin sheen of off-white film, the water bordered on chilly, and my hands and feet needed a shot of Botox. Grabbing a peach-colored towel, I wrapped it around my body and stepped into the bedroom.

We saw each other at the same time, instantly belting out simultaneous screams. Virginia howled in unison.

"Margaret! It's me."

I blinked, trying to focus without my glasses. "Willie?" I opened my mouth to scream again.

"Shh. Margaret," he whispered. "Margaret, don't scream. I can explain," he pleaded, holding up his hands, palms facing me. "Shh, please."

By degrees, my racing heart slowed to a sprint. Virginia leaped from the bed and into my arms, turned and barked once at the offending intruder, then buried her face in my heaving bosom.

"What the hell are you doing in here, Willie?" I hissed from between my chattering teeth.

"I followed you here from Tiffany's. What are you doing here? I thought you lived on the other side of town."

"I have . . . two places," I quickly lied, and saw the momentary gleam of appreciation in his eyes. "But that's beside the point. The real question is what in the hell are you following me for? We know *you* don't live here."

"I just needed some place to hide out until morning."

"Hide out? Hide out from who?" I almost didn't want to know.

"If you promise not to scream, I'll tell you," he said.

I stared into his beady eyes, trying to see the little Willie that I remembered from preschool. Not the burly man who'd turned up on Tiffany's doorstep dressed in a FedEx delivery uniform or the crazed madman who was in the middle of Chantel's bedroom, ready to kidnap me, hold me hostage in some undisclosed location, demanding millions of dollars for my safe return.

The television cameras would do a close-up of Grandma's pitiful tear-streaked face. "All I have is a hundred-dollar bill. Brand-new, but it's all I got," she would say. "But I'd give it to you in return for my granddaughter."

My mother would then step into the frame. Her face would be stern. And then she would launch into a string of cuss words and the camera would go to black.

Oh, Lawd, I'd never be rescued.

Breathing deeply, I took a cautious step backwards, easing toward the phone . . . just in case.

"You sit over there, where I can see you," I demanded, pointing to the lounge chair on the far side of the room. "And stretch out. All the way out."

"What?"

"You heard me. Stretch out, or I'll call the police." I figured if he was lying down, it would be pretty hard for him to pull any fancy moves.

"All right, all right." He stretched out on the lounge chair and looked to me for more directions.

"Now, put your hands under your butt."

"What!"

"You heard me." I made a move like I was reaching for the phone.

"Okay, okay."

He wiggled around until he had his hands securely fastened to his rear end. I almost smiled, wondering what else I could make him do.

I pulled up a chair from Chantel's vanity table and sat down, facing him. All I needed now was a bright light and a phone book, and I could make him talk.

"You ready to talk, or am I gonna have to call the police?" I asked.

"I said I would tell you everything. You don't need to call anyone. This is all a big mistake."

"That's what they all say. So spill it."

"Well, it's like this. . . ."


By the time he'd finished, my head was spinning. Twinkie Willie a professional thief, a cat burglar? Who would have thought it?

"The thing of it is, I'm not really a thief. I sort of relieve wealthy folks of the 'extra' stuff they have and give it to those who really need it."

"So, you're like a Robin Hood, huh?" I asked sarcastically.

His face lit up. "Exactly!"

I frowned. "But you still haven't explained why you followed me here."

"I think the police may be on to me. Or at least want to ask me a few questions. I saw a couple of cops at the FedEx depot at the end of my shift. It's probably nothing, but I didn't want to go home, just in case. I was hoping to just hang out until morning, and I swear I'll disappear."

"Is there a reward out for you or for whoever they think this thief is?"

"Fifty thousand dollars, last time I checked," he said, a ring of pride in his voice.

Oh, really? Fifty thousand dollars would certainly make my life easier. "Fifty thousand, huh?"

His eyes widened with alarm—he could surely see the wheels turning in my head. "Listen, Margaret, please don't turn me in. I've never hurt a soul. I swear I haven't. I just slip in, take what I need, and slip out."

I cocked my head to the side. "How *did* you get in here?"

"I jimmied the lock. I have tools."

Tools, hmmm?

"Okay, look. For old times' sake, you do me a favor, and I'll do you one. I won't call the cops."

"You name it."

I stood and picked up the diary from the bed. "Can you get this off without damaging it, without making it look like it's been touched?"

He looked it over from his supine position. "Piece of cake."

My heart pounded with excitement.

"I left my tool bag by the door."

"Okay, you can get up. But don't try anything funny."

I followed a few paces behind him to retrieve his bag; then we returned back to the bedroom.

Willie whipped open his tool case, and I'd swear the lineup of instruments looked like bizarre surgical equipment. I was sure there was something in his bag of tricks that would get through the lock.

He wiggled a few instruments in the lock. "This says it belongs to Chantel Hollis," he commented as he twisted a thin scalpel-like thing in the opening. He looked up at me. "*Chantie* Chantel?" he asked.

My pulse raced just a little. "Yes."

"Why are *you* opening it? And if this is your place, why is her diary here?"

"You ask a lot of questions for someone who's potentially on the run from the cops. You want me to call the police, or do you want to open the diary? Your choice."

"Gotcha." He went back to work, and moments later the lock popped open with a soft click. "Here ya go." He proudly handed it to me. "Told you it would be a piece of cake."

Reverently I took the treasure from his hands, walked across the room, and sat down on the bed, eager to dig in. I opened the first page.

"What's in there?" Willie asked, stepping around to look over my shoulder.

I shut the book with a thud.

"None of your business." I looked him up and down. "You know, you ask an awful lot of questions."

"Sorry," he said sheepishly.

I moved to a safe distance. Willie sat on the side of the bed and stared at me. It was obvious that I was not going to be able to read the diary with Willie staring me in the face. I put the book down and folded my arms. "Can I ask you a question?"

"Sure," he said.

"How did you ever get involved in this, anyway?"

"Sort of by accident, actually. I'd been driving for Federal Express for about three years, and some of the stuff I saw in these homes just turned my stomach when I went back to the old neighborhood and watched folks live from hand to mouth. So I took a couple of courses."

"In breaking and entering?" I asked incredulously, wondering what reputable college offered a B.A. in burglary.

"No. Locksmith. I'm licensed."

"Did they give you those tools as a graduation gift?"

He chuckled. "No. I picked them up along the way."

"What kinda stuff do you take?"

"Televisions, radios, clothes, jewelry, silver—things like that," he said, as if he were running off a grocery list.

"So how do you get rid of the stuff? A fence?" I asked.

"Friends," he said. "The less you know, the better."

"Just how long were you planning to stay here?" I asked.

"Just until daybreak."

"Well, you certainly can't stay in here with me."

"I'll sleep in the living room."

"Fine. Go. Good night."

He looked at me for a long moment. "Thanks, Margaret. I really appreciate you not turning me in."

"Good night."

He turned and walked out, closing the bedroom door softly behind him.

I walked to the door and locked it; then for good measure, I stuck a chair beneath the knob. After all, he was a skilled burglar.

Now that I had the privacy I needed, I borrowed one of Chantel's nightgowns and slipped between the cool sheets and set the alarm for 6 a.m.

Propping myself up on pillows, I opened the diary and started to read.

The next thing I knew, the alarm was blaring and Virginia was licking my face. With great effort, I opened my eyes, looked around, and for a moment was totally disoriented. Then in bits and pieces, the events of the previous day came rushing back. Who would believe it? I thought.

As I sat up, the diary fell from the bed to the floor. I hadn't gotten past the first page.

I got up, and every bone in my body creaked as I picked up the diary and padded off to the bathroom. Then I remembered—Willie.

Pulling the chair from the door, I unlocked it and tiptoed down the hall to the living room.

"Willie," I called out. Silence. I went to check the kitchen. Empty. Then I noticed a note on the table.

Dear Margaret,

Thanks for everything. By the way, I reset your alarm on the way out. You have to be careful these days—there are some pretty unscrupulous people out there. Take care.

*W.*

P.S. You looked really great in that towel.

Me? Great in a towel? Humph. Only Twinkie Willie would say something like that, and I wondered if he remembered that fateful day in kindergarten as clearly as I did. Probably not.

Virginia whimpered at my feet. (My cue for the morning stroll.) I threw on my outfit—what was left of it—and headed outside.

While Virginia did her doggy thing, I mulled over my options for getting to work on time and wondered if Willie had made a clean getaway or if he'd be ducking behind a raincoat on the eleven o'clock news.

I caught my reflection in a store window and was horrified by my appearance. I looked like a survivor of a rock concert gone bad. How could I go to work like this? I certainly didn't have time to go home and change and then get Virginia back to Tiffany's before heading to the office. Mr. Fields, my boss and associate publisher, was what my grandmother called "a real pain in the ass." To be honest, everyone on staff thought the same thing but was too terrified of him to say anything—myself included. The last thing I wanted on a Monday morning was to get to my desk late, looking like a refugee to boot and spend the better part of the morning being browbeaten by Mr. Fields. I'd taken enough abuse in the past forty-eight hours. Hmmm. This was what was called in some circles a conundrum.

I was pretty sure Chantel would never know that I borrowed an outfit for the day, and I could leave Virginia until I got back. No big deal. "What difference does it make where you stay for the day, right? After all, you're still just a dog."

Virginia, still in search of utopia, trotted down the street, pulling me dutifully along behind her. She finally came to a stop near a tree. I turned my head to give her some privacy. There was one high point. I had the diary, and the minute I had some free time at the office, I was going to dive right in.

As I imagined the wondrous treasure trove of information I would glean from the pages, something warm and liquid splashed across my feet. I leaped back. Too late. I'd been doused.

I looked down, and Virginia glanced up at me with what almost looked like a gleam in her eyes and trotted down the street.

Humiliated, I walked five paces behind her, and if I didn't know better, I'd swear she was laughing.

# Just Another Day
# at the Office

*B*efore I entered Chantel's building, I took off my wet shoes and dumped them in the trash can, then proceeded barefoot up the concrete steps to the front door. Now I needed to add shoes to my list of must-have items. I looked down at Virginia and bared my teeth. She ignored me and proceeded to march off to the bedroom.

It was nearly eight o'clock. I took a quick shower and prayed that when I got out, I wouldn't have any more drop-in guests. When I emerged, I took a good look around just to be sure before going in search of an outfit. Confident that I was alone—except for you know who—I slid back the doors of Chantel's closet.

There was a Versace suit that I'd been salivating over for months. I knew I could never afford the real thing, and the knockoffs looked just like that—knockoffs. I figured I'd have to be content imagining myself in the aqua blue two-piece number spiced up with some high-tech fabric that shimmered when it hit the light just so. Until today. I pushed aside a fire-engine red dress, and there it was.

With reverence, I took it from the closet, hurried over to the full-length mirror, and held it in front of me. The reflection that stared back at me was a woman who was brick-house shapely, flawlessly coiffed, makeup perfected with a wicked knowing smile dancing on her lips.

Thankfully, Grandma always told me to wash out my undies at night, which I'd done. Unfortunately, they were still a bit damp, but they'd have to do. I unwrapped the towel, slipped into my bra and panties, took the jacket from the hanger and then the skirt.

I wiggled, I inhaled and exhaled, I meditated and then resorted to prayer before the skirt fought me tooth and nail on its way up and across my behind and hips. Sweating from exertion, I put on the jacket and tried to zip the skirt.

Now every woman knows that if you hold your breath and put the waistband just above the waistline, you can generally squeeze into a skirt at least one size smaller than your norm, two if you're agile and lucky. Well, I held my breath so long, I became faint. White dots danced in front of my eyes, and I felt the room begin to sway until a tearing noise snapped me out of it.

Startled, I twisted around to see the damage. The entire right side seam of the skirt had ripped completely open, while I simultaneously ripped the underarm seam of the jacket on the left side.

Chantel's feigned cultured voice rang in my head: "I paid fifteen hundred dollars for this suit," she'd boasted one Friday night. I'd almost chocked on my clam chowder. "Don't you just love it?"

"You're kidding," Tiffany had said with wide-eyed wonder. "That's a steal." She turned to me. "Don't you agree, Maggie?"

All I could do was nod.

Now look at it, I thought, staring with horror at the damage I'd caused. What was I going to do?

First things first, I decided. Hide the evidence. I'd have to worry about it later. What was most pressing at the moment was finding something to put on and getting to work.

I quickly disposed of Exhibit A in my trusty shopping bag. At this rate, I thought, heading back to the closet, I'd need a steamer trunk before it was all over. Deftly rifling through the row of clothing, I noticed another row in the back. I pushed aside a Halston original, and lo and behold, an entire rack of girdles—and body shapers!

Let me just say this: There were girdles and body shapers in every style and color known to women—zip up, button up, slip on, see through, long line, short line, leather, bejeweled. You name it, and she had it. It was a get-in-shape jamboree! No wonder Chantel always looked so perfect, not a lump, bump, or bulge. She had help. There had to be one of those bad boys in there that was perfect for *moi!* I ran my hand along the rack and finally selected something basic but with the control I felt I needed.

It was a struggle, but when I stood before the mirror, I was amazed at what I saw. My 36Bs were amplified to cup-runneth-over proportions. My never-before waist magically appeared tapered and tucked, my stomach was ripple-free and smoothed out, and my hips flaring and daring. In other words, I was b-a-d. I couldn't stop grinning. As an added plus, this little number had garters. No ninety-nine-cents-corner-store pantyhose today. I was going to slip into some real live stockings.

Pulling open Chantel's top dresser drawer, all lined up in a row were silk stockings in a variety of shades and textures. I selected a pair of off black and couldn't believe how delicious silk felt sliding up my legs. Feeling daring and suddenly sexy, I didn't simply walk; I strutted, with attitude, back to the closet, confident that any outfit I selected would be happy to drape itself over this new and improved *bodilicious*.

I selected a baby blue jersey knit dress that fastened with tiny white buttons from cleavage to just above my knees. I took another peek in the mirror. I looked good. But my hair was scary, so I resorted to an old trick my grandmother taught me as a child. I wet my hair, found some gel (it would have been hair grease or Vaseline back in the day), slicked my hair back to the nape of my neck, and fastened it with a pearl-studded barrette from Chantel's accessory tray. Then I put my size nines in a pair of navy blue size eight and a half pumps. All the while that my feet screamed and protested, I convinced myself that once I got to work and at my desk, I would take them off.

Grabbing my everyday bag, keys, and shopping bag with the evidence, I headed for the front door, with Virginia hot on my heels.

"Look Virginia, I know this isn't your place," I said, bending down and looking her in the eyes, "but keep it nice until I get back. Okay?"

She stuck her nose up in the air, just like Tiffany, and walked away. Now there's nothing worse than a dog with an attitude.

I set the alarm, sniffed the air for smoke, and shut the door behind me.

Fortunately, I was still in the upper-crust vicinity, and catching a cab was pretty much a snap. I was downtown in twenty minutes and sitting at my desk when Mr. Fields walked in.

He muttered something under his breath at my greeting then

told me to have Margaret come into his office when she decided to show up for work.

He was kidding, right? For a moment I sat there, a bit perplexed. I knew that Mr. Fields didn't pay me much attention unless there was a deadline, an emergency, or if I'd done something wrong. But I did think he knew who I was. Perhaps he was just being his usual obnoxious self. I decided to just go see what he could possibly want at 9:06 a.m.

"Mr. Fields, you wanted to see me?" I asked as I stood in his doorway.

He glanced up over the morning edition of *The New York Times,* returned to what he was reading, then looked up again. He frowned and then put on his glasses. "Margaret?"

"Yes, Mr. Fields."

Slowly he put down the newspaper, and I could feel his eyes roll up and down my body, up and down, up and down, until mercifully, his gaze settled on my face.

I wanted to snap my fingers and yank him back to reality. I saw his Adam's apple working overtime in his throat. "Was there something that you needed, sir?" I lifted my chin just a bit, and I'd swear I saw a line of perspiration break out across his hairline. Deliberately I let a subtle smile ease across my mouth.

"Uh. No. Never mind." He swallowed hard. "You can, uh, go back to your desk."

"Yes, sir." I started to leave.

"Uh . . . Margaret . . ."

"Yes, sir?"

"New hairdo?"

"Something like that, sir."

"Hm. Very nice, very nice."

"Thanks." I turned and left. By the time I reached my desk, my knees were knocking, my toes were throbbing, and my heart was racing—but something else was happening to me, as well. I felt a rush, a surge of electric energy. I felt totally female, full of feminine powers I never knew I had. I recognized it in Mr. Fields's eyes and the way he looked at me, not through me. I had it, too!

I sat down at my desk and smiled. Maybe it was the silk stockings or the girdle or the dress or all three, but there was definitely something to the old saying, "clothes make the man." Well, they make the woman too. Yeah, there was definitely something to it. But just to be sure, I figured I'd try it out around the office. Taking a stack of folders so that it would look as if I were doing something more than simply walking around aimlessly, I began my stroll down the corridor en route to the employee cafeteria.

Thankfully, the hallway was carpeted—because as you may have guessed, my feet were in an all-out state of revolt. The bottoms of my soles burned as if I'd been walking on hot coals, which kind of gave my walk a pretty neat salsa flair—short, fast steps with a little swivel in my hips to keep my balance. If you can put that all together in your head, you'll get the picture.

Anyway, I kept going down the corridor. No one approached me directly or asked the silly questions they usually asked me. For the most part, I got quite a few curious looks in my direction, as if they couldn't believe what they were seeing, several comments about my banging outfit, a few whispers, or, like Mr. Fields, they didn't know who the hell I was.

"What did you do to yourself?"

I turned toward the sound of the familiar voice and put on my best hot-mama smile, expecting to be greeted with wide-eyed admiration.

"Good morning, Lawrence," I cooed, trying to ignore his appalled expression.

He pushed his mail cart closer and stopped about a foot away. "It *is* you," he murmured, and not pleasantly.

I pursed my lips and remembered something my grandmother always swore by: "If you don't have nothing good to say, get it off your chest anyhow." I propped my hand on my hip and rolled my neck one good time. "What's that supposed to mean?"

"Just that you don't look like yourself or walk like yourself."

"Are you saying there's something wrong with the way I look and the way I walk?"

He frowned, then shook his head. "Sort of. Hey, forget it. What do I know?"

I tugged in a deep breath, swore I wouldn't cry, then stuck out my chest and my upswept boobs. I cocked my head to the side and gave him a long up-and-down look. "You're right about that. What do you know?" With that, I spun on my heels, rocked unsteadily for a moment, and turned down the first available corner.

My vision blurred from withheld tears. If I could only make it to the ladies' room, I could pull myself together before having to face the gauntlet of onlookers as I returned to my desk. But just as I approached the ladies'-room door . . .

"Margaret? Is that you?"

I sniffed and blinked rapidly to clear my vision. Beverly. Inwardly I groaned. "Hi," I murmured.

"You look . . . different," she muttered. "Nice outfit. Get it on sale?"

"Thanks, and no, I didn't get it on sale. It's an original."

Her brows rose in surprise. "Well . . . I didn't mean anything. It's just that—"

"I know what you meant. Excuse me." I sashayed past her and continued down the hall. The only thing on my mind was getting to my desk. I didn't need to have Beverly telling everyone within hearing distance any calamity that might befall me in the ladies' room.

By some miracle, I managed to get back to my desk without being waylaid any further. The instant I sat down, I tried to take my shoes off. At first, I couldn't. My feet were so swollen, they were wedged in. I looked down, and I'd swear I heard them singing, *"Let my people go."*

The intercom buzzed.

"Yes, Mr. Fields," I answered, wincing over every word.

"Come in. I want to discuss this last reader's report you submitted."

Groaning, I pushed myself up from my seat and hobbled toward his office. But just as I reached his door, a dictum from one of the books ran through my head. *A true Diva never lets them see her sweat.*

I straightened my spine, smoothed my dress, patted down my hair, took a deep breath, and knocked.

"Come in."

"You wanted to see me," I said.

"Have a seat."

*Amen.*

For several moments, he simply stared at me.

"Is there something wrong, Mr. Fields?"

He shook his head as if waking from a dream. "Uh, no. I wanted to see you about—"

I tilted my head to the side and smiled sweetly. "Yes?"

"You did a wonderful job on this report," he said.

Say what? I'd been working at University Press for eight years. And never once had Mr. Fields said anything remotely nice, least of all to me. "Um, thank you."

"You know, Margaret, we've never really had a chance to talk. I know nothing about you."

Uh-oh. I shifted in my seat. "I'm not sure what you mean, sir."

He leaned forward. "I was thinking that perhaps we could . . . say . . . have lunch one day."

"Lunch? You and me?"

"Yes, talk about where you want to go in the company, things like that. How does that sound?"

What would Tiffany or Chantel do? I wondered. "I'm sure it will be fine."

"Good." He shuffled some papers around on his desk then looked across at me. "That's all." He smiled, and went back to reading.

Gingerly I stood and got out of there as quick as my swollen feet would take me. Back at my desk, I wiggled out of those shoes, and my eyes rolled to the back of my head as each little toe hollered, *"Hallelujah!"*

Once the throbbing subsided to a dull ache, I turned on my computer, dug in my shopping bag, and pulled out Chantel's diary. I stuck it inside a bound galley that I had to read and flipped open to the first page.

# Mondays Should
# Be Abolished

*Dear Diary . . .*
      "Meez Margareet, is that you?"
      I glanced up. It was Maribel, the mother hen of the
custodial staff. This could take a while. Maribel was renowned for
her ear-numbing dissertations on the state of everyone's lives. She
had a remedy for anything that ailed you, real or imagined.
      "Morning, Maribel. How was your weekend?"
      "Very nice, and yours?"
      "You really don't want to know."
      She laughed. "You are so funny, Meez Margareet. You move for
a minute. I get under your desk with the vacuum."
      I did as I was ordered and stopped cold when she let out a cry. I
thought she'd seen a mouse.

"Your feet." She stared at them with a mixture of concern and amazement. "What happened?"

"It's a long story." I tried to tuck them back under the desk, but she wasn't having it. She swung my chair around until the two throbbing puffs that were now my feet faced her.

"Oh, dis eez not good. Not good." She shook her head sadly. "Something bit your feet?" she asked, bending down to get a better look.

"No. Nothing that exotic. My shoes were a little too tight."

She made a clucking noise with her tongue. "I fix you right up," she said, standing, and then hurried away.

Oh geez, this was going to take even longer than I thought. But the truth of the matter was, there was no way I was getting back in those shoes. And it would be pretty hard to explain why I was walking around barefoot all day. Sigh.

Moments later, Maribel returned with a bucket from the supply room and a pitcher of ice from the employee lounge. "I have just the thing. We had to soak *mi madre*'s feet every night when she come home from working at the hospital." She put the bucket under my desk, dumped the pitcher of ice in it, reached in her smock pocket, and pulled out a small box of Epsom salts.

"Do you always carry around Epsom salts?" I asked, amazed.

"Of course. Don't you?"

I didn't bother to answer.

"I keep a box in the supply cabinet. It's good for everything."

She stirred the concoction around for a few minutes and then instructed me to stick my feet in the bucket.

I did as I was told and nearly leaped out of my chair when my burning feet hit the ice. By degrees, the shock slowly wore off and a numbing chill spread slowly up my legs.

"Keep your feet in there until ice melts. The salt will do the rest." She bobbed her head with authority. "I'll be back to check," she said, wagging a finger at me.

Well, since I couldn't very well get up and track water all over the freshly vacuumed floor, I returned my attention to the diary.

The first few pages were mostly Chantel's ramblings about how she had to wait on line for twenty minutes at the bank even though she had a VIP account. (Big deal.) Then she went on and on about a new suit that she just had to have. (Boring). I skipped a few pages, hoping to find something of interest. I thought my quest was hopeless until I saw a page dated six months earlier.

*Dear Diary,*

*I really had no idea the club would be so thrilling. I have to admit, I was terrified at first. All the men were thugs. The kind you see on street corners, on videos, and leaning on expensive cars shouting out lewd remarks to every woman who passes by. Tiffany let me borrow one of her outfits from her secret closet so that no one would recognize us. Part of our indoctrination into the Corporation was to periodically immerse ourselves in the lives of the less suitable to ensure that we would never accidentally slip and fall into mediocrity. Tiffany had a knack for finding some of the most outrageous dives. I always wondered how she found them, but she's never told me.*

*I was totally fascinated. It's amazing how the other half lives— anything goes. I felt out of my element when I went to the bar and asked for a white wine and the bartender looked at me as if I had two heads. He told me all that he served was beer and mixed drinks. Can you imagine that? Tiffany didn't seem to mind. When I looked around, she was all cuddled up with someone who looked like he could murder his own mother. I was appalled. I wanted to leave. But I didn't want to seem like a drip, and I certainly didn't want Tiffany to spread the word about me to the other Sisters, so I struck a pose like some of the other women in the place, and before I knew what happened, this guy grabbed my hand and pulled me onto the dance floor. The name Duke was stitched on his shirt. I tried to get away, but the floor was so packed with sweaty, writhing bodies that I was pressed against him. All the way against him—if you know what I mean. I tried to pretend that I wasn't getting turned on, but I was. I really was. I felt so decadent—so scandalous. The music changed, the crowd thinned, he let me go and disappeared into the crowd without saying a word. How rude! I spent the rest of the night looking for him, to give him a piece of my mind, but he was nowhere to be found. I dreamed of him, and for the next few days I kept looking for him on the street. I couldn't seem to get Duke out of my mind. I wanted to tell Tiffany about my fantasy, but I couldn't. A guy like Duke was totally unacceptable. It goes against all the Diva rules. "We need to see how the other half lives," Tiffany would say, "but we don't want to be a part of it." She swears that she'd never be caught dead with one of "them."*

*But one night when she pleaded a headache, I decided to go back to the club to see if I could find Duke myself, and who did I see all hugged up but Tiffany and Duke! She never saw me. And I never told her. That will be my little secret. One of these days I may get to use it.*

And now it was *my* little secret. Who would ever think that Ms. Manners would have a thing with a "common" man? I flipped a few more pages.

*Dear Diary,*

*I finally met the Grand Diva herself! She was old. Can you believe it? Old enough to be my grandmother, for heaven's sake. But everyone was bowing and scraping like she was royalty. It was true that she did have that certain something that made you stand up and take notice. But her hair was gray. Didn't she ever hear of Miss Clairol? But that didn't seem to matter to anyone. They all sat at*

*her feet like good servants, listening to her outrageous stories of con-*
*quest—from jobs to men. "There are only a select few of the female*
*species who are born Divas, endowed with the aptitude to breeze*
*through life on the backs and toes of others," she'd said, and the*
*women nodded and murmured in approval. "Using nothing more*
*than charm, her looks, and attitude, a true Diva has the power to*
*make others believe whatever she wants them to believe." She then*
*started on an incredible story about how she met her first of four hus-*
*bands. I stopped listening. It was just so hard for me to swallow*
*that this old woman was the brains behind the entire operation. But*
*I suppose anything is possible. I wonder what she would say if I*
*slipped her a note about Tiffany and Duke.*

It seemed that Ms. Chantel had a naughty streak beneath her
carefully crafted facade. I'd have to keep that in mind. I flipped a
few more pages.

*Dear Diary,*
 *It's too bad that we will miss the soiree this year. Last year was*
*fabulous and well worth all the money I spent on clothes and*
*makeup. Everyone who is anyone was there, even the ones who had*
*that musical show named after them. You had to have a special invi-*
*tation to attend and a password. I felt honored to have received mine.*
*This year Tiffany wanted to go to Europe instead. She convinced me*
*that the men in Europe were much more exciting than American men,*
*and she'd heard that there were some great clubs that we could visit.*
*I can't wait. Perhaps I will find a European version of Duke. . . .*

Nothing else was of major interest other than some references
to her job and the women who hated her. The list was long and
lengthy. I flipped to the end and was just about to close it when

my eyes landed on one word written in small block letters on the last page of the diary: MARGARET.

Margaret? Why would Chantel have my name in her diary? Was it a note to remind me to do something? Just jotting down my name for the heck of it or . . .

I swung my chair around to face my computer, fired up the Internet, and typed in *www.divalicious.com.* When it prompted me for a password, I typed *Margaret.* I held my breath. After a few buzzes, screen changes, and advertisements for push-up bras, the Divas, Inc., homepage opened.

I was in!

# Tools of
# the Trade

*I* was so excited, my hands were shaking—or maybe it was because of the icy water. In any case, I was thrilled. The homepage was very simple but elegant, in soothing colors of mint and salmon. Smack in the center of the page was a black-and-white silhouette of a woman with a wide-brimmed hat that dipped down and covered her right eye, putting the rest of her face in a shadow. Beneath the image were the words GRAND DIVA. I tried to get a better look. There was an air of familiarity, but I just couldn't place it. Oh, well.

On the left was a long line of links. I clicked on the photo gallery page, and what emerged were photographs of fabulous parties, what looked like women's conferences, and dinner parties all populated by incredible-looking women and even more incredible men. Not that their physical looks were showstoppers, but their body language and attitude made them appear outstanding. I caught glimpses of Tiffany and Chantel in several of the shots, looking as if they were having the time of their lives.

I then clicked on the BIOS link, and there was a list in alphabetical order of apparently all the Divas registered with Divas, Inc. They were women from all over the world, in every profession. There were so many names that I recognized, from radio personalities to television and movie stars, singers, magazine editors—the list was endless. It included the dates that they were admitted, and there was also a list of who'd been banned, with strict instructions on not associating with these fallen women or risk the consequences.

That was all very interesting, but what I was really hunting for was information on the soiree. I scrolled down and found the link SOIREE 2004. I clicked, and it immediately asked for my diva registration number. Diva registration number? Can't a girl get a break? Where was I supposed to find that? I stared at the screen for several moments, trying to will it to let me in with my mind. Nothing. Zip. Apparently my psychic powers had been numbed by the ice water.

Maybe there was something in the diary that I'd missed. I flipped the book back open.

"Why are your teeth chattering?" Larry asked, dropping a bundle of mail in my in-box.

I glanced up. Maybe that was what was causing my headache. "The air-conditioning must be on too high," I chattered.

"You're shaking all over. Are you ill?"

"No. I'm fine. Really."

He looked at me suspiciously. "You've been acting odd all morning. First the outfit, then the attitude, and now this. You're probably coming down with something. Maybe I should go and get Maribel. She knows everything."

"No!" I squawked. "I mean, no. That's fine. I'm fine. Forget it."

"Hey, listen." He stepped a bit closer. "About this morning—"

I tried to look up at him, but my neck kept bobbing like one of those car toys that you set on your dashboard. So I opted for looking up with my eyes only.

"I was kind of hard on you this morning. That was out of line." He shrugged a little bit. "To be truthful, you look . . . really nice today, Margaret. I guess I was just surprised. You know."

"No, I don't know. Not really."

"Hey, forget it. It's not important. Anyway, I'm sorry, okay?"

"Sure, Larry."

"Are we still on for lunch?"

"I'll try to make it. I'm kinda underwater here with work."

"Okay. I'll save a seat for you, just in case."

"Thanks." I watched him as he pushed his mail cart down the hallway, and even though he did simultaneously insult and dismiss me, I couldn't avoid taking my daily assessment of his buns.

Finally he turned the corner and was out of hindsight—I mean *eyesight*. A shiver ran like a bolt of lighting up my body. I didn't care what Maribel said. I couldn't stand it any longer. I was sure I would catch pneumonia. Just as I was about to take my feet out of the frozen depths, Maribel came around the corner.

"How you feel, Meez Margareet?" She came behind my desk and looked down into the bucket.

"I am freezing, Maribel. I think my feet may have actually fallen off by now."

She waved her hand and laughed. "You are so funny, Meez Margareet. Come, take them out and let's see."

My legs felt like cement sticks, and I had to use my hands to lift them up and out of the bucket.

She smiled proudly. "Oh, Meez Margareet, your feet are back to normal."

I glanced down, and sure enough, they were back to normal all right, except that I could barely move them. They were as stiff as plywood. I tried to stand but quickly changed my mind. I couldn't feel my toes.

"It will be all right, Meez Margareet. Just give them some time to thaw out. Try to walk, Meez Margareet. You need to get the circulation going. You know."

I rolled my eyes. Gingerly I pushed myself up from my seat. Maribel put her arm around my waist until I was upright.

"Can you walk now?"

I took one step then two and imagined how some Chinese women must have felt to have their feet bound and able to take only itty-bitty steps. Maribel helped me walk around my desk about three times until I could finally feel some sensation in the bottoms of my feet.

My intercom rang.

I hobbled over to the phone. "Yes, Mr. Fields?"

"I'm waiting on your reader's report for the *Flight of Insects in the Sahara*."

"Yes, Mr. Fields." But he'd already clicked off.

"Well, I go now," Maribel said. "I come back later to check on you."

"No thanks, Maribel. I'll be fine."

She waved her hand and laughed again. "Oh, Meez Margareet, you are so funny." She chuckled all the way down the hall.

I failed to see the humor. My life was in some sort of downward spiral.

The intercom buzzed again.

"Yes, Mr. Fields?"

"I'm waiting." Click.

Grrrr. What happened to the man who seemed hot for me only hours ago? I looked down at my feet and wondered how much time I would get for murder if I pleaded insanity. I could already hear the news reports: *Mild-mannered book editor cracks and kills custodian after bizarre foot incident. Cults may be involved. Details at eleven.* They'd probably trot out Wayne as a star witness who would testify that I was prone to sudden spasms and that perhaps they'd gotten to be too much for me and I snapped.

I opened my file drawer next to my desk and pulled out the manuscript in question. Boring with a capital *B*. Turning to my computer, I found the evaluation, printed out a copy, and attached it to the manuscript. I stood, ready to walk into Mr. Fields's office, when I realized I didn't have on any shoes.

I stared at the cursed shoes. Well, I wouldn't be intimidated by a pair of Manolo Blahniks. Boldly I shoved in one foot and then the other and went to Mr. Fields's office.

Taking a deep breath and straightening my spine, I knocked.

"Come in," said the spider to the fly.

"Here is the report, Mr. Fields," I said, inching across the carpeted floor.

Mr. Fields, always the eagle-eye, watched my every move. I was certain he was going to ask me why I was walking that way. I handed him the evaluation and the manuscript with my notes.

"Are you all right?" he asked.

"Just fine, sir." My eyes roamed the room, looking at everything but him. "If there's nothing else, I'll be getting back to my desk." I made a move to leave.

"Just a minute, Margaret."

"Yes, Mr. Fields."

"About this morning . . . I . . . um, hope you didn't take what I said the wrong way."

"Which way should I have taken it, Mr. Fields?" I asked in a moment of bravado borne of the unnatural turn of events in my life. I folded my arms defiantly and titled my head to a "come on with it" angle.

His tawny complexion darkened with embarrassment or outrage at my presumptuousness—I didn't know which. And I didn't care. I figured everything that could possibly happen to me in the span of a few hours already had, and getting fired would simply end my misery. I should have been so lucky.

Mr. Fields suddenly made a jerky move to adjust his tie as if he was having a hard time breathing. His eyes began to bulge, and he grabbed his chest seconds before collapsing across his desk.

As I watched the paramedics wheel Mr. Fields out of the office, a moment of manic hysteria swept through me, and I began to laugh uncontrollably. Perhaps this was all some bizarre dream, an episode of *The X Files,* and any moment I would wake up and everything would be fine.

Heads peeked out of every doorway, their curious looks inspired by my laughter. Out of nowhere, Maribel appeared and gave me one good smack. My head did a complete 360. And I swear to you, I saw stars.

"You feel better now, Meez Margareet. *Mi madre,* God bless her soul, she get hissterical, too. A good smack works every time." She smiled brightly. I saw two of her.

"Thank you, Maribel," I whispered.

I glanced around at the onlookers. What were they thinking? Did they believe that I had something to do with what happened to Mr. Fields? That now with him out of the way, I could soar to power and cast out all those who'd slighted me? Hmmm. Sure, I'd wished him a slow and painful death on many occasions, but I never really meant it. I swear I didn't. "Be careful what you wish for," Grandma always said. " 'Cause what you ask for is never what you get nohow. There's always a twist to it." I had to agree with her on that one.

In a daze, I shuffled back to my desk and spent the rest of the afternoon explaining what I thought was so funny and then what happened to Mr. Fields.

If this was indicative of what the rest of my week would be like, they were going to have to have me committed.

"It's just awful about Mr. Fields," Beverly said, sidling up to my desk once the crowds had dispersed.

I barely glanced up. "Tragic."

"You seemed to take it pretty hard."

"Did I?" She missed my sarcastic tone.

"What did the EMS folks say?"

"Not much. They were pretty busy, if you know what I mean."

"So who's going to run the office?"

"I have no idea." And even if I did, I would never tell Beverly.

"I guess you don't know much more than I do," she said, smiling.

*That's what you think.* "Listen, Bev, I'd love to chat, but I have a ton of work to do."

She waved her hand just like Maribel. "Margaret you are too funny. Who works when the boss is away?" She chuckled as if she'd just heard the best joke and sashayed down the corridor.

Beverly did have a point, I thought as I watched her until she turned the bend. There was no telling when or if poor Mr. Fields would return. And the show must go on. Bolstered by that thought, I pulled out the diary. If the registration number was in there, I was going to find it.

As I scanned the pages, I realized that the girdle was no longer cutting off my circulation. I could actually breathe without fear of bursting open or cracking a rib. I smiled triumphantly. It was a small victory, but it was mine, damn it. Things were finally looking up, at least for the moment. But of course, the day wasn't over yet.

# Wonders
# Never Cease

By the time my day ended, I felt like jumping in front of a moving cab. I had a pounding headache, one I was sure was brought on by the events of the day and the slap across the face from Maribel. And unless the registration number was in some kind of code in Chantel's diary, there was no mention of it.

The hospital called to inform us that Mr. Fields was resting comfortably but wouldn't be returning to work any time soon. At least he wasn't dead. I still needed to get to Chantel's house, pick up Virginia, drop her off at Tiffany's, and have dinner with the folks—in no particular order.

One thing I did know, at some point I needed to take a look at the videotapes and do some more reading of the manuals. Hopefully the handbook would turn up eventually.

Larry stopped by my desk with the last mail delivery of the day. "Crazy day, huh?" he asked.

"You think so?"

He chuckled. "Did anyone ever tell you that you are one funny lady?"

I gave him a wide-eyed innocent look. "No. Not once."

"Well, you are. Listen, I'll meet you in the parking lot at five."

As much as I could have used a ride, I knew I wasn't up to a half-hour interrogation by Larry on the trip home.

"Thanks, but I think I'll take a cab."

He frowned. "A cab? Oh, I get it—you're still pissed off about this morning."

"To be truthful, I'd forgotten all about it until *just now*." I gave him a hard stare.

"Fine. See you tomorrow."

"Sure. Have a good night."

I turned off my computer, put my pilfered items back in the shopping bag, grabbed my purse, and limped out.


At least it wasn't raining, I thought as I stood on the corner of Fifth Avenue and Twenty-third Street, trying to hail a cab at rush hour. Folks were pouring out of the buildings along the avenue with the same intention as me unless they were opting for mass transit. I worked in the Flatiron Building, considered in some circles to be a historical landmark or at the minimum a building of some unique importance. So every now and then—more now than then—tourists would be so busy looking up at the flat design they'd run right into me and then apologize in a variety of accents.

Mercifully, a cab finally squealed to a stop in front of me, and just as I jumped in from one side, the opposite door was pulled open, and another passenger got in.

"Hey, this is my—!"

"What the—?"

"Calvin?"

"Maggie, is that you?"

"Where to, folks?" the cabbie tossed over his shoulder even as he'd already sped out into moving traffic.

"Yes, it's me, and you're in my cab."

"I think you're in *my* cab. I've been standing out here for the past twenty minutes and I—"

"Look, Calvin," I said, cutting him off, "I've had a *really* bad day. You have no concept of the kind of day I've had. And the last thing I want to do at this very minute is get into a debate with you about this cab! Now you can either shut up and come along for the ride or get out."

He held up his hands. "All right, all right. Take it easy." He settled back in the cab then cut a look at me from the corner of his eye. "Tell the man where you want to go," he said.

"That's better," I muttered. "I have three stops, driver."

"Three stops!" Calvin squawked.

I ignored him. "First stop is Eighty-sixth and Park," I called out to the driver. "What are you doing over here, anyway?" I asked.

"My car is in the shop, and I had a meeting with a client around the corner. What are you doing over here?"

"I work here," I said haughtily. "In the Flatiron Building," I added to give my tidbit of information some panache.

His brow quirked, but just barely. "Hmmm," he murmured. "Landmark." He turned and stared out of the window.

For the next few minutes, we drove in silence, which was fine with me. But that wasn't long lived.

"Have you heard from Tiffany?" Calvin asked in a stiff voice.

I turned to glance at him, and I could see how stoic he was try-ing to be. "No, actually, I haven't."

"Hmmm. Still no idea when she will be back, I suppose."

"No, not really."

"Look, about yesterday at the apartment, I'm . . . sorry for act-ing like such an ass. But sometimes she makes me crazy, you know."

"I certainly do."

He sighed. "Maybe this is all for the best," he said in a resigned voice. "I never could figure out what would make her happy, any-way. Obviously it's not me."

"Well . . . I wouldn't go that far."

He snapped his neck in my direction. "Why? Has she told you something?"

I wished I could say something to make him feel better, but I couldn't. "No. Not really. Sorry."

He shrugged. "It's okay. I guess I was kind of prepared for this. But I didn't expect her to just walk away without a word and stuff my things in a box." He turned and looked at me. You know the kind of look of kid gives a parent when they are sure the parent has the answer. "What kind of woman does something like that?"

*Women like Tiffany and Chantel,* I wanted to say, but didn't. He'd already been dealt a hand of nasty news. "People go through all sorts of ups and downs," I said instead. "They make good and bad decisions, change their minds, and make mistakes. Unfortunately people get hurt in the process." Who knew that better than me?

"I guess you're right." He angled his head. "I know this may sound . . . out of place . . . but you look . . . different."

"I've been getting that a lot today."

He smiled, and the usual hard lines of his jaw softened and crinkled his eyes. "What do you do again?" He turned in his seat and focused all his attention on me. It was a bit unnerving.

I cleared my throat. "I'm a senior editor at University Press."

"That sounds interesting."

"It does?" I asked, wondering if he meant it or if he was just pulling my leg.

"Yeah, it does. You sound surprised. Don't you think what you do is interesting?"

"Not most days."

"Then why do you do it?"

He had me there. I thought about it for a minute and then another. "To be honest, I really want to be a writer," I finally blurted out. "I had some foolish notion that working for a publisher would somehow get my foot in the door. But I do so much reading of other people's work, I can't think about writing when I get home." *Why did I tell him all that?* I'd never revealed that to anyone. The last time I did was years ago, in Tiffany's teenage bedroom.

"That's too bad. If more people truly pursued their dreams in life the world would be a much better place."

I looked at Calvin from a new perspective. He suddenly didn't sound so pompous—but actually thoughtful, almost philosophical. "Are you really doing what you want?"

He chuckled. "Most days."

We both smiled.

Somehow the conversation veered to music, and curiously enough, Calvin was a blues buff, of all things. It was hard to imagine straitlaced, Mr. Corporate America enjoying anything other than opera. He actually had me cracking up, pretending to sing some hilarious blues lyrics. I had to wonder if he ever sang for Tiffany.

"Eighty-sixth and Park," the cabbie said, cutting off Calvin's rendition of "Gutbucket Blues."

Calvin jumped out and opened the door for me. I got out and was almost flush against him. I held my breath.

He looked down at me and smiled as if he'd discovered a treat. "Look, I'd love to ride with you all over town, but I have an early day tomorrow."

I nodded, not knowing what to say.

"This has really been—"

"Eye-opening," I said, filling in the gap.

He nodded. "Yes, it has."

Pause. Silence. Pause.

He cleared his throat. "I'd better let you go. I can get another cab."

"Okay."

He stepped back, and I squeezed by him. I tilted my head toward the driver's window. "I'll be right back."

He shrugged. "Meter's running."

"Take care, Calvin," I said, and started away.

"You . . . uh . . . look really nice," he called out as I rushed toward Chantel's front door.

I almost tripped but didn't. I turned around at the door, struck a vogue pose, and said in my best Mae West voice, "You're not lookin' too bad yourself, big boy."

He tossed his head back and laughed as I slipped inside.


The instant I crossed the threshold, Virginia was on me like white on rice. She growled at me then started barking and pacing in front of me like a father who'd caught his child breaking curfew.

"I'm sorry, I'm sorry. I got here as soon as I could." I tossed my purse on the hall table. "You have no idea the kind of day I've had."

She growled some more.

"That's not the kind of attitude to take. My feet were swollen because Chantel's shoes are too damn small. Then they froze solid when I kept them in a bucket of ice for too long, my boss had a heart attack, and Maribel the custodian smacked me in the face."

All of a sudden, Virginia started howling, howling like a were-wolf in a B movie then rolled onto her back. If I didn't know better, I'd swear she was cracking up laughing.

"I'm glad you find all this amusing." I walked past her. "We have to get out of here. I still have a full night ahead of me."

I pulled off the cursed shoes and padded to the bedroom. Chantel had to have a pair of regular old house slippers that I could borrow until I got my own shoes. I scanned the bottom of her closet and found a pair that looked as if they'd do the trick. As long as they didn't suddenly transport me to Munchkin land, they were cool with me. I slid my feet in and sighed out loud. It was like stepping onto a cloud. For a moment I closed my eyes, savoring the moment.

"Okay, let's go. I have a cab waiting outside. And you better be-have," I warned, wagging a finger at her.

She pranced out of the room to the front door.

Virginia was the reason I had fish. I grabbed her leash, checked the alarm, and locked the door behind us.


The driver was a little pissed off that I'd brought a dog in the car, but I promised him that Virginia was a good dog and wouldn't cause a moment of trouble. I should have known better. Virginia started whining halfway between Chantel's place and Tiffany's, and before I could react—yes, you guessed it—she'd peed all over the cab floor. Determined not to have another pair of footwear ru-ined in one day, I braced my feet up on the back of the driver's seat and prayed he didn't smell anything before we got to our destina-tion. In the meantime having relieved herself, Virginia took a seat on the opposite side of the cab and looked out the window, cooing periodically if she saw a Doberman go by.

The ride over with Calvin certainly *was* eye-opening, I thought as the yellow cab zigged and zagged around the traffic. He didn't come across as the snob that I'd always taken him for, but a rather decent, pretty good-looking man, who unfortunately got tied up with Tiffany Lane. I wondered what her real plan was when it came to Calvin. Did she intend to continue to play games with him, string him along? What if her plan backfired? He did say he'd been expecting this. Maybe it's what he wanted, too. But then again, he did seem upset about what she'd done. I sighed. Now if I had someone like Calvin . . . I would . . . I really didn't know what I would do. The opportunity had never presented itself before. But it would, and soon. I was going to get this Diva thing down pat, and when I did, hundreds of Calvins would be groveling at my feet.

The cab came to a stop in front of Tiffany's town house. When I took a look at the meter, I knew I'd have to eliminate my next stop. All I had in my wallet was thirty dollars. I dug in my wallet and pulled out my last twenty and didn't even wait for my ten cents in change.

I scooped up Virginia, my purse, my shopping bag and high-tailed it out of there before he realized that ten cents was his entire tip and that the back floor of his cab had a bit of a puddle.

And just when I thought my day was coming to a reasonable end, who do you suppose was waiting for me on the steps? Right. Wayne.

"Wayne, why are you here?" I asked, stepping around him so I could get to the front door.

He stood and walked up behind me. "I was waiting on you."

"How did you even know I'd come back here?" I turned the key in the door and pushed it open.

"I know Virginia likes to go for her walks at seven. It was a little after, and I got worried."

I spun around so fast, I almost knocked him back down the stairs. I frowned. "Do you watch Tiffany all the time?"

He shrugged. "I wouldn't say all the time. But I pretty much have her routine down. Besides, whenever she gets in a jam, I take care of Virginia." He bent down and scooped her up. "Right, girl?"

I looked from one to the other. "You two deserve each other," I grumbled from between my teeth.

"What happened to your shoes?" he asked.

I glanced at him over my shoulder. "You don't want to know."

We stepped into the foyer. I dug down in my bra and pulled up the slip of paper with the code. Wayne walked by me and pushed the numbers before I had a chance to blink. I looked at him askance. He shrugged.

"It helps to know these things," he offered. "We don't want another incident like yesterday."

"Thanks for reminding me. I suppose I don't need to ask you if you want to come in," I said, and I was sure he missed my sarcasm.

"Thanks."

I just shook my head and went inside. "You can't stay long, Wayne. I have things to do."

He took a seat in the living room. "That's what you always say. Did you water the plants?"

"No. Would you take care of that for me? I need to feed Virginia."

"Sure." He got up from the couch and filled the water can from the kitchen faucet. What's for dinner?"

"Say what? I know you don't think you're staying for dinner."

"I could fix us something."

I planted my hands on my hips. "Have you taken a good look

around here? Unless you plan to fix cobwebs and shriveled vegetables, you are out of luck."

"Tiffany isn't one for food shopping. But I could fix us something at my house."

"Do you have a girlfriend, Wayne?"

He momentarily lowered his head. Embarrassed? I couldn't tell.

"Not at the moment. My work keeps me kind of busy."

"Yeah, I know what you mean." And I did. "You know what, Wayne, dinner sounds great. But I need to make one more stop. Will you look after Virginia until I get back?"

"No problem." He grinned like he'd won something.

"Great."

I headed for the bedroom, stashed the shopping bag in the closet, and hurried back out front.

"I should be back in about two hours."

He waved at me from the couch, with Virginia sitting on his lap. "We'll be waiting," he said with a grin.

*That's what I'm afraid of,* I thought, shutting the door behind me. But as we have already discovered, in Margaretville, things could always be worse. However, I was pretty certain that dear old Wayne knew much more than he let on. If I played my cards right, he would spill the beans eventually.

Now, off to Grandma's house.

# Off to Grandma's House—
# Or Not

As you all know by now, Grandma is a very nutty lady. She's always good for a few laughs and a few raised eyebrows. I figured that an hour at her house, between my mother's rantings about the post office and my grandmother's time travels, and I would be sufficiently brain dead after my life-altering day.

I emerged from the subterranean depths of the A train station and shuffled down the two blocks to Grandma's house. All along the thirty-minute ride from Manhattan to Brooklyn, people on the train gave me queer looks about my footwear. But quite frankly, I could not have cared less. I smiled, looked at the advertisements for everything from learning English to beautiful skin via Dr. Zizmore and acted like wearing fluffy slippers with a $1,500 designer suit was quite the rage.

When I reached the house, Grandma was perched in her usual seat watching E! her favorite evening TV channel. "This is where you get the real news," she would always say. "That other foolishness is nothing but political propaganda." Funny thing is, she was probably right.

"Nice getup," she said instead of hello, giving me a quick once-over. "But don't go getting too comfortable, 'cause I need you to run to the store. I need a small box of sugar."

"I don't think so, Grandma. Not today."

She reared back and looked the way I must have when Maribel slapped me. "You tellin' me you can't do your old grandmother a good turn?"

I walked over to her chair and looked down into her crafty eyes. "The jig is up, Grandma. I know what you've been up to all these years."

She squeezed her eyes together and bunched up her face like she was going to cry.

"This is the thanks I get for all I've done for you. Back talk!"

"Don't try it, Grandma. I'm on to you."

"Humph." She straightened up.

"Admit it. You've been scamming me for years—and Mama before that."

"Can't an old lady have a few laughs?" she whined.

I just shook my head. "Where's Mama?"

"You're so smart, Sherlock, *you* figure it out," she said, folding her arms beneath her breasts like a petulant child.

Dismissed, I marched off to the kitchen. "Hi, Mom."

"It's about time. That woman is about to drive me crazy," she muttered as she whipped a pot of potatoes just short of death. "You're going to have to take over tonight. I can't tolerate another minute."

"Say what?"

My mother spun around. "You're going to have to look after your grandmother tonight. I'm beat, and I can't take any more of her foolishness."

"No way! Nope. Can't do it. Sorry." I shook my head vigorously. Taking care of Grandma for the night was not on my agenda. I had plans.

My mother's eyes suddenly filled with tears. "Do you want to see your mother's face plastered all over the late news, on the cover of every newspaper? Because that's what's going to happen," she screeched, her voice rising in octave. "I swear it, Margaret." She tossed down her spoon, whipped off her apron, and stormed past me. "I left twenty dollars in the coffee jar," she tossed over her shoulder.

The next thing I heard was the slamming of the front door. I ran behind her, but I was too late. By the time I got to the door, my mother jumped into a Mercedes-Benz and whizzed away. A Mercedes?

*"This can't be happening!"* I yelled.

I spun around, and Grandma was right behind me. "Ready?" she asked with a big grin.

I looked down. She had her overnight bag in one hand and her everyday purse in the other.

I'd been duped again!


The entire ride back was spent in silence—at least on my part. Grandma, on the other hand, was a nonstop fountain of chatter. She ran her mouth about everything from the cracks in the sidewalk to the hard times of '29. (That was the current era she was visiting.) I tuned her out for the most part and just pouted.

How did I let my mother do this to me? She was even craftier than Grandma. The whole thing happened so damned fast, I didn't see it coming. Now I was stuck with my nutty as a fruitcake grandmother for an entire night. I'd finally concluded that in a former life I must have been a serial killer—or worse, a lawyer.

"When did you figure it out?" Grandma asked, right in the middle of her monologue about Teddy Roosevelt and his alleged proposal to her. ("I was a pretty hot mama in my day," she'd said. "He thought I was royalty.")

(I'd nodded my head. There was no way I was going to entertain the idea of Grandma as a hot mama being proposed to by a dead president.)

"Found what out, Grandma, the fact that you've been scamming me for years with the hundred-dollar bait-and-switch game? Is that what you mean?"

She giggled, and her eyes sparkled with mischief. For a scary minute, I could actually see her cozying up to Teddy.

"It was only to teach you a lesson," she said matter-of-factly.

"Oh, really. And what lesson might that have been?"

She leaned over in the cab and looked me square in the eye. "To pay attention to the least obvious."

"What?"

She turned away and continued to stare out the window. "You'll figure that out, too. One day."

The cab pulled to a stop in front of Tiffany's town house.

"How much?" I asked, already reaching into my purse.

"Twenty-eight dollars," he said, pointing to the fare on the meter.

I pulled out my wallet with my last ten and the twenty from the coffee jar, but Grandma, suddenly lightning fast, stopped me with her hand on mine. She dug in her bra with her free hand and pulled out the hundred-dollar bill.

"All I have is this, sugah," she said in a husky voice I'd never heard before. She slipped the bill into the little Plexiglas door.

"I don't have change for a hundred," he said, somewhat miffed.

She slid to the front of her seat. "It's all we have," she cooed sweetly. "Maybe we could ride around for a while and find some change." She lowered her lids like a smoky barroom cabaret singer and then leaned back and crossed her legs, exposing a surprisingly smooth knee and shapely leg.

I didn't know whether to be appalled or to crack up laughing. I watched the metamorphosis of Grandma from an eccentric old bat to a Mata Hari. All she needed now was to whip out a cigarette with a gold holder. Either that or her head could spin around.

The cabbie started babbling in frustration. His Adam's apple bobbed up and down, and his eyes rolled over Grandma like a train on a railroad track. They didn't miss a spot.

She proceeded to fan herself with the bill as if it had suddenly grown unbearably warm in the air-conditioned cab. Then she actually winked at him. Winked!

The next thing I knew, he'd jumped out of the car, rounded the hood, and opened the door—on Grandma's side, of course. Grandma got out with the grace of Marilyn Monroe stepping onto the red carpet on premiere night. She smiled up at him, and I'd swear he blushed.

Grandma squeezed his bicep and made a little pouty thing happen with her lips.

"Hmm, hard, the way a man should be."

She made a big deal of stuffing the hundred back down into her bra and sauntered past the cabbie like she was on the runway.

Before he snapped out of it, I hurried after her, afraid to look back. I had that awful sinking sensation of being on the brink of getting away with the goods, having eluded all the store detectives and clerks. You breeze by the lingerie, cosmetics, and per-

fume counters. You can smell freedom on the other side of the re-
volving doors. If you can only make it before someone stops you.
Your heart is racing. You know everyone is watching. The door is
only a few feet away. Look straight ahead. A line of sweat breaks
out across your hairline just as your big toe touches the threshold.
But just as you step across, a big clammy hand grabs your shoulders, and the damning voice of the guard says . . .

"Hey, who's that?"

I jumped three feet into the air. When I landed, I whirled
around to find myself nose to nose with—of course—Wayne.

I stomped my slippered foot in utter frustration. "What is wrong
with you?" I yelled. "Do you want to give me a heart attack?"

"Sorry," he mumbled.

Grandma was bent in half, laughing, and even Virginia—the
traitor—seemed to find the whole scene amusing. Finally she
pulled herself together and stuck out her hand. "I'm Grandma."

"Grandma?"

"That's what everyone calls me."

He grinned. "Makes me feel like family," Wayne said proudly.
"My name is Wayne. Everyone calls me Wayne," he added with
a wink.

Grandma giggled like an ingenue. "And what does a handsome
man like you do for a living, Wayne?"

"I'm a chiropractor."

Grandma's brows rose to Mount Everest heights. "Really, a
doctor—sort of." She glanced at me then back at Wayne. She slid
her arm through Wayne's as he helped her up the steps.

I had a good mind to slam the door in everyone's faces and simply disappear for all eternity into Tiffany's secret closet—which reminded me that I had to find the password so that I could go to
the soiree. I had a very strong feeling that it was somewhere in
Tiffany's house.

"I thought you were fixing dinner, Wayne," I said, suddenly famished.

"It's all done. I can bring everything here, or you two can freshen up and join me at my place." He looked at Grandma and gave her a Colgate smile.

"A man who can cook," Grandma said coyly. "Of course, we will make it easy for you and join you at your place," she graciously offered in our behalf. "Won't we, Margaret?"

*Who is this woman?* I gritted my teeth and stomped off toward the bathroom to "freshen up." While I looked at my tormented face in the mirror, I wondered how I was going to make it through the night with me and Grandma under the same roof—and what the penalty was for murdering your own mother.

# Light at the End
# of the Tunnel

*I*t was pretty clear after the first ten minutes at Wayne's place that Grandma must have spent time as an expert interrogator in one of the elite units of the CIA. Before he had a chance to finish setting the table, she'd uncovered his views on Republicans, gentrification, cholesterol, same-sex marriage; his fear of flying; and his penchant for praline ice cream. It was quite frightening.

"So you grew up in North Carolina," Grandma stated, popping a curried shrimp into her mouth.

"How did you know that?" Wayne asked, a look of astonishment on his face.

"I have a good eye and a better ear." She smiled benignly and took a long swallow of her iced tea.

"That's an amazing talent you have there, Grandma."

"The better to eat you with, my dear," she replied in a very sorry imitation of Red Riding Hood's big bad wolf.

From there, it was a classic Grandma interlude. She had Wayne practically falling on the floor with her incredible tales that included everything from being a psychic for Scotland Yard, assisting Harriet Tubman, her fling with Winston Churchill, her days as a Black Panther leader, and how she'd spent the summer of her seventeenth year being a midwife at a brothel on the outskirts of New Orleans.

And through her entire monologue, she didn't crack a smile. She'd only periodically punctuate her tales with, "You may not believe this, but it's all true. I was there."

Mercifully dinner finally ended—or should I say, Grandma momentarily ran out of stories to tell—and Wayne walked us back to Tiffany's place.

"Your grandmother is an interesting woman," Wayne whispered to me at the door. "Does she really believe half of what she's saying?"

"I try not to think about it too much."

"Has she always been so . . ."

"Looney?" I said, filling in the obvious blank.

"Well?"

I looked down the hallway, and Grandma was merrily chatting with Virginia and asking for a tour. "I realized a long time ago that my grandmother wasn't like other grandmothers, and I've learned to live with it."

He grinned. "You're a funny lady."

"So I've been hearing. Anyway, Wayne, thanks for dinner and for looking after Virginia."

"My pleasure." He paused a moment. "Well, uh, will you be around tomorrow?"

"More than likely."

"What are you going to do about Grandma tomorrow?"

Grandma? Tomorrow? I hadn't gotten that far. All I wanted was to get through the day. "I guess I'll have to get her back home before I go to work." I sighed heavily.

"If you give me the address, I can drop her off for you."

I glanced up at him. "You would? But why?"

"Why not?"

I thought about his offer for all of two seconds. "Sure. That would be great." I reached in my bag, pulled out a piece of paper and a pen, and jotted down the address.

"I'll get her there safe and sound."

"Thanks, Wayne."

He tucked his paper in his pocket. "What time?"

"Around eight. I'll be back from walking Virginia by then."

"See you at eight." He took a step back out the doorway. "How's your acting coming?"

"Huh?"

"Your acting. Remember you told me—?"

"Oh . . . yes . . . uh, well, you know how the entertainment business is."

"No, not really."

I blinked rapidly and made the fatal mistake of jutting my nose in the air. In a flash, Wayne had me in a viselike grip, ready to re-align my vertebrae.

"Wayne!"

It was too late. Snap, crackle, pop.

"What's going on?"

Wayne set me on my feet and turned to Grandma. "Margaret has a bad case of sudden spinal spasm. A relatively new diagnosis," he added.

Grandma put her hand on her hip and cocked her head to the

right. "A bad case of what? Girl, what foolishness are you telling this man?"

*She* had the nerve to question anyone's ridiculous story? I shook my body like a wet cat. "I'm not *telling* him anything." I glared at Wayne. "Say good night, Wayne."

"Good night, ladies. It was great meeting you, Grandma."

She smiled sweetly as he walked out. "Pretty nice place your friend Tiffany has here," she commented, heading for the living room. "I always knew that one would do well." She began watering the plants.

I wanted to ask her what she saw in her crystal ball for me, but decided it was best not to know.

"You can spend the night in the guest bedroom," I said. "It's at the end of the hall."

"Yes, I know," she answered, not looking up from her self-imposed task. Then suddenly she turned toward me. "You could get used to this," she stated. "Just remember when you look in the mirror, the face you see may not be your own."

I didn't want to hazard a guess as to what that meant.

"Sure, Grandma. Let me get you settled. It's getting late."

She waved me off. "I can take care of myself. You go ahead and finish doing what you came over here to do." She gave me a wink and turned back to the plants.

Although I was reluctant to leave Grandma unmonitored, I couldn't very well watch her for the entire night. After all, she wasn't dangerous in the Merriam-Webster sense of the word.

I returned to the bedroom and decided to watch one of the videos. I dug in the shopping bag and pulled out the first of three and popped it in the VCR.

After a rolling of credits, the screen filled with a room full of women who appeared to be at some sort of seminar. The camera zoomed in on the woman on stage who was a dead ringer for a Motown songbird who left her partners for a mega solo career. The woman's lecture was about "flaunting."

"No one knows what you have, what you think, or what you are capable of doing unless you show them and show them that you are better at it than anyone else even if you aren't," she shouted like a Baptist preacher.

The audience applauded loudly, as she strutted back and forth, flipping her weave from one side to the other.

"The key," she said, "is illusion. You can make the seer believe whatever you want them to see—if you believe. Say it with me. I believe!"

The crowd roared back its response, and the very uppity meeting turned into a down-home revival, complete with foot-stomping organ music.

Women in the audience jumped up and began testifying about how they'd gone from wallflower to fly girl, from office aid to corporate honcho, from submissive in bed to getting theirs. At any moment, I expected them to break out and sing, "We Are the World."

The tape came to a rousing end with a close-up of the speaker, who looked directly into the camera and said, "If not you, then who? If not now, then when? Do you have what it takes?" Fade to black.

"Yes! Yes!" I cried, jumping to my feet.

Virginia barked as if to say, *Relax.*

I stuck my tongue out at the dog, aimed the remote at the television, and turned off the set. I felt revitalized, invigorated. I believed I could beat this Diva thing. I would get the hang of it. I would become that which I had only dreamed of becoming. Putting the tape back in the shopping bag, I headed for the shower.

When I finished, wrapped in a towel and determination, I went straight for Tiffany's computer in her small office. While luxuriating under the water, I was hit by an idea about the registration code to access the soiree application.

With nimble fingers, I navigated the murky waves of the Internet until I reached the Diva Web site. After a few keystrokes, I typed the sign-in name and the password: *Margaret*.

When I arrived at the registration page, and I was asked for a registration number, I typed in 36-26-36. And there it was!

Tiffany was always bragging about her figure. And knowing her as I did, it made sense that she would dole out those numbers at any given opportunity.

I filled in all the required information and added my name as the new recruit and hit SEND. Moments later, I received my confirmation.

Margaret Drew was going to the soiree.

# You Just Never
# Know How Things
# Will Turn Out

*I* was up with the sun, totally traumatized, having had Technicolor dreams of my big day with the Divas. I saw myself arriving to a throng of admirers who applauded, marveled at my stunning attire, and parted like the Red Sea as I strutted my stuff down the white carpet. At the end of it, perched on a throne was the Grand Diva herself. Her face, as always, was shadowed by her hat, which dipped down almost to her mouth.

"Maggie, darling, welcome," she said in a sultry voice befitting someone of her stature. "Come and sit beside me. I've been waiting for you."

I heard the murmur of voices—all those malcontents who wished they were me. Ha! I approached the steps that led to the throne, careful not to trip, when out of nowhere appeared Virginia, who darted between my legs, tangling me in her leash until I tumbled down the stairs to the jeers and laughter of all the Divas.

I woke up shaking. I couldn't let that happen. Their laughter still rang in my ears, but I would not be defeated. Hoping out of bed, I took one look at Virginia and growled with determination. Maybe the dream was a sign of some sort. A vision of what would happen if I wasn't prepared.

Armed with determination, I dressed quickly in one of my own nondescript outfits and took Virginia for her morning constitutional. Upon my return, I found Grandma up, dressed, and having miraculously found enough food to whip up breakfast.

"Where did all this come from?" I asked, perplexed, as I sat down at the kitchen table.

"There's always a way to make something out of nothing when you know how," she said, classically cryptic. "I made friends with the storekeeper around the corner," she admitted, and then winked.

I eyed her suspiciously but didn't comment, just as the doorbell rang. "That must be Wayne. He's going to take you home."

"How nice. We can have a chance to chat. I really like that boy."

"Hmmm," I murmured as I answered the door.

"Good morning, Margaret. Rest well?"

"Not really," I said, recalling my nightmare. "Come in. Grandma's in the kitchen."

"Warm tea a half hour before bedtime will help that," he offered.

"Thanks for the tip."

He sauntered past me and into the kitchen. "Grandma! Aren't you looking lovely this morning."

She blushed. "That's what a woman needs first thing in the morning, a complimentary lie from a man." She winked at him. "Have some breakfast."

"I'd love to, but I've already eaten. Looks good, though," he said, eyeing the spread of hash browns, eggs, biscuits, and sausages.

Grandma finished off her food and stood. "Ready when you are."

Wayne hurried around the table and took her by the arm. "Your chariot awaits."

My stomach rolled—so did my eyes.

They both turned to me at the door. "Have a good day," they said in unison, beaming identical smiles. And I had a sudden, frightening flash of Grandma and Wayne as a couple on the front page of *Entertainment Weekly*. I shook my head to rid myself of the disturbing vision and quickly shut the door behind them.

Returning to the bedroom, I faced my next task, getting ready for work. If I was going to ease into the role of Diva, I definitely had to look the part, and I knew that none of my outfits fit the bill. But after my horrific day yesterday, too-small shoes were not on the menu. I'd been wise enough to bring a pair of my own from home, which would have to do in the meantime. Sliding open the closet door, I selected a teal blue two-piece suit by Vera Wang, put on the prerequisite girdle pilfered from Chantel's place, and finished dressing. I took a look in the mirror. I had no ideas about makeup and hairdos, and now was not the time to experiment. I opted for lip gloss and a Halle Berry–styled wig from Tiffany's secret closet. Another look in the mirror, and I was transformed. Wow, I even felt different. Grabbing my purse, I bade Virginia a fond farewell and headed out.

The moment I arrived at work, everyone I passed looked at me with raised brows and suspicious glances. Something was afoot. When I reached my desk, there was a note from Amy, the editor-in-chief's secretary, telling me to come to his office by 9:30 sharp. I didn't like the sound of that.

Would I be interrogated about Mr. Fields's sudden heart attack? Did they somehow believe that I was involved? What could they possibly want to see me about? The questions ran rampant through my mind. I had visions of bright lights beamed into my eyes while I was handcuffed to a chair, pleading my innocence.

I jumped at the sound of the ringing phone, and banged my knee on my desk.

"Margaret Drew," I said by rote, gritting my teeth and rubbing my sore knee.

"This is Amy. Mr. Savage will see you now."

*Savage.* How appropriate. "I'll be right in."

There are those you meet in life who don't fit their names in the least, and you wonder what the parents could possibly have been thinking when they looked down at their precious little bundle and hung the handle on them.

Well, let's just say that Thor Savage was not one of those parental mistakes. His folks knew just what they were doing. At six feet six and an easy three-hundred-plus pounds butt naked, Thor Savage could put fear in the heart of the Terminator. He had the kind of voice that preceded a major thunderstorm: heavy, booming, and terrifying to little children and adults alike. For someone who had the responsibility of dealing with employees, he was the least personable human being I'd ever encountered. I was not looking forward to the meeting.

Everyone I passed as I walked down the corridor averted their gazes or sadly shook their heads. I felt as if I were walking to the guillotine.

"I'm here to see Mr. Savage," I said to Amy. My voice shook.

She looked at me with something akin to pity on her pinched face. "Go right in," she whispered, and snatched a terrified look over her shoulder.

I walked forward on wooden legs and timidly knocked on the door.

"Come in," the voice boomed from behind the door.

I swallowed hard.

I opened the door and stepped inside. Thor Savage rose from his seat and rose and rose until I was no more than a speck on the carpet. He looked way down on me from scary blue eyes.

"Sit," he commanded, and I nearly fell down in the chair from the blast.

He put on his glasses and peered at me. Then he flipped open a folder on the desk and looked at me again suspiciously.

"Margaret Drew?" he asked, as if he weren't expecting me but someone else instead.

I nodded.

"You've been here for how many years?" His voice bounced around the room like Zeus on Olympus, and for a minute I couldn't remember.

"Well? How many?"

"Uh, umm. Six . . . eight."

He glared at me. "Long enough. As of today, you will be taking over the duties of Mr. Fields until his return."

Coming from Thor Savage, the promotion, albeit temporary, sounded like a life sentence without thought of parole.

"Y-yes, Mr. Savage," I stammered.

"The support staff will report to you. I'll send out a memo."

"Yes, Mr. Savage."

"I'm sure you understand how important it is that we keep the editorial department running smoothly. We cannot disappoint our clients."

"Yes, Mr. Savage."

He nodded, and the room rocked from side to side.

"Any questions or problems, you come to see me."

*I doubt it.* "Sure thing, Mr. Savage,"

"Is there anything you need clarified . . . Ms. Drew?"

"No, sir."

"Good." He stood and extended his hand.

Gingerly I put my hand in his, and it immediately disappeared in his grasp. I felt my teeth rattle as he shook it up and down.

"Thank you, Mr. Savage," I mumbled, checking with my tongue for any loose teeth.

He grumbled something unintelligible as I scurried out of his office. It certainly wasn't quite so horrific as I'd imagined, I thought as I returned to my desk, letting the news of my temporary promotion settle in. A slow smile eased across my face. *Margaret Drew, Executive Editor.* Yes, I liked the sound of that. I already had ideas in mind for redecorating Mr. Fields's office when I was waylaid in the corridor by Beverly.

"The rumor mill has it that you're going to be the new executive editor," she said in a conspiratorial whisper, as if we were really good friends. Then she giggled and tapped my shoulder in that "old pal of mine" gesture. "But of course that can't be true."

I stopped walking and turned to face her. "And why not?" I drew out every syllable.

"For one thing, I've been here longer than you have."

"But did it ever occur to you that maybe I know what I'm doing, and you don't? That I was already senior editor and that maybe I actually deserved it?"

She reared back as if I'd slapped her, which I'd been meaning to do for years. But the stunned expression on her face was almost as satisfying.

"By the way, the rumor is true. And while we're on the subject of work, I have three galleys that need to be read by the end of the week." With that, I flounced away, leaving dear Beverly with her mouth hanging open.

I returned to my desk feeling all-powerful—able to slay my enemies with a stroke of my pen or at least a heavy workload. I glanced at the meager personal possessions on my desk, dropped them in the shopping bag, and marched off to Mr. Fields's office.

How many nights had I dreamed of sitting in *the* seat, making decisions that could ruin weekends or change lives. Now here I was in the inner sanctum. They would all have to come to me for the slightest thing, and I had the power to deny them!

I walked behind the desk and sat in the high-backed soft leather seat. Leaning back, I put my feet up on the desk and my hands behind my head, and I surveyed my empire. This was going to be fun. At least I hoped so.

# This Could Be
# a Problem

For some inexplicable reason, my day proceeded without any major incident. All my plans for firing off orders and crushing underlings beneath my pumps went unfulfilled. Everyone carried on as usual, as if Margaret Drew being elevated to executive editor was an everyday occurrence.

I suppose the highlight of my day was during Larry's mail delivery. That's when I knew the tides had definitely turned.

"Congratulations," he said without much enthusiasm as he dropped Mr. Fields's mail—now mine—into the in-box.

"Thank you." I puffed out my chest, waiting for more accolades about my who-would-have-thought-it rise to power. Nothing came.

"Have a good day, *boss,*" was the next thing he said. Larry turned and started down the corridor.

I was deflated. I'd expect that kind of attitude from Beverly but not from Larry. And now that I was part of management, it was inappropriate for me to associate with hourly-wage employees. So I ate lunch at my desk and watched the clock slowly count down the day.

The instant the clock struck quitting time, I gathered my things and made a dash for the parking lot, certain that, as always, Larry would be waiting. But I was batting zero with Larry. His beat-up Honda was nowhere to be found.

Miffed and hurt by the obvious slight, I walked back through the building to the front entrance, resigning myself to the train ride home. When I stepped out among the masses, I stopped cold when I spotted Calvin waving to me from in front of a sparkling black Mercedes Coup convertible.

"I haven't heard from Tiffany," I said instead of hello.

He half smiled. "I didn't come about Tiffany."

"So what are you doing here?"

"I was in the neighborhood, and I thought you might like a ride to wherever you needed to go."

After I picked my mouth up from the sidewalk, I said, "Now let me get this straight—you're offering me a ride?"

"Yes, is that so hard to believe?"

I frowned. "Sort of, yes."

"You're funny, Margaret."

I gave him a slight smile.

"So how about that ride?"

I shrugged. "Sure."

Gallantly he pulled open the door, and I slid onto the plush leather seats that still smelled like the showroom.

"So where to?" he asked as we pulled into traffic.

"I need to stop off at Chantel's and check on things. . . . Tiffany's, as well," I added, and glanced at him from the corner of my eyes. His expression remained unmoved by my evoking the name of his sorta ex-beloved.

"You must be some kind of friend to run around like this every day," he said. "How long have you known Tiffany and Chantel?"

I thought back to those early days in the bassinet. "For a while."

We stopped for a red light, and he turned to me. "I, um, have an extra ticket to a Knicks game tonight at the Garden. Tiffany hates the Knicks, and my buddy couldn't make it. Would you like to come with me?"

I hiccuped, I was so startled. I hiccuped five times in a row.

Calvin looked stricken. "Maybe I should pull over and get you some water or something."

I tugged in a deep breath and willed myself to get it together. I pressed my lips shut, and when the next wave attacked, it sealed my eardrums shut. Panicked, I turned to Calvin. His lips were moving, but I couldn't hear a damned thing. The whole world was a rushing mass of color, activity, and silence. Oh, Lawd!

I tried to read his lips, but they were moving too fast. I tried sign language to let him know that I couldn't hear. Finally after my poorly performed attempt at charades, wide-eyed expressions, and tears, he got the point, pulled to a stop at the curb, and reached into the glove compartment. An array of everything from AA batteries, condoms, assorted fruit-flavored lip balms, to road maps fell into my lap. He sifted through the rubble on my lap and dug out a pen and a tollbooth receipt.

*Are you ok?* Calvin scribbled on the scrap of paper.

*No!* I mouthed, pointing to my ears.

He hunched over and scribbled again. *Yawn.*

*What?*

*Yawn.*

He opened and closed his mouth to demonstrate. I noticed that he had several fillings in his back teeth and the rest were in good shape.

I followed his instructions, and one ear popped and then the other, but there was definitely a dullness to everything, like hearing the world through a sponge. But at least I wasn't deaf.

"Better?" he asked, and I actually heard him this time, but as if it were from far away.

I nodded.

"Whew. You had me scared for a minute." He chuckled nervously. He looked at me for a few more minutes, I guess to be sure that nothing else bizarre happened before he pulled off.

I spent the better part of the drive opening and closing my mouth in exaggerated movements which must have been pretty interesting to look at based on the array of bemused expressions I'd get from passersby when we stopped for lights.

We finally arrived at Chantel's without any more episodes, but I was still wrestling with Calvin's offer. It wasn't a date in the true sense of the word. I was only filling in for his absent friend, I reasoned as I collected Chantel's mail, did a quick look around the apartment, watered her plants, and darted back outside. *It might be fun,* I thought while I locked her doors and walked back to the car where Calvin was waiting. But after the hiccup episode and my subsequent loss of hearing, I figured the last person he'd want to spend any length of time with would be me. Ha! Wrong again.

"Everything okay?" he asked as I buckled my seat belt. His voice still sounded like it was underwater, but at least I could make out what he was saying.

"Everything's fine."

He laughed.

"What's so funny?"

"You're yelling," he said, and pulled off.

With that bulletin, I decided to remain mute for the balance of the trip.

Coming in?" I asked, careful to control my volume, when we stopped in front of Tiffany's town house. I watched his lips.

"I think I'll wait here."

I nodded and started to get out.

He grabbed my arm. "You never did give me an answer about tonight."

"Uh . . . okay. Sure."

"Great." He beamed as if he was really happy. "Dress casual."

I looked him over. Designer down from his perfectly cropped hair to his Gucci loafers. Calvin Russell did not look like the casual type, even on a bad day. I was sure Tiffany had something suitable for a night at the Garden.

"I'll try to hurry, but I have to walk Virginia first and change," I said as quietly as possible.

"Then why don't I dash home and take care of a few things. I'll come back for you in say—" He shot his cuffs, revealing a gold Rolex. "—about an hour."

"I'll be ready."

"Great. See you in a few." He pulled off again.

I stood on the curb until he disappeared around the corner. I checked my Timex. Fifty-nine minutes and counting. I darted up the steps and stuck the key in the door.

"What were you doing with Calvin?"

I whirled around. "What did I tell you about sneaking up on people?" I snapped at the ever-present Wayne.

He smiled down at me. "It's worth it to see the look on your face."

I took a deep breath and held it.

Wayne tossed his head over his shoulder. "What were you doing with lover boy over there?"

I peeked around him, pretending to look for "lover boy." I raised my brows in naive ignorance. "I don't know who you're talking about."

He twisted his lips and glared at me from behind his glasses. "You know who I'm talking about. Calvin . . . Tiffany's boyfriend, Calvin. What were you doing with him?"

"I don't like your tone," I said, tossing my head haughtily up into the air and bracing my hand on my hip. I tapped my foot with impatience.

"Sorry," he muttered in a cracked voice, and without another word, he turned away and double-stepped down the street.

Satisfied that I'd momentarily put a halt to his relentless questions, I turned the key in the lock. Virginia was barking on the other side of the door. I'm sure she figured I was just going to whisk in and take her for a walk. I opened the door, set the alarm, and strutted inside.

I looked down at Virginia and rolled my eyes. Ignoring the pesky creature, I walked past her and into the living room, where I began watering the forest of plants.

I didn't have time to worry about Wayne or Virginia, I thought as I watered the aloe. I had bigger, more pressing problems to deal with—a date with Calvin.

Finishing my nightly chore, I darted into the bathroom for a quick shower and realized that the shower-gel bottle was empty. Searching the under-the-sink cabinet as well as the medicine chest for more proved fruitless. Naked, I hurried back into the bedroom, sure that Tiffany would have an extra stash somewhere.

I checked the dresser, the top shelf of the dreaded closet. Nothing, nada, zippo. By then I'd resigned myself to bathe with plain old soap when for the first time I noticed a small pale-pink designer shopping bag against the wall. I supposed I must have missed it, since it almost blended in with the walls.

It looked like the kind of bag that Tiffany would have filled with expensive purchases for the bath. I walked over, picked it up, and lo and behold—it wasn't a shopping bag at all, but a book designed to look like a bag—a handbook!

Wayne, Virginia, and Calvin, even Grandma forgotten, I held the treasure to my chest. The hunt was over. In all my almost glorious nakedness I pulled up a chair and flipped open the book.

# I Can Do This

The first page was a hit list of what appeared to be ten commandments.

1. Me first above all others.
2. Attitude is everything.
3. Associate only with those who can help you look good and get ahead.
4. Appearance counts: Wear only the best, even when you can't afford it.
5. Know a little bit about a lot of things.
6. The only person you can truly trust is no one.
7. A hair stylist is a woman's best friend.
8. Get everything you can for as little as possible.

9. Don't hesitate to take the credit if it makes you look good.
10. The only obstacle in life is a small mind. Think BIG.

Each commandment had a chapter dedicated to it. The book wasn't thick, and it could easily be stashed in a nice-size everyday bag for quick reference. Briefly I browsed through it and was amazed at how simple it all was. Ultimately, to reach the heights of Divadom, a woman must believe that she is the be-all to end all—she must live it, breathe it, and convince everyone else of that fact, whether it was true or false. Once the "outsiders"—as Divas called those outside the inner circle—saw you as the quintessential woman, they would envy, admire, and long to be you, to be in your company. Men would desire you and do all they could to have you.

I closed the book and stuck it in my purse. I would study it the same way I studied science and math equations. I would make the commandments a part of my life. I smiled. And what better person to test it out on than one who craved a Diva himself—Calvin. Between the handbook, the tapes, and Chantel's diary, there would be no stopping me.

Showered and dressed in one of Tiffany's white silk blouses with a light blue stripe and a pair of navy pleated pants, I added a gold chain from her jewelry box and matching gold studs for my ears. I looked down at my feet and my plain black pumps. *Hmmm.* I guess I could manage to squeeze my feet into a pair of Tiffany's shoes for a couple of hours. As for makeup, I knew I had a long way to go and opted for the fresh-face look—lipstick and a couple of strokes of mascara. I pulled my hair back into a pearl-encrusted barrette and took a look in the mirror. *Hmmm.* I opened a couple of buttons on the blouse. No point in wearing a push-up bra if you didn't use it to your advantage.

Scanning the top of the dresser, I selected Chanel No. 5 and dabbed it behind my ears and my wrists and between my recently developed cleavage. I gave myself another once-over and smiled.

I snatched my purse from the bed with the handbook tucked inside and left the bedroom.

The doorbell rang in concert with the telephone. I darted into the kitchen to pick up the phone. "Hello?"

"Maggie? Is this you?"

Oh, no. *Tiffany.* My heart started to pound. "Hi, Tiffie." I glanced at Virginia, and I'd swear she had a smug look on her face.

"How is everything? We've been so busy. Didn't have time to call. How's Virginia?"

"Uh, everything is fine."

"Did you remember to water the plants and pick up the mail?"

"Of course. I said everything was fine."

The doorbell rang again.

"Was that the bell?"

Supersonic hearing. "Uh . . . yes. Probably someone selling something. Listen, I was just getting ready to leave . . . and go home. I'll check on my way out."

"Let me talk to Ginny."

"Who?"

"Virginia."

I held out the phone toward Virginia. "She wants to talk to you."

Virginia trotted over to the phone. When she heard Tiffany's voice, she wagged her tail, looked up at me, and barked several times into the phone before walking away.

I put the phone to my ear.

"What's going on with Calvin? Has he been by to pick up his things?"

I snatched a look at Virginia. Had she turned on me? "Uh, yes. He dropped by the other day. I gave him the box like you said."

"What did he say? Anything?"

"Not really."

"He was probably too shocked. He's probably wallowing in sorrow." I heard Chantel giggle in the background.

"Well, I should be going. Chantel and I have dates tonight." Chantel giggled again. "Two gorgeous Frenchmen. They promise to show us the sights . . . at night, of course." She laughed. "I'll check back later in the week. Don't forget the housekeeper will be there on Saturday."

"Sure."

"Oh, Maggie, you haven't bothered anything in the apartment, have you?" Her voice seemed to be suddenly laced with suspicion.

A "B" movie version of the past few days of catastrophes ran through my head. "Of course not."

"Good." She sighed heavily. "We mustn't keep Jean and Pierre waiting."

"Have f—"

The line went dead. I pursed my lips, hung up the phone, and headed for the door. I took one look back at Virginia, who shook her head at me, turned, and walked away. I would not have a dog make me feel guilty. I set the alarm and shut the door defiantly behind me. What was the number-one Diva tenet? *Me first above all others*. Well, for once in my life I was going to think about me first! What could possibly be wrong with that?

Fortified by that and Commandment Number Two: *Attitude is everything,* I stepped outside—with attitude. All my preparation was worth it when I saw the look of appreciation in Calvin's expression. For a moment I was taken aback. I couldn't remember any man looking at me that way. Ever. He did a real-live double take when I stood for a moment on the top step of the town house stoop. Slowly and deliberately, the way I'd seen the women on the tapes walk, I approached him with one of those "take my picture now" smiles pasted on my face.

Calvin hustled around to the passenger side of the car and opened the door for me.

"Sorry to have kept you waiting," I murmured before sliding into my seat.

He leaned down before closing it. "It was worth it."

I felt like giggling but thought better of it. I fastened my seat belt instead.

Calvin hopped behind the wheel, beaming like what was happening was a real date or something. But it wasn't. It couldn't be, because if it was—well, I didn't want to think about it.

We listened to John Coltrane, a definite switch from the blues he'd played earlier. I always believed that any time a man wanted to impress a woman, he played jazz as if that somehow validated his taste, whether he had any or not. There were two schools however. The true lovers would call Coltrane, Davis, and Rawlins by their first names. And the others believe that Kenny G invented jazz. That's how you could tell the difference. Then there were the others, who thought that cool was a car stereo system that could take out a square block and believed that anyone within earshot wanted nothing more than to listen to the noise blasting from their speakers.

"Coltrane," I said offhandedly.

A smile spread across his face. "The man," he said. "No one can blow like John."

*Hmmm. First name.* But here came the true test. "You have any Kenny G?"

His face crumbled like a crushed cookie. He turned and almost sneered at me. His brows knitted into a single line. "Sorry. No." He sounded disgusted; maybe *disappointed* was a better word.

"Glad to hear it," I said, adding a touch of smug to my voice. "It's the easiest way to separate the fakes from the real things."

He tossed his head back and laughed. "You are a funny lady, Margaret."

I smiled, and then the images and the message on the training video flashed in my head, and one word beamed like a neon sign: *Flaunt*.

"John was a genius, but so was Miles," I said, and began unfurling all the info I could remember from having read the manuscript, *Miles from Home—The True Miles Davis Story,* for University Press.

Inwardly I smiled as I rattled off facts, figures, and anecdotes, surprising myself with my monologue and obviously impressing Calvin, who smiled and nodded for the entire trip to the Garden.

"You sure know your stuff," he said when we pulled up to the parking garage. He helped me out of my seat and handed the attendant his keys. "I hope you enjoy the game as much as you enjoy music."

"I'm sure I will."

He took my arm and guided me inside the historic Madison Square Garden. Maybe this was a date, after all.

# Sports Wrap-up

Of course, those lousy Knicks lost again, but being in the Garden for a live game was thrilling nonetheless. I cheered and booed with the best of them, forgetting all about being a dignified Diva, and just enjoyed myself in the company of a handsome, very attentive man.

"How 'bout those Knicks?" Calvin said as we headed uptown on Eighth Avenue.

"Houston is a waste of money and manpower," I replied. I'd read enough of the sports pages and heard enough complaints from the guys in the mailroom to be able to add my two cents.

Calvin took a quick glance in my direction. "That's an understatement."

"He's a streak shooter," I added, remembering it was something Larry often said.

"And tonight wasn't one of those streak-shooting nights."

"Humph. They should trade him."

"That's what everyone says; everyone but management."

We chuckled.

"Hey, I know it's kind of late, but you've got to be hungry. I am."

"Maybe a little. But I can pop something in the microwave when I get back."

"Do you like soul food?"

"Love it. Why?"

"There's this great place. I know you will like it. It's called Brothers. I usually go there after a game, toss back a few beers and have some ribs. How 'bout it?"

My stomach growled, demanding that I do its bidding. Hopefully he didn't hear it over the strains of Nancy Wilson on the radio. I wondered if this was someplace that Tiffany and Chantel wouldn't be "caught dead in." Although I found it hard to imagine either of them eating anything with their fingers—which everyone knows is the only way to eat ribs.

"Hmmm, sure. Why not. Sounds like fun."

"Great."

He made a quick right and then turned onto Seventh Avenue—in some circles known as Fashion Avenue and headed downtown.

Brothers wasn't what one would call a five-star establishment, but it had character: leather booths, sparkling wood floors, the appropriately dim lighting, a mammoth bar that took up one side of the restaurant, and of course the prerequisite large-screen color television permanently set to the sports channel.

Even at 11 p.m., the place was still crowded. The waitress seated us at the last available booth. We ordered a plate of ribs to share (ain't that cute?), a bowl of collard greens, and two sides of slaw.

Let's just say that my impressions of Calvin were tossed out with the trash. He was truly down to earth, intelligent without being pompous, and had a good sense of humor. I had to wonder why Tiffany didn't want to be bothered.

Dinner lasted a good hour, and we talked nonstop, licking our fingers in between dialogue.

"Should I take you home, or are you staying at Tiffany's?" he asked when we got back in the car.

"I'll be going to Tiffany's. I have to walk Virginia at seven in the morning."

"Oh, yes, Virginia," he said, not too kindly.

I laughed. "Do you have a problem with Virginia?"

He gave me a twisted smile. "Let's just that the dog is a little too human for my tastes. Kinda spooky."

*If you only knew.*


W ell . . . here we are," Calvin said, pulling in front of Tiffany's place. He turned in his seat to face me. "I had a really good time tonight, Margaret. Thanks for coming with me."

"So did I. Thanks for the invite."

He glanced down at his hands, then at me. "Look, I don't want to put you in an awkward position with you being a friend of Tiffany's but . . . I was hoping I could see you again."

My breath caught. "See me again?" I repeated inanely, my voice having taken on a Mickey Mouse quality.

"Yes . . . see you again."

"Well, I, uh . . . Can I think about it?"

"Sure." He dug in his pocket, pulled out his wallet, and handed me his business card. "Call me when you decide."

"Okay." I opened the lock on my side. "Thanks again for tonight. I really had a good time."

"Can I walk you to the door?"

That's generally the prelude to the good-night kiss. "Uh, no need. I'll be fine."

"Then I'll wait here and make sure you get in safely."

I was just about to get out when Calvin grabbed my arm. I turned, and he kissed me lightly—on the forehead. And I found myself strangely disappointed.

"Good night, Margaret."

"Night."

I almost ran to the house. I punched in the code for the alarm, locked the doors behind me, and reset it. *Whew.* I stood with my back against the door, trying to wrap my mind around what had just happened when I looked down and saw Virginia looking up at me.

"I had a very nice time, if you must know. Calvin is a really decent guy. Tiffany doesn't deserve him."

Virginia just turned and padded away.

I fixed myself a glass of ice water—there wasn't much else to choose from—then got ready for bed.

With the covers tucked under my chin, I did a mental rundown of the events of the past few days. I was now the acting executive editor at University Press, perhaps not the most prestigious house in the literary world, but it would still look good on my résumé. I had two full designer wardrobes at my disposal, a handsome bachelor was apparently interested in me, I'd found the handbook, explored Tiffany's secret closet, uncovered Grandma's scam, and I'd wiggled my way to an invitation to the soiree. I had training tapes, workbooks, and Wayne at my disposal.

I flipped over on my side and turned out the light. I was on my way! My last thought before drifting off to sleep was finding out where my mother went in that Mercedes.

———

The following morning I was awakened by the ringing telephone. Bleary-eyed, I peeked at the digital clock on the nightstand— 6:00 a.m. Somebody better be dead.

"Hello?" I snapped.

"Is that any way to answer the phone?"

"Wayne! Do you have any idea what time it is?"

"I most certainly do. I waited up for you last night."

"You did what?"

"I wanted to hear how your 'date' with Calvin went."

I sat up in the bed. "I really don't see how that's any of your business, Wayne."

"Tiffany, for all her uppity, snobbish quirks, is my friend—sort of—and I thought she was yours, too."

"Your point?"

"How can you date your friend's boyfriend?"

"It wasn't a date, I'm telling you."

"It looked like one to me."

"Looks can be deceiving."

I heard him sigh on the other end. "Is he there now?"

"What is this really about, Wayne?"

"Never mind. Have a nice day." He hung up.

I flopped down on the bed and pulled the sheet over my head, determined to put Wayne out of my mind and catch a few more winks before I had to walk Virginia.

No such luck. Wayne's question bugged me. There was a part of me that knew what I did the night before was suspect at best, and a part of me that enjoyed it immensely. I had two choices: (1) feel utterly guilty or (2) utterly enjoy my guilty pleasure for as long as I could. I chose number two. After all, it wasn't forever. Just a few weeks. What could be the harm in that?

# Large and
# In Charge

*I* figured if my first day as acting executive editor was a breeze, day two would be a piece of cake. As usual, I was wrong.

The moment I walked into the office, I sensed trouble. There was an icy chill in the air, the kind a spy must feel when he's come in from the cold and all his colleagues suspect him of betrayal. Eyes that can barely meet yours, those who once greeted you effusively suddenly can't remember your name. That was the atmosphere at University Press. I had no idea what I was up against, how many enemies lurked in the corner offices. But like any good spy, I would uncover the truth and vindicate myself.

I spotted several conspiratorial secretaries huddled by the water fountain, talking in harsh whispers that quickly dropped when I approached. *Interesting.*

"Good morning, ladies. Lovely day, isn't it?" The best offense is a defense, I thought, eyeing each of them.

"Depends," Shaniqua said while popping a wad of gum.

Her water-cooler sidekicks giggled their support.

Fine. I continued down the hallway toward my *new* office. I made a mental note to request a temporary assistant from personnel. But when I arrived at my office, none other than Beverly was sitting behind my old desk, casually filing her nails. I stopped dead in my tracks.

"Can I help you with something?" I asked—no, *demanded.*

She rolled her eyes before responding. "According to Mr. Savage, that's what I'm supposed to be asking you." She pursed her berry-tinted lips as if she were ready to spit on my shoes, then looked me up and down.

I blinked and shook my head to clear it. "Excuse me?"

"I'm your new temporary assistant. Didn't you get the memo?"

Not to appear as if I was out of the loop, I replied, "I'm sure it's in my basket, and I haven't gotten around to it yet." I straightened my shoulders, remembering the second commandment. "I'll have your assignments for today ready shortly." I looked down at her over the bridge of my nose, as I'd seen Tiffany and Chantel do to those whom they believed were "beneath" them. "Did you finish up the manuscript I gave you the other day?" I arched a brow for added effect.

For a moment she looked flustered, and I almost smiled, but she quickly pulled herself together. She lifted her chin, and for a hot New York minute, I wished Wayne were around to snap her back in place. She picked up her nail file and continued to groom her nails.

"Nope," she said calmly, then examined her left hand.

"Then I suggest you get started," I said with as much authority as I could summon, then spun away shutting *my* office door solidly behind me.

On shaky legs, which were being precariously balanced on Tiffany's three-inch Prada heels, I teetered to my desk and sat down. For several moments I sat perfectly still, trying to gather my wits. Obviously there had been some twisted mix-up. I couldn't work with this woman. It was apparent that Beverly's presence in my life was set to thwart my rise to power. She was the Dr. No to my 007. And as we all know, Bond always came out on top—literally. I pulled out the handbook and quickly read the chapter dedicated to the tenth commandment: *The only obstacle in life is a small mind. Think BIG.*

The chapter described a situation similar to mine. A young, promising, capable woman (that would be me) was given a promotion over another woman in the office. We'll call her woman B. All the other women in the office sided with woman B and did everything in their power to sabotage the other woman (me). Initially she cowered under the pressure until she turned the tables.

So I would turn the tables. Think big, bigger than them. They wouldn't beat me.

I smiled a sinister smile and pressed the intercom.

"Yeah?" Beverly responded, and I cringed.

"Hey, girl. Listen, I was thinking maybe me and you could take a long lunch break together. You know, since the both of us have moved up in the ranks, we may as well take advantage of it."

"Say what?"

"Yeah, girl, how 'bout it?" I asked, throwing in the whole sisterfriend routine.

"Well . . . is it on you?"

"Of course. Well, let's just say it's on University Press." I laughed, and so did she.

"Sure. Okay."

"Great. Noon sound good to you?"

"Sure."

"See you then." I let go of the intercom. Round one.

There was a light knock on my door.

"Come in."

The door eased open, and Maribel stuck her head in. "Meez Margreet, I come to clean up."

"Come in, Maribel."

She came in, pushing her buckets and brooms in front of her. "Congratulations, Meez Margreet, on your promotion."

"Thank you, Maribel."

Then she looked up at me, her eyes suddenly filling with water. "Now that you beeg boss, you not have me fired for slapping you? I really need my job, Meez Margreet."

Commandment number three: *Associate only with those who can make you look good and get you ahead.* Now who knew the inner workings of an office better than the custodian? The custodian was the equivalent of a bartender or a taxi driver. People tended either to bare their souls or totally ignore them and continue with the most intimate conversations as if they weren't there.

I came from behind my desk, stepped up to her, and put my arm around her shoulders.

She glanced at her shoulder then up at me.

I smiled. "We both know you did what you had to do, Maribel. I would never hold that against you. You have nothing to worry about from me. And I never properly thanked you."

"It . . . was nothing," she said in a halting voice.

"No, no it was something . . . You can believe that." I squeezed her shoulder a little tighter. "Why don't you come and sit down for a minute so we can talk. We never really had a chance to get to know each other."

"But I have so much work—"

"Work! Ha. I'm the new boss now. And I said you can take a break."

She eyed me skeptically but finally sat down.

"That's better." I took my seat. "I have to confess something to you, Maribel." I lowered my voice and leaned forward. "This new job . . . It's kind of frightening, you know. Especially when," I dropped my voice even lower, forcing her to lean closer, "you don't know who your friends are." I forced my eyes to well up with tears. "That makes it so hard to do my job. And I want to do a good job, Maribel. I want Mr. Fields to come back and be proud of me. I feel so lost. There's no one I can turn to." I covered my face with my hands for effect.

"*Ay,* Meez Margreet, don't cry. I would do anything to help you do a good job."

I slowly lowered my hands. "Anything?"

"*Sí.*" She bobbed her head enthusiastically up and down.

My smile glowed with gratitude. Quickly I pulled myself together. "Well, it would help me a great deal if you could . . . well, listen to what people are saying about me . . . I mean my promotion, how I'm doing my job, things like that. So that I can be even better."

Her eyes widened with excitement. "You want I should be a secret agent?" she eagerly asked.

For a moment I saw Maribel as my very own Carmen Sandiego, complete with her floppy wide-brimmed hat and belted trench coat. Maribel was perfect for the job.

I smiled. "Yes, a secret agent."

She popped up from her seat. "When do I start?"

"Today," I shot right back, pumped by her enthusiasm.

"I do a good job for you, Meez Margreet."

"I know you will, Carmen—I mean—Maribel."

She gathered her tools and headed for the door, then stopped. "Do we need a secret place to meet?" she asked in a hoarse whisper.

"No. Why not just bring me up to date when you come in each morning?"

She bobbed her head up and down again and then scurried out.

Now that I'd secured a loyal ally, it was only a matter of time before I learned everything I needed to know about the staff at University Press. Things were going to work out, after all. But then my intercom buzzed.

"Yes, Beverly," I said evenly.

"There's a James Blake on the phone. He says it's urgent."

My eyebrows rose. Chantel's boyfriend!

"Tell him I'll be right with him," I said, needing a few minutes to gather my thoughts. What was he doing calling me, and how did he get my number? Well I'd just give him the bare minimum and get him off the phone. I pressed the flashing red light.

"Margaret Drew," I said into the phone as if he didn't know. "Oh, James, yes. What can I do for you?"

"I don't mean to put you on the spot or anything, but have you heard from Chantel? I've been calling her for days, and all I get is her machine. I went to her office today, and they said she was on vacation."

"Uh, yes, she is."

Silence.

"Hello?"

"Sorry, Margaret, I was trying to put it together in my head. Why would she pick up and leave and not tell me?"

"Gee, James, I don't have a clue."

"Did she tell you where she was going?"

"Uh, yes."

"Well, where is she?"

"Last I heard she was in Paris."

"What!"

"Look, James, I really have an awful lot to do. . . . I was just promoted and—"

"I bet she's with that damned Tiffany and her sidekick, Calvin."

Interesting. Did I sense some animosity here?

"Never could tolerate either one of them."

"Oooh, reeeally?"

"Look, would it be okay if I stopped by your office after work?"

"Say what?"

"I have a meeting to go to, and I really need to talk to you. You're Chantel's friend—maybe you can help me understand."

"But—"

"Say I meet you out front at five. I'll be in a silver Lexus. Thanks, Margaret."

Click.

"Shit. What just happened here?"

*Knock. Knock.*

"Come in."

"Morning, boss," Larry said. "Seems like you've made yourself right at home." He took some mail from his cart and put it in my in-box. "Even got yourself an assistant."

"I don't remember you bringing Mr. Fields's mail into his office. You generally leave it out front."

He gave me an odd look. "Wanted to see you in your new digs. And it looks like you fit right in. Have a nice day, *boss*."

I stared at the closed door. Men. They're just like buses. For hours you don't see one, and then they come in bunches.

# Things Get Curiouser
# and Curiouser

*I*t was only ten o'clock, and it looked as if my day was going to be a humdinger. Now I wished I hadn't invited Beverly to lunch. But to uninvite her would be bad form. I would have to make the most of it.

I reached beneath my desk and extracted one of the manuals from my trusty shopping bag—*Training Manual Two*. I flipped it open to the table of contents. What immediately caught my attention was the section called "Excelling in the Workplace with Little or No Effort." I turned to page ninety.

*I*t is important for every Diva, especially those in training, to perfect the art of being important, even if you are the lowest woman on the totem pole. Obviously, if you don't think you are important, no one else will either. You must work at positioning yourself for promotions, raises, and added perks. How is that accomplished with the minimum amount of effort on your part?

- Always keep your ears open for gossip. One of the best places to glean information is in the stalls of the ladies' room. Make it a point several times per day to hang out in the ladies' room. Enter one of the stalls, and lock the door behind you. Stand up on the bowl's rim, and listen to the conversations people have when they think no one is listening. This is especially effective during holiday parties.

- Come in each day at least ten minutes before your boss does and leave ten minutes later. Always have several open folders on your desk, and have your computer on. For an added kick, have the phone to your ear and scribble irrelevant notes as your boss passes by. It gives the illusion that not only can you multitask, but that you are a dedicated employee, as well.

- Compliment higher-ups on the great job they are doing. Pay attention to the postings for those who have been promoted or shifted to different departments. Be sure to mention your heartfelt congratulations when you see them.

- Know the names and birthdates of your immediate boss, his or her spouse, and their children. Send personal notes on holidays and birthdays. (Cheaper than sending gifts that won't be used.)

- Find out who in your department is good at certain tasks. Learn to delegate early on. This gives underlings the impression that you are important and gives higher-ups the impression that you have what it takes to be a manager.

- Always look busy, even if you have nothing to do.

Those were easy enough to implement, I thought, reviewing the list one more time. And I was really intrigued by the whole bathroom stall thing. That one sounded like a real winner. I closed the book, stuck it back in the shopping bag, and took out my extra shoes. I'd learned my lesson. Slipping my comfortable pumps on, I decided to survey my domain and see what everyone was up to. I thought it prudent as the executive acting editor to make sure that folks knew I was on top of things. It might also be an opportunity to show some goodwill. I smiled, tugged on the hem of the borrowed Vera Wang two-piece pantsuit, and strutted into the outer office, where my *assistant* sat.

"Beverly, I should be back shortly."

She glanced up from taking notes on the manuscript I'd assigned to her. "Sure."

I started to walk away. I figured the secretary pool would be a good bet.

"Uh, Margaret."

I fixed a smile on my face and turned. "Yes, *Bev.*"

She arched a brow. "Are we still on for lunch?"

"Sure. Is there a problem?"

"Uh, no, not really. It's just that I realized I had a . . . nail appointment today."

I waved my hand in a friendly but dismissive manner. "Girl, if you need to have your nails done, then get them done. No problem. We can always do lunch."

"Really?"

"Yes, really." I laughed lightly. "As a matter of fact, take an extra half hour. Nothing like getting yours nails done and then have them get messed up because they aren't dry."

She pursed her lips in agreement. "I know what you mean. Especially your toes."

"Exactly. So don't even worry about it. Do your thing."

"Thanks, Margaret." She smiled a genuinely surprised smile, and for a moment I almost felt bad for pulling her leg. Almost.

I continued down the corridor, listening for any sounds of dissent in the ranks. I ran into Larry just as he was coming out of the personnel office. "Hey, Larry. How's it going?" I walked up to him.

"Everything's fine on my end. What about you?"

I shrugged. If there was one thing about my relationship with Larry, it was that we were pretty honest with each other most of the time. I felt this was one of those times. "To be truthful, it's kind of scary."

"Why?"

"It's one thing to sit on one side of the desk, in your little part of the world, and do your little job. It's a completely different story when you are responsible for everyone else's little part of the world, too."

"I guess you're right. But at least you're dressing the part. Funny how everything sort of came together at once."

I glanced down at my borrowed outfit. "What do you mean?"

"You know. You come in with a new look, a new attitude, and suddenly Mr. Fields has a heart attack and you are elevated to his job—even if it is only temporary."

"I guess it's about being in the right place at the right time. And being able to do the job when you get there, which, from what I'm gathering, not many think I can do." I planted my hand on my right hip and eyed him for any signs of the truth in my words.

He shrugged slightly. "There will always be someone putting the badmouth on you. The bottom line is, as far as everyone is concerned, you're no longer *us,* you're *them.*"

I titled my chin at a haughty angle (seeing as Wayne was nowhere in the vicinity). "And what do *you* think, Larry? Do *you* think I don't deserve this job and that I'm just a face in a fancy suit with a head full of air?" I kept my voice cool and even, the way I'd heard Chantel and Tiffany dress down an opponent without raising a brow.

At least he had the decency to look duly chastised. "I think you got a lucky break. I just hope that it doesn't turn you into the kind of woman who everyone loves to hate—that's all. Look, I gotta get the rest of this mail delivered. Have a good day." He started down the hall.

"Meet you at five?" I asked, just to see what he would say.

He turned and looked at me over his shoulder. "I don't think that would be a good idea, Margaret." With that, he pushed his mail cart down to the next office and disappeared inside.

For a few minutes I simply stood there, taking in what Larry had said. I was now a *them.* I wasn't welcomed in the cafeteria with the rest of the staff, most people thought I couldn't handle the job even though I knew I could and could probably do a better job than Mr. Fields, Larry no longer wanted to be seen with me outside of work, and the rest of the staff stayed away from me as if I had the plague. Was this the reward for climbing the ladder of success?

I smiled. Fine! They'd left me with no choice. I'd have to go true Diva on them.

# It's Raining Men

*I* spent the better part of the day going through the manual, picking up tips. In between, I read excerpts from Chantel's diary and how she managed to pull the wool over the eyes of everyone at DKNY. Apparently Chantel was quite adept at the bathroom-stall thing and constantly picked up inside information about other employees' marketing ideas, which she then modified and turned into her own, ultimately garnering her account executive status.

A trip to the ladies' room was in order. I went out front and informed Bev that I would be back shortly. I made a comment about how lovely her nails looked and told her we'd have to make a rain check for lunch.

I entered the ladies' room and found it empty. Great. I chose a

stall at the end of the line, stepped inside, and locked the door behind me. I stood up on the seat, precariously balancing myself,
and waited. I didn't have to wait long.

Shaniqua and her water-cooler buddy Tashana came in.

"So what's on for the weekend?" Shaniqua said.

"I'm going to the Easy Does It lounge up on One Hundred
Thirty-fifth."

One of the stall doors opened and then closed.

"So what do you think of that doofy Margaret being in charge?"
Tashana asked.

"Girl, pleeze. She won't last a week. She thinks 'cause she put
on some fancy clothes, she's all that now."

"I hear ya."

They both laughed. The toilet flushed.

"I got a trick for her," Shaniqua said.

"What?"

"I have to key in changes for three manuscripts." She laughed.
"By the time I'm done with them, so will she."

"Oooh, you wouldn't," Tashana said, then giggled.

"Just watch me."

The bathroom door opened and then closed. I eased down from
my perch. I didn't know whether to be elated that I'd overheard
her plan or heartbroken that they thought so little of me. For as
long as I could remember, I'd been overlooked and underrated.
Well, in the famous words of Glenn Close in *Fatal Attraction*, "I
will not be ignored!"

I returned to my area and stopped at Beverly's desk. "I need you
to send out an e-mail to design and editorial. There will be a staff
meeting tomorrow morning at nine fifteen. No one is excused.
Everyone must come prepared to bring a list of all current projects."

"A staff meeting?" Her eyes widened in surprise. There hadn't

176 ★ DONNA HILL

been a staff meeting since Mr. Fields took over, nearly eight years ago.

"Yes. And please get that out right away." I turned, entered my office, and shut the door firmly behind me.

I stood in the center of my office and folded my arms. *The end of me . . . I don't think so.*

I pulled up the production sheet on my computer for all the manuscripts that were currently scheduled. I printed it out. Then I went through all Mr. Fields's files to bring me up to date on the projects, the authors, their previous works, their publicists (internal and external) and their agents. My ability to speed-read and memorize came in handy. I jotted down notes for the staff-meeting agenda and stuck them in my purse.

By the time I'd finished, it was five on the dot. I shut down my computer, locked the office, and headed out.

"Good night, Beverly. I just wanted you to know that I think you're doing a great job. That's going to mean a lot, real soon," I added with a smile, then walked away, leaving Beverly with her mouth partially open.


As promised, James was waiting out front.

I took a deep breath and walked over to his car. "Hey, James," I said, leaning down and talking to him through the open window.

"Margaret? Is that really you?"

"Were you expecting someone else?" I opened the door and slid gracefully onto the plush seat. "You wanted to talk. So talk."

He blinked several times, put the car in gear, and pulled out into traffic.

"Can we go somewhere for a drink?" he asked.

I hoped he didn't plan on getting me drunk and then plying me for information. I'd watched enough James Bond movies not to fall for that old trick. I checked my watch. "I have a little time, but not much." I thought of Virginia's evening stroll and the plan to confront my mother about her disappearing act.

"I really appreciate it, Margaret."

"Not a problem."

He tuned the radio to the R & B and classic soul station 98.7 KISS FM. My all-time favorite Marvin Gaye tune was playing— "Distant Lover"—the live version, and before I knew it, James was singing along, and he was quite good. I held my applause until the song ended.

"You're really good," I said, and meant it.

"Thanks. I sing with a band on weekends."

"You?"

He kind of blushed. "Yeah, I know. I don't look the part with this getup on."

His getup was a gray pin-striped Brooks Brothers suit, a pearl-gray shirt and gray-and-burgundy tie. No, he didn't look like a member of any band, except maybe the Wall Street Quartet.

"No offense, but you don't. What do you sing?"

"Mostly covers of R and B from the sixties and seventies, some do-wop for a change of pace every now and then."

I looked him over. "Get outta here."

He laughed and nodded. "That's pretty much what Chantel says. She won't come to any of my shows, says she doesn't want to be in that kind of environment."

So then I guessed he knew nothing about Chantel's secret crush on Duke or her and Tiffany's clandestine rendezvous to the after-hours spots. Funny how Tiffany and Chantel presented this elitist front, when underneath it all, they were really two homegirl wannabes. And I had all the evidence I needed to out them.

"Which clubs do you play at?" I asked.

He turned and looked at me for a moment. "Hmm, Lenox

Lounge and Jimmy's Uptown in Harlem, Pumpkin and Akwaaba in Brooklyn, some spots in New Jersey."

"I'd really like to see you perform sometime," I said.

"You would?" He sounded truly surprised.

"Yeah. I love R and B."

He beamed like a street light. "I have a gig this Saturday at Freddy's Cove in the West Village. Come on down. I'll get you in for free."

"Thanks—I just might take you up on that."

He pulled up in front of the Sidewalk Café on Avenue A.

"They have really great margaritas here," he said, putting quarters into the meter. "We can sit outside if you like."

"Sure."

The waitress showed us to a table. I ordered a jumbo pink margarita, and James ordered a regular one.

"So when did the dynamic duo leave?" James asked while we waited for our drinks to arrive.

"Saturday."

He slowly shook his head. "She could have told me, ya know. Makes me think she's up to something." He looked me in the eye. Fortunately I hadn't had my drink yet, so my lips were still sealed. "Why didn't you go?"

"I just got a promotion to executive editor and couldn't take the time off," I said as smooth as butter. Of course he didn't have to know that my windfall had nothing to do with skipping the Paris trip. "So I offered to look after their places until they got back." That added tidbit made me sound magnanimous.

"And when is that?"

"A little more than a month."

"A month!"

"Yep."

He frowned. "I don't believe her." He was silent for a moment.

"Fine. If that's the way she wants to play, so be it. If she can have her fun, so can I."

I didn't know what to say, and fortunately I didn't have to say anything. Our drinks arrived, and I dived right in.

For the most part, we drank in silence until James asked the million-dollar question: "You really don't seem the type to hang out with those two. So why do you?"

"What do you mean, I don't seem the type?"

"How can I put this without sounding like a jerk?" He paused. "You're actually nice."

What was I to make of that? "I have a better question for you."

He leaned forward and put his drink down. "Ask away."

"I get the impression that for whatever reason, you don't think very highly of your girlfriend, so why are you with her?"

He chuckled. "Margaret, you have no idea how many times I've asked myself the same thing. I guess I was originally attracted to the glamour of Chantel. She's the kind of woman who knows people, looks good on your arm, and can carry a conversation."

"Is that all it takes?"

He at least had the decency to look ashamed. "It shouldn't. But I guess I got caught up in the whole image, you know."

I shrugged. "I suppose."

"Don't get me wrong," he said. "Chantel can be really sweet when she wants to. . . ."

*She can?*

"And I do care about her. . . ."

He didn't sound too convincing to me. "But?"

He glanced up from the depths of his drink. "Never mind. I shouldn't be telling you all this anyway. Forget it."

We finished our drink, and James asked if I wanted to order dinner. "They have great food here."

"No, thanks. I've really got to be going."

He signaled for the waitress and paid for our drinks. "I really appreciate you talking with me," he said as we walked to the car. "I didn't mean to put you on the spot or anything. I guess I was hoping you had some answers about Chantel." He opened my door. "Is she seeing someone else?"

"I . . . really don't know, James. If she is, I've never met him." At least that much was true.

"Where to?" he asked, getting behind the wheel.

"Tiffany's. I have to walk Virginia by seven."

"You are some kind of friend. I hope Tiffany appreciates you."

"I'm sure she does," I murmured.

He turned on the radio, and we spent the balance of the drive singing along with the Temptations and James Brown.

"Hope you'll think about stopping by the club this weekend," James said when we pulled up in front of Tiffany's place. He reached into his jacket and pulled out his wallet, took out a card, and handed it to me. "My office, cell, and home phone numbers. Call if you decide to drop by. It would be great to see you again. Get to know you better. As a friend," he added.

I looked at him for a moment before taking the card. "Thanks." I got out of the car. "Keep up the singing," I said, heading toward the front door. "You just might get famous one day."

He laughed. "Maybe. See ya, Margaret."

I waved as he drove off into the sunset.

Well, as the old folks would say, when it rains it pours. One minute I had a total drought when it came to the male species; now it was raining men. Go figure.

# Large and
# In Charge

By some miracle, I was able to avoid Wayne. So I took Virginia for her walk, came back, checked the mail, watered the plants, and ordered us something to eat from the Italian restaurant—on Tiffany's account, of course.

While I waited for the food to be delivered, I decided to go on another expedition into Tiffany's secret closet and pick out a few outfits. I had a plan in mind and needed the proper attire to pull it off. A night out on the town was in order.

I laid the outfits on the bed and shoved one of the videos into the VCR. This one was a workshop called *Assuming the Position—Rising without the Fall*.

"In order to build your personal empire," the speaker said, "you must first cultivate the resources necessary to achieve your goals.

Examine your strengths and weakness, and look around you to the people who can make you even stronger: coworkers, relatives, friends, shopkeepers. *Everyone* has something that you can use. Cultivate these people, find out who they know. Everyone knows someone of importance. You must know them, too."

The women in the seminar were asked to stand up and name one person that could be used as a stepping stone to success. The list ran from the managers of restaurants to ticket clerks at movie theaters to bouncers at nightclubs, attorneys, GYN doctors, to the mailman.

I made a list of everyone they'd named and added a few of my own.

"The world runs on favors," the woman stated, "and you must be prepared to secure as many favors as you can, and make them feel good about doing it for you—that is the key." The room erupted into applause just as the doorbell rang.

I pressed STOP, hopped up from my prone position on the bed, and went to the door, with Virginia trailing behind me. My mouth was already watering for the veal parmesan I'd ordered. But instead of the delivery man, I found Grandma!

"Grandma, what in the world are you doing here?" I looked over her shoulder to see if there was any sign of my mother, but all I caught were the taillights of a Mercedes.

She smiled and breezed by me. "Your mother had to go out and didn't want to leave me in the house. So I suggested she drop me over here. Isn't that nice?"

"No. It isn't."

She ignored me and proceeded into the living room. I stomped off after her. "Where is Mother, and whose Mercedes is that?" I demanded.

Grandma shrugged her shoulders and sat down on the couch.

"She didn't say where she was going or who that lovely car belongs to."

I frowned. This was getting to be too much. One night was bad enough, but two was too many. Now I was stuck again.

"Where is that wonderful young man—Wayne?"

"Please don't talk him up."

But no sooner had the words left her mouth than the doorbell rang again. Yeah, you guessed it—Wayne.

"Come on in," I grumbled without preamble.

"I saw your grandmother pull up in a fancy Mercedes. I just had to come by and say hello."

"Oh, did you, really?" He totally missed my sarcastic tone.

"Grandma! How are you?" he bubbled as if she were his long-lost relative.

Grandma's face lit up like the Fourth of July. "Wayne, you darling boy. So glad you could drop by."

They embraced like old friends.

"Sit and tell me about your day," Grandma said, patting the space next to her on the couch. Wayne sat down, and so did Virginia.

"Well . . . I had this patient who came in with . . ."

I watched the scene from the doorway of the living room. Why do these things happen only to me? But then something from the video hit me: *Everyone has something you can use.* Well, looking at Grandma and Wayne, I couldn't imagine what that could be, but I was willing to give it a try. After all, it was Grandma who'd been able to run the hundred-dollar-bill scam for years without getting busted. That took ingenuity. Wayne seemed to have a detective's eye when it came to spotting even the slightest thing out of the ordinary—like my jutting nose, for instance. Well . . . maybe that's not such a good example, but you get the picture. Even the Roman empire started small.

I headed for the living room with a new attitude but was stopped once again by the doorbell. Fortunately it was the food this time.

"Hmm, something sure smells good," Wayne said as I tipped the delivery person.

"I slaved over a hot stove for hours," I replied, hauling the piping-hot bags into the kitchen.

"Isn't she funny?" Wayne said.

"You think so?" Grandma asked, following me into the kitchen. "I never thought she had much of a sense of humor."

"Thanks, Grandma." I put the bags on the table. "Can you help me serve this up?"

"I'll do it," Wayne offered. "You two ladies just relax."

"See how sweet and thoughtful he is?" Grandma said, pinching his cheek.

*Grrrr.* I flopped down into the first available chair while Wayne busied himself taking out plates and utensils, chatting merrily about his day at the office and describing the string of patients who came in for his care.

I have to admit, I was stunned to find out who some of his clients were. They made up some of the who's who of the upscale New York celebrities: everyone from actors to singers to models, doctors, dentists, and Indian chiefs. Maybe Wayne wasn't such a crackpot after all.

What was even more mesmerizing to watch was Grandma, who appeared to make Wayne feel like he was the most important man in the world. She hung on his every word and encouraged him to elaborate on each detail, especially the technical terms. She got a big kick out of that.

"You are so fascinating, and you get to meet such interesting people. You see them at their worst, and then you heal them," she cooed. "They must tell you so many of their secrets." She patted his thigh, and I'd swear he blushed.

His eyes brightened. "Sometimes they do," he said in a hushed whisper, and glanced at me as if I was not supposed to hear.

Grandma slid her arm through Wayne's. "You will definitely have to tell me all about it one of these days."

Wayne grinned like a schoolboy realizing he had a crush on his teacher.

"Can we eat?" I said breaking up the lovefest.

"That's what's wrong with young people today," Grandma said, taking the seat that Wayne held for her. "Always in a hurry." She looked pointedly at me. "Patience, my dear," she said, as if she were imparting the secret path to the promised land. "You will always be surprised what it will get you." She wagged her finger at me for emphasis, and for some reason I was actually embarrassed to be chastised by my grandmother in front of Wayne.

I pouted for a minute until I realized neither of them noticed or seemed to care. Besides I needed to be open-minded as I culled for information to build my empire. So I watched, ate, and listened. And you know, Grandma and Wayne might not have been as crazy as I thought.

I made a mental list of some of Wayne's clients for future reference, because as the good Diva book says, it's all about who you know. And I watched with utter fascination as my grandma cooed and wooed Wayne, laughing gaily at his lame jokes, alternately including me in the conversation with a question or a comment, but keeping her eagle eye focused on the center of her attention, Wayne. It was almost as if she were holding court, entertaining the troops. I'd seen Tiffany and Chantel do that when they entered a room. As much as you may have disliked them, you couldn't help but be fascinated by them and inwardly would long to be noticed by them. Geez, Grandma would have made a great Diva in her day.

"I could talk to you all night," Grandma said with a smile, "but

186 ★ DONNA HILL

an old lady needs more beauty rest than this young thing here."
She turned to me and patted my hand, giving me a sidelong wink.

Wayne immediately stood and extended his hand to help her
up. "Old lady." He laughed. "You have got to be one of the most
fascinating women I've met in ages. Men of any age would love to
be in your company." He lowered his voice to a teasing note. "And
you're kinda cute."

Grandma giggled and pinched his cheek. "You know just what
to say." She looked at me. "Good night, my dear. And thank you
for a lovely dinner."

I had to smile. "Good night, Grandma. See you in the morning."

"I'll be by to pick you up about eight, Grandma," Wayne said.

"Thank you, my dear. Now you two behave yourselves." She
ambled off to the guest room.

Wayne and I looked at each other for an uncomfortable moment, and naturally both of us starting talking at once.

"Sorry . . ."

"You first . . ."

"I . . . thanks again for offering to take Grandma home. I really
don't know what's gotten into my mother lately."

"Like I told you before, it's not a problem. I don't mind." He let
his finger brush my chin. "And neither should you. Good night,
Margaret."

As I watched him leave, I got that sticky, gooey feeling inside
and quickly shook it off. Wayne was not listed under the descrip-
tion of the men you wanted on your arm, according to the Diva
handbook. James and Calvin were the perfect types. They knew
how to look and act the parts, even if underneath there were issues
that could raise a few eyebrows. Those were the men you wanted
to be seen with. Wayne was the guy you went grocery shopping
with or let walk your dog or run errands for you. He wasn't the
guy a true Diva settled for, even if he was sort of a doctor.

Then why did I feel so twisted up inside, knowing what I knew? Perplexed by very disturbing emotions that were in total contrast to my agenda, I decided a nice hot bath would clear my head, but I still hadn't gone to Chantel's, so the bath would have to wait.

I walked into Tiffany's bedroom, checked my wallet, and noticed how low I was on funds. I already knew that my checking account had about fifteen dollars in it and my savings account wasn't much better. All the running around and jumping into and out of cabs was beginning to take its toll. I checked my jacket pockets and was truly disturbed to discover that I had only a little more than two dollars' worth of change.

Momentarily daunted by this latest annoyance, I flipped through the mail I'd placed on the dresser and noticed the monthly bill from Parking Unlimited. Now, why hadn't I thought it before? Tiffany's Jaguar was parked in the garage around the corner. Of course, since I had access to her apartment, I couldn't *imagine* that she hadn't meant to tell me that I had use of her car, as well. I'm sure it was an oversight on her part.

Totally energized, I grabbed my purse, darted down the hallway, and snatched the car keys from the hook by the kitchen door. I spun toward Virginia, who was hot on my trail, as usual.

"Look, I have to go out for a little while. I need you to behave yourself and keep an eye on Grandma. Got it?"

Virginia angled her head to the side and looked me up and down. She barked.

I patted her head. "Thanks, Virginia." I set the alarm, tiptoed out, and hustled down the street to the garage. *This should be a breeze,* I thought. I'd dart over to Chantel's in style and dart right back, take my hot bath, and turn in. What could possibly go wrong? I should have known better than to even entertain the question. I started to get a feeling that things were going south when I approached the parking attendant.

"Hi," I said cheerily. "I'm here to pick up Ms. Lane's car." I dangled the keys with the parking lot reserved number on them.

The attendant gave me an odd look. His thick brows drew into an ominous line. "You're not Ms. Lane." He squinted his eyes at me and shifted his cigarette from the right side of his mouth to the left.

"I know," I said, holding on to my smile. "My name is Margaret Drew—I'm Ms. Lane's friend. I'm here to pick up her car."

He shook his head vigorously. "You're not Ms. Lane."

"Yes, I know," I said through my teeth. "I only want to pick up her car."

"Where is she?"

Now we were getting somewhere. "She went away on a long trip. That's why I have her car keys." I jiggled them in front of him again. But it was clear from the blank look in his eyes that he didn't catch a word I was saying.

He slowly shook his head. "Nope, can't give the car to you. That would spell big trouble for me."

The direct approach was obviously not working. And then, I flashed on an image of Grandma and the surly cabdriver and Grandma winding Wayne around her finger. If my century-old grandmother (and I'm being generous with the age) could morph into a cat on the prowl, so could I.

I stepped closer to him and played with the top button of my blouse. His eyes turned into laser beams. "You can trust me," I said in a come-hither voice. "I know you're worried about your job, but you have nothing to fear." I inched closer and deftly opened one button while keeping my fingers in place. I watched his breathing become labored. "Tiffany Lane is my dear friend. She would want you to loan me the car—" I fingered the name tag pinned to his chest. "—Stanley." I inhaled and exhaled deeply, and he nearly fell down into the valley. I bit my lip to keep from laughing.

"Well . . ."

I inhaled again.

"Okay." He finally looked me in the eye.

I smiled sweetly and stroked his cheek. "Thank you so much." I held up the keys, and he took them from my fingertips.

I released a sigh of relief when he went scurrying off in search of Tiffany's car. I was rather proud of myself. This stuff was pretty easy.

Moments later, Tiffany's midnight-blue Jag cruised to a stop in front of me. The car was gorgeous. Stanley hopped out, holding the door open for me. I brushed his jaw with my fingertip.

"Thank you. I'll be back later tonight." I flashed him a suggestive look. "Will you be here?"

He bobbed his head up and down so rapidly, I was sure he'd give himself a migraine.

"Great. See you later." I gave him a wink and slid behind the wheel.

Now I know firsthand why they call certain automobiles luxury cars. You had no choice but to have attitude when cruising around in a Jaguar. And of course Tiffany had one at the top of the line, with everything in it but the kitchen sink. It was equivalent to driving around in your living room. Lush, plush, and it smelled good! I was looking and feeling special. Rather than use the air-conditioning, I rolled down the windows so that the summer breeze could blow through my borrowed shoulder-length wig . . . from the Beverly Johnson collection. The only item missing was a pair of shades. I'd made a mental note to pick up sunglasses and a couple of more girdles from Chantel's drawer.

I made it over to Chantel's in about fifteen minutes, parked, and dashed to her apartment. I did a quick inventory of the place, watered her plants, and put the mail in the wicker basket on the kitchen table. It was then that I heard a noise. Now if I had good sense, the thing to do would have been to haul ass out of there. But . . . need I say more.

I tiptoed down the hallway toward the bedroom, forgetting all the movies I'd seen where the black folks are the first ones to get the ax. I slowly pushed open the bedroom door, and it creaked just like the doors in the haunted-house movies. I saw a shadow dart across the room and toward the closet. I screamed and turned on the light switch.

"Willie!"

# Who Would Have
# Thought It?

*W*illie! What the hell are you doing here again?" I
yelled, stomping my feet in time to my voice.

"Take it easy, take it easy." He held up his hands
to halt my tirade.

By degrees I settled down and began to pace. "You shouldn't be
here, Willie." I spun toward him. "Are they still looking for you?"

"Don't think so. They finally caught up with me at work, asked
a few questions, and left. Either they've lost the scent or interest,"
he said.

I sat down on the bed and propped my head up on my hands;
then I looked at him. "So . . . what have you been doing?" Once
the question was out, I wasn't sure if I wanted to hear the answer.

He grinned. "Since I work for FedEx and have a regular route, I generally know when folks are in town or out. Know what I mean? Folks tell me things, ya know."

"So if the cops are not looking for you, and you've been going to work, then why don't you stay in your own place?" I asked, perplexed.

"This is more fun. Makes me feel like Capone." He laughed, and so did I.

Then an idea hit me. "Hey, Willie, who are some of the people on your route?"

"Rich types, mostly. My route is the Upper East Side. Dons and divas, if you get my drift."

"Oh, really. Do you ever, uh, get invited to any of their parties?"

"A few of the ladies have asked me to escort them when they were at loose ends for a date. Why?"

"So you can hold your own with the upper crust."

"I do okay. But you didn't answer my question."

"Oh, nothing—just asking." I stood up with my hands on my hips. "Are you planning on staying here tonight?"

"Probably not. Actually, I have a hot date later on. I brought my clothes over here to change."

"You sure go to a lot of trouble when you could just as well do all this at home." The cops don't really know who you are, anyway."

"Like I said, it keeps the adrenaline flowing and my skills sharp. Plus I get to see you." His eyes rolled up and down over me. "You sure are looking good these days, Margaret."

I took a step back. "Is that right?"

The corner of his mouth curved up. "Yeah, that's right. You're nothing like I remember."

"Neither are you."

He slid his hands into his pockets. "I know."

"Now that we've gotten that out of the way—"

"What are you doing next weekend?"

"I beg your pardon?"

"You heard me. What are you doing next weekend?"

I blinked several times to get him back in focus. "Why?"

"I thought maybe we could hang out."

"Me and you?"

"Why not? I think it would be fun."

I shook my head to clear it and thought back to the days in kindergarten when I put my little heart and pride on the table and he crushed it like a bug. Now he was actually asking me out on a date. What next?

"I'll have to check my calendar and get back to you."

"Can I call you?"

"I guess so . . ." I dug in my purse, pulled out a piece of paper and pen, and jotted down my office number.

He took the paper and stuck it in his shirt pocket. "I'll call."

"Okay."

We looked at each other for a few minutes.

"I guess I'd better be going."

"Uh . . . I only have a few things to pick up, and then I'm leaving. I suppose you can stay here if you really need to."

"Just long enough to change, and then I'm gone. Promise."

I angled my head to the side. "If you have such a hot date, then why are you asking to take me out, anyway? Seems like you would want to stick with your 'hot date.' "

"To be truthful, it's another one of those 'Will, can you please go with me tonight?' kind of dates," he said in a terrible falsetto. "I'm doing a lady friend a favor. Free food, free drinks, and you never know who you will meet." He shrugged. "So why not."

"Sounds pretty mercenary to me."

"Why? Women do it all the time," he said casually. "They never seem to have a problem with a man paying for a night on the town. It's standard operating procedure. But when a man goes for the gold, eyebrows get raised. Double standard." He grinned and brushed off one index finger with another in a tsk-tsk motion. "I don't do anything someone doesn't ask me to do."

"You mean anything other than breaking into homes and stealing?"

"Even that's a service."

I had to laugh. "You really have this all figured out, don't you?"

"Not really. I just know what I know. The rest I fake."

"There's a lot of that going around," I mumbled.

"Anyway," he hitched his thumb over his shoulder. "I'm gonna jump in the shower and get dressed." He checked his watch. "I have to pick my lady friend up at nine."

"Well don't let *me* keep you."

He grabbed a garment bag from the chaise longue and strolled off to the bathroom. "I'll call you," he said before shutting the door.

Standing there, I had the weirdest sensation that somehow Willie was the one who belonged in Chantel's apartment and I was the one uninvited. Well, I didn't have time to dwell on it—or rather I preferred not to do so.

While Willie was in the shower, I picked out a couple of body shapers and stuffed them deep into my bag. A dazzling pair of earrings on the dresser caught my eye, and I scooped them up, as well. I knew they would go great with something. I figured since I was there, I might as well take a quick perusal of the closet. I found a suit by Liz Claiborne that I'd salivated over when I'd seen it on Chantel. Covering it in a garment bag, I put it on the bed, just as Willie stepped out of the bathroom.

You know that line from the romance novels about how the

heroine's heart began beating like tribal drums in her chest when she saw the hero? Well, that's exactly what happened.

For a moment I couldn't catch my breath, and I would have sworn my eyes were playing tricks on me. Willie was *f-i-n-e!* He'd shaved and trimmed his mustache. The navy suit with the wide-legged pleated pants jump-started my libido. The jacket was open, and so was the stark white shirt beneath, revealing an enticing line of chocolate flesh. He even walked differently as he strode out of the bathroom, exuding a certain kind of swagger that only men fully confident in their masculinity possessed.

Fortunately he didn't notice me staring with my mouth open, which gave me a moment to pull myself together. He looked up from adjusting the belt on his pants and smiled. Damn if he hadn't suddenly developed a dimple in his left cheek. When had that happened?

"Hey, I see you're ready to go," he said, motioning to the bag on the bed.

I swallowed over the dryness in my throat. "Uh, yes."

"You okay?" he asked, stepping a bit closer. "You look a little . . . shook up or something."

"No. I'm fine. Listen I have to go. I'm sure you can find your way out." I turned to leave.

"Talk to you soon, Margaret. That's a promise."

"Have a nice time tonight," I tossed over my shoulder and walked out.

As I returned to my borrowed Jaguar, I made an important decision. Willie was the man who would accompany me to the soiree, if he didn't land in jail first.

# Getting the Hang of It—
# And Liking It!

The Jag drove as smooth as fine silk. If I closed the windows, it was as if I were riding in a soundproof booth. The obstacle course of New York City potholes had no effect on the incredible suspension. I didn't feel a thing. I should have thought of using Tiffany's car days ago. It would have made my life a lot simpler. But from here on out, my intention was to live the way I intended to grow accustomed to.

This was the life, I mused as I pressed a button and opened the sunroof: great apartment, fabulous clothes, deluxe car, gorgeous men, good credit, and a philosophy that espoused that I deserved it all—and more. This was what I'd been missing all these years. Now it was in my grasp. I was getting the hang of it.

As I cruised along the busy Manhattan streets, my thoughts

segued from the lap of luxury to the memory of seeing Willie
*GQ*'d. I still could not quite get over his transformation, but then
again, I suppose many could say the same about me. Little more
than a week earlier, I was a nondescript assistant to an obnoxious
editor. I couldn't remember the last time I'd gone on a real date or
purchased clothes that weren't on sale. Now, I was banging. I had
the clothes, the accessories, the wigs, the tapes, the handbook, and
now the ride. I smiled. Life was indeed good, and good things
came to those who waited and waited.

My thoughts shifted back to Willie. Did clothes really make
the man, as the old adage said? In Willie's case, apparently they
did. He was a completely different man. Or perhaps it was his
FedEx uniform that camouflaged the real Willie beneath. In any
event, Willie had everything necessary to get into the soiree. All I
needed to do now was talk him into going. And on that note, I
didn't believe it would be difficult. He'd already confessed that he
was generally a willing and available arm for a woman to hang on
to when called in to duty.

I made the turn onto Tiffany's street then zipped around the
block to the garage. Stanley practically leaped up from his alu-
minum seat to greet me. I put my smile in place as he came
around to the driver's side of the car. He opened the door for me
and held my hand as I stepped out.

"Aren't you the perfect gentleman," I cooed sweetly before
pursing my lips as if I were going to give him a kiss for his efforts.
I stepped past him careful to brush a shoulder across his chest. He
looked as if he was going to faint or snatch me into a back room
and have his way with me.

"Are you okay, Ms. Drew?"

I shook my head to clear it. Pulling myself together, I dug in
my bag for my last few wrinkled dollars and pressed them into his

palm. "Thank you so much for taking care of me." I smiled and stroked his cheek. "I won't forget you." I watched a line of perspiration form on his top lip, so I inhaled deeply and followed his eyes as they dipped down into the danger zone. "I'll be back to pick up the car in the morning around eight. Will you be here?"

He bobbed his head up and down like one of those dashboard car toys.

"Wonderful. I'll see you then . . . Stanley."

"Absolutely."

"Good night, Stanley."

Well, you would have thought I told him he won the lottery, the way his face lit up, or that I'd babbled something more suggestive than good night. He started speaking to me lightning fast, smiling and beaming like Times Square on New Year's Eve. I knew it was time to go. I'd lost track of the conversation the instant he opened his mouth. I waved and hurried out of the garage and around the corner.

I stuck the key in the door, flipped on the hall light, and set the alarm. I was sure I would see Virginia trotting down the corridor to greet me. But nothing.

"Hello! Where is everyone?" I headed for the kitchen, then the living room and bedrooms. Not a soul to be found.

I checked my watch. It was nearly ten. Grandma never stayed up beyond nine thirty. Where in the world could she be? I'd told that Virginia to keep an eye on her. I tell you, you just cannot get good help anymore.

Before going truly crazy, I hunted around in hopes of finding a note. Again, nothing. The only place they could be was over at Wayne's house. One more time, I grabbed my bag, reset the alarm, and headed to Wayne's place.

When I walked up to Wayne's front door, I heard music coming from inside. I peeked in the window, and it was at that point I knew I'd lost it. Dancing to the beat of Beyonce's "Crazy in Love" was Wayne and Grandma boogying! Grandma? Wayne? I adjusted my glasses and looked a bit harder. It was them, all right.

I pressed the bell, determined to get to the bottom of their odd behavior. What in the world was going on between those two? And a better question was; Where had Grandma learned to move like that?

The music stopped, and I watched Grandma take a seat while Wayne came to the door. "What's going on around here?" I demanded the instant he opened the door. I brushed by him and went inside before he could answer.

"Grandma was lonely. She called me, and I went to get her," he said, following me inside. "I was only looking after her until you got back."

I whirled toward him, pointing a threatening finger in his face. "You call this looking after her, dancing to Beyonce!"

They both looked at me like I was insane.

"What?" they echoed in unison.

I stormed over to the stereo, determined to find the evidence. I pressed open the CD changer and found all eight slots empty. I checked the cassette box and found that empty, as well. Then I pressed the radio and chamber music filled the air. I turned toward the culprits.

They both smiled benignly at me. Virginia trotted over and looked at me askance, too. "I think you're working too hard," Wayne said.

"Poor girl," Grandma offered. She walked up to me and put her hand on my shoulder. "You need some rest."

I tugged in a breath. Something was definitely awry, but I couldn't put my finger on it. Maybe they were right and I did need some rest. It had been a trying week, and I did have the staff meeting the next day.

"Fine. I'm going to bed, and so are you, Grandma." I took her arm. "Good night Wayne."

"Thank you, darling boy, for keeping an old lady company," Grandma said to Wayne.

"Don't even think about it. I enjoyed myself."

"Hmmm," I grumbled.

"See you in the morning, ladies."

"I'll be ready," Grandma singsonged.

Walking back to Tiffany's house, I couldn't shake the images of Grandma and Wayne dancing together in his living room. Well, the entire series of events for the evening put a serious damper on my original plan—to visit one of Tiffany's and Chantel's hot spots. It would have to wait for another time. My main objective at that point was to tuck Grandma safely in bed and get some rest myself. I wanted to be in top form when I confronted the staff.

"You really should loosen up," Grandma said, cutting into my thoughts as we walked up the steps to Tiffany's town house.

"I beg your pardon."

"You heard me. You need more fun in your life. You take it all much too seriously. If the old saying is true that you have only one life to live, then live it up every chance you get." She cackled at her own humor.

I stuck the key in the door, and Virginia scurried past me. "Do you really think I live a dull life, Grandma?"

"Do you?" She winked at me and shuffled down the hall to the spare bedroom and closed the door.

I stood there for a moment, taking in Grandma's cryptic comments. Dull? That may once have been my middle name, but things were changing. And if I had my way, my life would never be dull again. After all, didn't I put the moves on the parking-lot attendant, get Maribel to spy for me, get Willie to crack open Chantel's diary, and figure out the codes to get invited to the soiree? Dull! They ain't seen nothing yet.

# And Away
# We Go

Always Johnny on-the-spot, Wayne arrived promptly at 7:45 to pick up Grandma and take her back home. I made a note to myself to call my mother at the post office and find out just exactly what she was up to.

Today, I sported a Naomi Campbell look with a full shoulder-length wig complete with bangs. I borrowed a raspberry lipstick from Tiffany's array of cosmetics and wore Chantel's Chanel suit, a dynamite two-piece number in raw silk that was an incredible shade of pale blue with peach piping.

I took a look in the full-length, and I had to admit that I was looking good. I grabbed my bag, made sure I had my notes, checked the alarm, and headed to the parking garage.

Stanley met me at the entrance, smiling as if I was on a plate for breakfast.

"Good morning," he said in an exceptionally deep voice, and adjusted his blue tie.

"Good morning, Stanley." I handed him the car keys, and he scurried off to get the Jag.

While I waited, I ran over what I was going to say to the staff. If I was to be the new head sistah in charge, even temporarily, I needed to get everyone in line.

Stanley pulled up with the Jag, jumped out, and held open the door for me.

"All ready for you, Ms. Drew."

"Thank you so much, Stanley." I wondered if I should tip him. But since I didn't really have more than my usual pocket change, I decided it would be best to sidestep that. I didn't want to blow my newfound image.

"Will you be coming later?" he asked as he looked me up and down.

"Yes. Around six. Will you be here?"

"Sure will!"

I smiled. "Then I will see you later." I wiggled my fingers good-bye, slid into the Jag, and sped off.

I sashayed into the office, filled with confidence. If they thought for one minute that I was going to be doofy Margaret the pushover, they were sadly mistaken. I tapped my bag and assured myself that the trusty handbook was there for quick reference.

"Good morning, Bev."

"Good morning."

I smiled sweetly. "Can you order coffee from the cafeteria for the staff meeting and have it sent to the conference room?"

"Uh, sure. Should I put it on the department's budget?"

"Yes. Thanks, Bev." I walked into my office, shut the door, and noticed my message light flashing.

Coming around the desk, I set my bag down and sat. Who could possibly have called me before 9 a.m., I wondered as I pressed the flashing light.

"Hi, Margaret, this is Willie. I'm pretty sure you haven't arrived yet, and that's really the reason why I called so early. I wanted you to have time to think about what I'm about to say. Like I mentioned last night, I want to take you out, wherever you want to go, and I hope we can make that sooner rather than later. I, uh, don't think I've ever thanked you for not turning me in. So if there is ever anything I can do for you, just name it and consider it done. Well, I gotta get to work. Here's my number 555-1234. I hope you decide to call."

All right, just what I needed! I jotted down the number and made a mental note to call him later that evening. I checked my watch. It was nine on the dot. I had fifteen minutes to get ready. Well, twenty. I wanted to be sure that everyone was in place when I made my entrance.

I pulled my notes from my purse and quickly reviewed them. Beverly buzzed me on the intercom.

"Yes, Bev."

"The coffee has been ordered. Did you want to add doughnuts or bagels?"

"Sure, why not?"

"I'll call the kitchen and let them know."

"Thanks."

The phone rang again. I waited for Beverly to answer it. After all, what was the point in having an assistant if you didn't let them assist?

"There's a Mr. Hathaway on the phone," Beverly said through the intercom.

"Who?"

"Mr. Hathaway. He said he's a personal friend."

I thought about it for a moment. Wayne! What could he possibly want? Oh, my—maybe something had happened to Grandma. I pressed the flashing light.

"Hello. Wayne? What is it? What's wrong? Did something happen to Grandma?"

"Good morning, Margaret. No. Grandma is fine."

"Okay, so then why are you calling me? And how did you get my number, anyway?"

"Grandma gave it to me."

"Talk fast, Wayne. I have a big staff meeting in six minutes."

"I thought you were an actress."

"I am, in my spare time. Do you want to tell me why you called?"

"I thought we could talk about it over dinner."

"Excuse me? Talk about what? What dinner?"

"What you're *really* doing."

A hot flash raced through my body with lightning speed. "What?"

"I'll see you later, Margaret. Have a good day."

"Wayne, wait! I—"

Click.

I put down the receiver. My heart was beating so fast that my hands started to shake. What in the world did he mean? What was he implying? What did he know? I started to sweat.

The intercom buzzed again.

"Yes," I said in a shaky voice.

"Everyone is waiting for you in the conference room," Beverly said.

"I'll be right there."

I wouldn't let Wayne's phone call rattle me. No good Diva would. I'd deal with him later. Whatever he had up his sleeve or thought he knew, I would nip it in the bud. No one would hamper my plans to soar to the top of my game. Not even Wayne Hathaway.

I gathered up my notes and a pad and headed to the conference room.

When I entered, all conversation ceased and heads turned in my direction. I tossed my new locks over my shoulder and strutted to the head of the table. "Good morning, everyone. I'm glad to see that you all could make it. I know you have busy schedules, so I'll get right to the point," I said, taking my seat. I flipped open my notepad and flattened my notes.

"As you all know, Mr. Fields will be out for quite some time. As a result, I have been given the responsibility of managing the office and all the projects until he returns." I glanced from one face to the next, looking for any signs of dissent. Finding nothing but outright curiosity mixed with hostility, I continued. "Beginning today, each of you will complete a daily work report on each of your projects and submit it by four p.m. to your supervisor. I will expect reports from each of the department supervisors for their divisions. Therefore, it is up to each of the supervisors to ensure that their staff is on top of their projects. I have a list of all the projects pending which I will match up daily to the submitted reports."

Low grumbles rounded the table, but I cut them short with a Grandma look: one squinted eye and one closed. "I will post the reports every Friday outside my office. The department with the highest success rate per week will get an hour off work the following week for their department." I paused and looked around the room. "I firmly believe in rewarding a job well done. And I can't imagine anyone not wanting some time off."

Excited mumblings filled the room. I eyed Shaniqua and

Tashana, who looked startled by my announcement. I smiled nastily in Shaniqua's direction. This would stomp out her little plan to screw me, unless she wanted to screw her supervisor in the process.

I turned to Beverly. "Beverly will send out the new forms that you will use for your reporting. The forms are simple and easy to work with. If there are any questions, please set up a meeting with me via Beverly."

I tugged in a satisfied breath. "Enjoy the coffee and bagels." I stood. "Have a productive day, everyone."

The room erupted into a frenzy of chatter the instant I stepped on the other side of the door. *Let them fight it out among themselves,* I thought as I headed back to my office. This would keep the departments running smoothly, maybe better than usual. There was nothing like the incentive of outdoing someone else and then being rewarded for your efforts. A little healthy competition couldn't hurt.

No sooner had I sat down than there was a knock on the door.

"Come in."

"That was some meeting you pulled off in there," Beverly said, stepping in and closing the door behind her. "Folks are pretty stirred up."

"Really?" I turned on my computer. "I'm sure they will all get used to the new procedures."

Beverly folded her arms and looked at me sideways. "You know something, Margaret."

"What's that?"

"I had you all wrong."

"In what way?"

"I always took you for a shy, unassuming, no-backbone kinda woman. But you're not that way at all. You really have it together. You look different—you act different." She paused. "I'm really sorry for being such a bitch to you for so long."

Wow. "Forget it."

"Well, I know you must have tons to do." She started backing away. "I'll get right on sending those forms out as soon as you have them ready."

"Give me about an hour. I'm putting the finishing touches on them. I want you to take a look at them first and see if you notice anything that I may have missed, something that needs to be changed or whatever. Okay?"

She truly looked taken aback. "Sure, of course, whatever you need. No problem."

"Thanks, Bev." I focused on my computer screen as she opened the door. "Oh, I haven't forgotten about our rain check."

She stopped and smiled at me. "Whenever you're ready, boss."

*Boss.* I liked the sound of that.

Now that I had the staff whipped into shape, I just needed to get my life in order. I opened my purse, pulled out my phone book, and looked up my mother's number at the post office. The phone rang about forty times before someone finally answered. No wonder the city agencies were going down the tubes.

"Can I help you?" a man asked, sounding as if the last thing he wanted to do was help someone.

"Yes, may I speak with Mrs. Drew, please?"

"Drew? She don't work here no more."

"You mean she doesn't work in that department anymore, that building?"

"No. She don't work for the P.O., period."

I frowned, totally confused. Obviously he must have my mother mixed up with someone else. "I'm talking about Madeline Drew—she's been working at the Thirty-fourth Street station for almost twenty years."

"Look, miss, like I told you, she don't work here no more. Now, is there anything else I can help you with?"

"Uh . . . no. Thank you."

Click.

Slowly I hung up the phone. *My* mother was no longer working for the post office. What was equally disturbing were the two big questions: Where was she going every day if not to work, and where was she going at night?

# Is Everyone a
# Double Agent?

For several moments I sat perplexed, in my very expensive leather seat, surrounded by state-of-the-art equipment, with a competent assistant only a few feet away, and I wondered if all the people in my life were not at all the people I'd thought they were. In less than a few weeks, the masks were being removed one by one. I should be afraid, very afraid. Terrified. No one was who they appeared to be. Who else's duo identity would be uncovered?

At no other time was the sixth commandment more relevant: *The only person you can truly trust is no one.*

What was a Diva to do?

*Caution* was the operative word. I would have to be very careful from here on out and follow the rules to the letter.

There was a knock on the door.

"Come in."

"Good morning, Meez Margreet."

"Maribel. Good morning. Have any news for me?"

She looked over her shoulder as if expecting someone to ease up behind her with a noose. She closed the door and actually tiptoed across the room. "I hear from some of the staff that they are very happy about your new rules. But"—she lowered her voice—"some are not happy. Say you throwing around your weight. And they not like it one bit."

"Why are they unhappy?"

"More work, no more money." She bobbed her head up and down. "They like things the way they were. Say you won't be here long. When Mr. Fields returns, everything back to normal."

"I see. Well, with new management come new changes. They will get used to it."

"I no want trouble for you, Meez Margreet. You nice lady—a little strange, but nice."

Strange? Me? "Thank you, Maribel. Well, keep your ears open for me."

"I will. I clean your office now."

"Go right ahead. I'm going to get some coffee."

I left Maribel to her tasks and walked down the corridor to the employee lounge. Larry was sitting on a side chair, reading the paper. He looked up when I walked in.

"Hello, boss lady."

"Hi, Larry." I poured a cup of coffee and turned to face him. "How are you?"

He shrugged. "Can't complain. I hear you are shaking things up around here."

"I think it will make things run more efficiently."

"So you're really taking this job thing seriously, huh?"

I straightened my posture and flipped the ends of my wig over my left shoulder with the tips of my fingers. "Of course. Why shouldn't I?"

"The job is only temporary, Margaret. Fields will be back, won't he? Or do you know something none of us do?"

"Yes, he'll be back, but that doesn't mean I shouldn't try to improve things in the meantime."

"It sounds to me as if you want to make being an editor your career. There was a time when all you wanted to be was a writer. What happened to that? Has the taste of power gotten to you?"

"You don't know what you're talking about, Larry. I thought we were friends. I thought you of all people would be happy for me."

"I would be if I believed this is what you really wanted." He stared at me for a moment. "You're not the same friend I knew. Everything about you is different, from the way you talk and act to the way you look." He stood. "But if it's what you want, I suppose that's what's important. Have a good day." He walked out.

*How dare he?* I thought. What right did he have to judge me? Did he know how long I'd waited for my moment in the sun, to be respected, envied, to have dates, money, clothes? This was my chance, and I was going to make the most of it. I didn't need Larry, and I didn't need his guilt trip.

I tossed the remains of my coffee down the sink and returned to my office.

"You have two messages," Beverly said. "I left them on your desk, and Mr. Savage wants to see you."

"Mr. Savage. Did he say what he wanted?"

"No. Just that he wanted to see you before lunch."

He probably wanted me *for* his lunch, I thought. "Thanks, Bev. I'll go down there now."

There was no one at the front desk when I arrived, so I went straight to Mr. Savage's office and knocked. His booming voice shook the door.

I stepped inside anyway. "You wanted to see me, Mr. Savage."

He looked up at me from the endless stack of files that always occupied his desk. "Sit down, Ms. Drew."

Immediately I did as I was told and tried to keep my knees from knocking,.

"I heard you initiated a staff meeting this morning and instituted some radical changes to the entire editorial department." His voice bounced and boomed around the room; my head started to vibrate from the aftershocks.

I swallowed over the sudden dryness in my throat. "Yes, I did, Mr. Savage. And I think it—"

"I didn't ask you what you thought."

My chair shook beneath me, and I held on to the arms to keep from getting thrown over the side.

"Any changes made to employees' time comes through personnel." He squinted his beady eyes and stared at me. "However, I think your plan is quite inspired. And I will give it my approval. But"—he wagged an enormous finger in my direction—"one screwup, one slipup, and I will hold you personally responsible, Ms. Drew. Understood?"

"Yes, Mr. Savage. I understand."

He nodded, and my stomach wobbled up and down. "Keep up the good work, Ms. Drew." His mouth did something that vaguely resembled a smile. I almost saw teeth.

I stood and began to ease toward the door. "Thank you, Mr. Savage." Faster than you could say *jackrabbit*. I hightailed it back to my office.

"Everything okay?" Beverly asked upon my return.

I hurled her a suspicious look. Was she really concerned, or was she looking for inside information? "Everything is fine, actually.

Mr. Savage is very pleased with the changes I've implemented and gave me his blessing."

Her left brow arched. "Really?"

"Yes. Really." I smiled triumphantly. "I'm going to send you the form to get out to the departments. Please hold all my calls." I'd always wanted to say that.

"Sure."

When I got back to my desk, I saw the two messages: one from Calvin and one from James. Hmm. Who should I call first? I did a quick eenie meenie miney moe, and came up with James.

"James Blake," he answered on the second ring.

"Hi, James. This is Margaret. I got your message."

"Margaret, hi. I'm glad you called. Listen, I have some extra tickets tonight to a club in the Village. I thought you might like to go. They have a live R and B band."

"Well . . . uh, what time?"

"Nine. I could pick you up."

"Why don't I meet you there?"

"So that's a yes?"

"Yes. What's the address?"

He gave it to me, and I jotted it down in my notebook. "So I'll see you at nine."

"I'll leave your ticket at the door."

"Thanks, James."

"No problem. I'm looking forward to seeing you."

"Great. See you then." I hung up.

Wow, a real date. I wondered what I should wear. Should I go casual or dressy? I'd figure that out later. I picked up the phone again and dialed Calvin's number. After being rerouted via a secretary, Calvin finally came on the line.

"Russell," he spouted in a very clipped tone.

"Hi, Calvin, it's Margaret. I'm returning your call."

"Hey, Margaret." I could hear the smile in his voice. *Sigh.*

"Is something wrong?"

"No, not at all. I was hoping you were free for dinner tonight. I thought if you were, I could pick you up after work."

"Today?"

"Yeah. If it's cool. Are you busy?"

"Well . . . uh . . . no." *Hee hee.* "Dinner sounds wonderful. But why don't you tell me where, and I can meet you. I actually drove Tiffany's car into work today."

"Tiffany's car? How did you manage that? She never lets anyone drive the Jag."

"Oh . . . I worked it out."

"Hmm. Here's the address. Say about six?"

"Perfect." An hour for dinner, run home, change, and meet James by nine.

"Hey, I gotta run. I have a meeting in five minutes. See you at six."

"See you then."

Slowly I returned the receiver to the base and eased back in my seat. Things were certainly shaping up. I had the troops at the office whipped into shape and two dates in one night waiting in the wings! Who would have thought that boring Margaret Drew could actually turn the tables and come out on top?

I switched on my computer, opened the file with the progress report form, made a few minor adjustments, and sent it off to Beverly. That should keep her busy for a while. My deeds done for the day, I could sit back and relax.

At least that's what I thought.

# Oh, What a Night

At five o'clock on the dot, I said my good-byes to Beverly, darted out to the employee parking lot, hopped into the Jag, and headed to Brooklyn. If I didn't hit any major traffic, I estimated that I would be at my mother's house in forty minutes. That would give me about five minutes to unravel her odd comings and goings, jump back in the car, and head to Midtown to meet Calvin for dinner by six or shortly thereafter. For reasons beyond my comprehension, I actually made it to Mom's in thirty. I pulled the Jag to a screeching halt in front of the house and jumped out.

Grandma, as usual, was in her favorite chair, cussing out the *Eyewitness News* anchor for some infraction or the other.

"Hi, Grandma."

She tore her attention away from the television and momentarily focused on me. "Well, the prodigal granddaughter finally returns home."

I chose to ignore the remark. "Is my mother here?"

"In the kitchen, burning up something, I'm sure. Are you staying for dinner?"

"Not tonight, Grandma. I have a date."

Her face lit up like a Christmas tree. "With that nice Wayne fellow, I hope."

"No, Grandma, not Wayne."

She frowned and gripped the sides of her chair. "Why in the world not? He's a wonderful young man with a promising future. Just the kind of man you need in your life."

I hardly wanted to tell my grandmother about the titillating feelings that skipped through my body when Wayne was around. Wayne wasn't a suitable candidate, according to the handbook and the tapes and the training manuals. He was the kind of man you saw on the side, in the dark, in out-of-the-way places. But Grandma would never understand all that.

"I have other plans for my life, Grandma."

"You young people never know a good thing when it smacks you." She looked me up and down. "Where did you get that outfit and that hair, anyway?" she asked, suspicion brewing in her query. She squinted at me. "I've been watching you." She wagged her finger at me and cackled. "Don't think that I haven't."

My heart beat a bit faster. Grandma was a crafty old coot. Who knew what she thought she knew or saw. I couldn't be too careful.

"They're mine," I lied smoothly.

"Humph, hardly." She turned her attention back to the show.

I shook my head in frustration and went in search of my mother. This time I was prepared for any of her swift getaways.

The Jag could catch anything. So if she thought she was going to make a run for it, she had another thought coming.

I checked the kitchen, and all I found was boiling pots, so I headed upstairs and knocked on her bedroom door.

"Grandma, I'll be down in a minute."

"It's me, Margaret."

I heard a lot of shuffling and scuffling before she finally inched the door open. All I could see was the tip of her nose.

"Hi, honey."

"Can I come in? We need to talk."

She glanced over her shoulder and then back at me. "Wait for me in the kitchen. I'll be right down." She slammed the door in my face.

Well! I checked my watch as I walked downstairs. I'd used up ten of the five minutes I'd intended to spend at my mother's house. Maybe this wasn't such a good idea.

By the time I entered the kitchen, my mother came in right behind me, walked up to me, and kissed my cheek—as if everything in the world were just peachy. "Hi, honey. It's so good to see you. I haven't had a chance to thank you for looking after Grandma. You have no idea how much I needed that break." She pulled out a chair and sat down as if she'd had an exhausting day at the post office—where she no longer worked!

"I called your job today. They said you don't work there anymore."

"I don't."

I'd expected more resistance, an alibi of some sort. "Why? What happened?"

"I resigned," she said calmly.

"Why? How are you going to pay the bills? What are you going to do?"

She smiled—one of those smiles people give you when they

know something that you don't. "I have it all taken care of. Don't worry."

"Don't worry! How can I not worry when you zip off in strange Mercedes and leave me with Grandma?"

She waved her hand in a dismissive fashion. "Oh, that. I do apologize. But I have that all worked out, too."

I planted my hands on my hips. "Whose car was that?" I probed.

"A friend's," she said.

"Fine." I gave her a hard look. "If you want to keep secrets, then so be it."

"A woman should always have secrets." She smiled brightly and winked at me.

My mother actually winked at me. My mother had never winked at me in all her natural life. What was going on? Who was this woman who suddenly didn't have a care in the world? She was certainly not the woman who ranted and raved against everything breathing that walked through the doors of the post office.

I looked at her for a long moment while she buffed her nails. It was apparent that I wasn't going to get any more information from her, and my time was running short. "I've got to go. I'll call you tomorrow."

"You're not staying for dinner?"

"No, I have a date."

"It's about time."

"Thanks mother," I grumbled. "Good night." I started for the living room to say good-bye to Grandma.

"Love that hair," my mother sang out.

I grumbled again.

Grandma was dozing in her chair. I tiptoed over and kissed her cheek. "Take care, Grandma."

"Two is always better than one," she mumbled without opening her eyes.

I jumped back as if I'd been smacked. "What did you just say?"

She opened her eyes and then winked at me. "I said, go out and have some fun."

I didn't have time to argue. "Thanks, I will." I hurried outside and back into the car. I had five minutes to get to Manhattan. Not humanly possible. My best bet was to get there as soon as I could, but the strange behavior of my mother's, and Grandma's cryptic remark, rode shotgun with me all the way to the restaurant. Something wasn't right. And at some point, I was going to figure out what it was.

In the meantime, I had two hot dates ahead of me. And I intended to make the most of them.

By the time I arrived at Le Cirque, a French restaurant on the East Side, it was nearly six thirty. A valet jogged over to the car, helped me out, handed me a ticket, and zipped away with the Jag before I could open my mouth. I must admit, I wasn't used to that kind of service, and I was momentarily halted in my tracks as I watched the car speed away. I imagined all sorts of horrible things happening to it, and me trying to explain to Tiffany how her beautiful car had been totaled.

Maybe that wasn't a valet at all, but a carjacker in disguise! Oh, my. I could almost hear myself pleading with Tiffany to spare me the firing squad as I tried in vain to explain. I started to sweat as my untimely demise took shape in front of me.

"Can I help you, madam?"

I turned to find a kindly old gentleman in a military-like outfit holding the door open for me. He smiled. Trying to assure myself that the car would be returned safe and sound, I stuck the little ticket in my purse and stepped into the lush environs of Le Cirque. The moment I entered, a hostess greeted me, asked if I had reservations or was meeting someone. I gave her Calvin's name. Before I could blink, I was whisked to his table. Being the perfect gentleman, he stood and held my chair for me as I sat down.

"So glad you could make it. I thought you might have changed your mind."

"No, just had to tie up a few loose ends. It took a little longer than I thought." I adjusted myself in my seat. My borrowed girdle was beginning to pinch, and I knew I had about another hour in the shoes before disaster struck.

There was an awkward moment of silence, and in that instant I wondered what I was doing. This was Tiffany's boyfriend, even if she said he wasn't. And here I was, as big as day, having dinner with him—a real live date.

"You look incredible," he said. "That color is great on you."

I felt my insides fill with a kind of elation I'd never known. This was a man who in my wildest dreams wouldn't give me the time of day. And now I sat across from him in a snazzy restaurant, soaking in compliments. That momentary attack of conscience evaporated in a finger pop. I was overdue. After all, it wasn't *really* a date in the traditional sense, I rationalized. We hadn't arrived together. We were simply two friends having dinner and getting to know one another.

I smiled graciously. "Thanks."

"How was your day as executive editor?" he asked, and signaled the waiter to pour the wine that was already sitting in a bucket of ice on the table.

"Not bad, actually. I was able to institute some new work rules."

His mouth quirked into a grin as he lifted the glass of wine to his nose, sniffed, and took a sip. "How did the staff take it?" he asked, and then nodded his approval to the waiter.

"There was some grumbling, but I'm sure it will be fine." I told him of my reward plan to offset the new rules, and he actually applauded.

"Now that is a stroke of genius. One thing I've learned along the way: It's always easier to get people to do what you want when you can offer them something that they want or need." He raised his glass to me in salute. "Congratulations on your first executive order. May there be many more."

We both laughed and touched glasses.

From somewhere deep within the cushiony confines of the restaurant, soft music was playing, underscoring our conversation, which went from politics to movies to sports to reality television. Calvin was well versed in a variety of areas and so easy to talk to. He looked into my eyes when I spoke, as if I was the most important person in the world. And I *felt* important. I could tell in the way my body moved, the way I tossed my head and hair back when I laughed, the way I held my fork or leaned forward to expose a teasing glimpse of warm flesh. I felt powerful, totally feminine, unstoppable.

Apparently it was all in my head, because Calvin asked if I was all right.

He leaned forward and put his hand over mine. "You look a bit flushed, and your eyes are enlarged."

I tried to smile, but the girdle was biting into my sides and cutting off my air. I knew I shouldn't have had the steak. And my feet were beginning to pound like tom-toms. My time was definitely up.

"Uh, I'm fine. Really." I checked my watch. "Oh, goodness—look at the time. Calvin, this has been great. But I've got to go."

"Leave? But you haven't had dessert."

"Oh, I couldn't." Believe me, I couldn't. I forced myself to stand without wincing.

He got up and came around to my side of the table. "Can I at least walk you to your car?"

"Sit, sit. Stay and have dessert. I'm really sorry I have to run out like this. Maybe we can have a rain check on dessert."

"Sure," he murmured, not sounding too certain. "Call me."

"I will. Good night, Calvin. And thank you for a wonderful evening."

He stepped up to me, and before I knew what happened, he kissed me, right there in the restaurant, right on . . . the cheek.

I gave him a half-smile and tried not to limp on my way out. What I needed to do (and quick) was get out of the shoes before my entire evening was spent with a bucket of ice.

I made it outside, handed the valet my ticket, and he brought back the car without a scratch. Whew. I eased behind the wheel, took off the too-tight shoes, and started across town. I needed to get to Tiffany's, get out of the damned girdle before I got asphyxiated, find something that could fit, walk Virginia, and get to the club to meet James by nine. The time on the dashboard read 7:45. Virginia would be pissed.

I decided to avoid Stanley for the moment, so I parked on the street across from Tiffany's town house and walked barefoot to the front door. I could already hear Virginia barking on the other side of the door.

"Look, don't start," I said, limping down the hall. I went into the bedroom, put on a pair of slippers, came back down the hall, and grabbed Virginia's leash. "Let's go."

I fastened her leash to her collar, and we headed out. No sooner had I hit the curb than we were waylaid by Wayne.

"What in the world are you doing driving Tiffany's Jag?"

"I'm staying here, aren't I?" I quickly tossed back in my defense. "She said I had full use of everything."

He looked at me with a megadose of doubt. "Tiffie's never let anyone drive the Jag—not even me."

"You and I are two different creatures. Maybe she didn't trust *you* with the Jag. Ever think of that?" I said with a smug smile, and walked a bit faster.

He clasped my upper arm, halting me in my tracks, and turned me around. "Just what are you up to? I think there's more to it than you simply watching Tiffie's apartment."

I cocked my head to the side and double-dared him to give me an alignment. "You know what you need to know, Wayne. It's as simple as that. Now, if you will excuse me, I have a dog to walk, places to go, and people to see."

He looked at me as if I'd just kicked him in the family jewels—stunned and hurt.

"Look, I'm sorry . . . I . . . I've really got to go." I hurried off down the street before what was left of my conscience went on the attack.

I couldn't very well explain to Wayne what I was up to, I rationalized as I waited for Virginia to find the perfect tree. I couldn't tell him what my real dream and ambition were. He'd never understand or accept the fact that I had every intention in the world of taking on Tiffany Lane's and Chantel Hollis's lives and making them my own in every way I could. I was off to a good start, and nothing and no one was going to stop me.

By nine fifteen, I'd pulled up in front of Down Home, the club James told me about over the phone. Being in the West Village, the locale didn't scream valet. I circled the block a few times and was unsuccessful in finding a parking space. Running out of time and choices, I opted for a garage about two blocks away. By the time I finally got inside the club, it was nearing nine thirty.

I looked around the dimly lit interior and finally spotted James at the far end of a very long bar, chatting with a group of guys. Confident in my hip-hugging, barely-touching-my-knees black wrap dress, I sauntered down the length of the bar to where James stood. He did a double take.

"Margaret." He looked me up and down none too subtly. "You look great. Glad you could make it." He stepped up and put his hand at the dip of my spine. "Fellas, this is Margaret. Margaret, the fellas."

The quartet chorused their hellos and introduced themselves: Lou, Henry, Phil, and Matt.

He stepped closer and lowered his voice. "This is the great R and B band I was referring to. I hope you aren't upset."

I arched a brow and gave him a pouty smile—then I turned to the group. "So you guys are the fabulous band that James was telling me about."

"He said we were fabulous?" Lou teased. "That's not what he tells us."

They all laughed.

"Very funny. You guys are gonna give Margaret the wrong impression of me."

"You mean she doesn't have one already?" Henry deadpanned, and they all cracked up again.

"Come on, Margaret, these guys are really a bad influence." He put his arm around my shoulder and ushered me away. "Thanks for coming. I promise you will have a great time. We're planning some new numbers tonight. Been practicing for weeks," he said, seating me at a reserved table in the center of the room. "Do you want anything? Name it, and it's on the house tonight."

"I'm fine, really. But a glass of wine might be nice."

"You got it." He signaled for a waitress and ordered two glasses of wine. "So how was your day?"

"Pretty productive." I told my story one more time, putting the right emphasis in all the correct places.

"You're amazing."

"Me?"

"Yeah. I think that's really cool what you did. Not many managers would have done the same thing."

I shrugged as if it were something I did every day. "Tell me about you. How was your day?"

He chuckled. "I'm just glad that it's over. If I didn't have my music, I would probably go crazy."

"Don't you like your job? Chantel is always bragging about how far you've come, the great job you're doing, new promotions, one of the youngest executives in the company." I looked at him the way I'd seen Grandma look at Wayne, as if he were the most important man in the world. "I can't imagine that all of it isn't true." I took a sip of my wine.

James lowered his gaze. "To be honest, there was a time when I loved what I did. But over the years, I suppose I've become jaded. At the same time, I've also become spoiled. Doing this." He waved his hand around the room. "This would never cover the lifestyle I've grown accustomed to." He laughed. "So I guess the real gig has its perks."

"You ever think about making the leap and just really doing what you wanted?"

He looked into my eyes. "Every day. I just need to get the balls to do it."

"Hey, James!"

He turned around in his chair. Phil was waving him to the back.

"Sorry, gotta run. We're on. Will you stay for the whole set?"

"I'll try. I do have a full day tomorrow."

"If you're not here when I'm done, is it okay if I call you to-morrow?"

"Sure."

He started to walk away.

"James."

"Yes?"

"Why didn't you just tell me that you were the group you wanted me to hear?"

He came back to where I was seated and braced his hands on the table. "Call it stupid pride or male ego. I just wasn't sure you would come out to see me."

I smiled and slowly shook my head. "Yeah, you're right; stupid pride . . . male ego. Break a leg—or whatever it is they tell folks."

He smiled and gave me a wink. "Will do."


I didn't stay until the end. That made it easier to say good-bye. I didn't have to offer excuses or explanations about anything. I was simply gone.

On the drive back to Tiffany's house, I ran through the events of the day. Without a doubt, it was definitely a highlight. And as horrible as it was to admit, I really liked James . . . and Calvin. I wanted to keep seeing them. They were the kinds of men that the woman I was becoming needed in her life. I wanted this game that I was playing to be real. I never wanted to go back to being plain, boring Margaret Drew ever again! And if I had my way, I wouldn't—ever.

# TGIF

*I*'m about finished compiling the weekly reports from the departments," Beverly said as I passed her desk on my way to stake out the ladies' room for any updates.

"Great." I checked my borrowed Cartier watch. "I'll need them completed before the end of business, and I want the list of anyone who has not complied." I leaned a bit closer. "I don't want anyone giving you a hard time. If they do, let me know. I'll handle them."

"You would?" she asked, duly surprised.

"We're a team, girl," I said to reinforce the whole bond thing.

A major footnote in one of the manuals stated that you must cultivate loyalties of those closest to you in order to get the job done. For what it was worth, Beverly was that person, and I needed to ensure that we stayed on the same side.

I gave her a wink and proceeded with my mission. En route, I gave the underlings a nod of acknowledgment as I passed them in the corridor. Dropped a few words of praise and encouragement on a select few. "Make them want to earn your favor," was another quotation from the training manual. "Shine the light on a select few, and others will clamor to bask in the glow."

As tired and as crazed as I'd been since stepping out of my life and into Chantel's and Tiffany's, I'd made it a point to read at least two to three chapters per day from the manuals and commit to memory everything that could possibly apply to me. Day by day, more and more was coming in handy.

When I arrived at "lookout point" (my code name for the ladies' room), there was only one woman from the print shop who was on her way out.

I checked under all the stall doors. Each one was empty. I picked one stall at the end, stepped in and up. It took a bit more work than last time, as I'd opted to wear one of Tiffany's 1940s outfits: padded shoulders, pinched waist, and tapered at the knees. It was the knee thing that made climbing and balancing a bit precarious, to say the least. I braced my hands on the side walls and waited. But after about ten minutes in a semi-squat position and no takers, I decided the stakeout was a bust, and I started to get down.

My knees locked. A cramp shot up my right thigh and locked in my right cheek. That's when my hands slipped and my left foot did a perfect high dive into the bowl. I was ankle deep in toilet water, and the heel of Tiffany's designer pump was stuck in the drainage hole.

Somehow I managed to get my foot out of the shoe, and just as I was about to push up my sleeves and dig out the pump, the bathroom door opened. I groaned inwardly as my mind scrambled for a quick solution. Then I realized it was Maribel doing her afternoon cleanup. I'd know the sound of her mops and buckets anywhere.

"Psst, psst, Maribel," I said in a high-pitched, harsh whisper.

"Meez Margreet, is that you?"

I spotted her white, thick-soled shoes beneath the stall door.

"Yes," I hissed. "I need your help. Quickly."

"Anything for you, Meez Margreet."

I opened the door.

Her hands immediately flew to her mouth. She gasped. "What happened?"

"I'll explain later. I need to get . . . my shoe out of the toilet before someone comes in."

"You have *mucho* trouble with your feet."

"Can we discuss that later? I really need your help."

"I'll be right back." Maribel hurried over to her tools, pulled out a CLOSED FOR CLEANING sign, and hung it on the outside of the door. I could have kissed her. She returned, armed with an industrial-strength plunger, and proceeded to extract the shoe. After several well-placed applications of the plunger, the shoe ejected from the bowl with a loud pop and gurgle.

Maribel whipped on a pair of yellow plastic gloves, and with two fingers, she help up the shoe for inspection like it was the Hope diamond. She beamed with triumph. "Here is your shoe, Meez Margreet."

Water dripped from it like Niagara Falls. Maribel turned it over and dumped out the remaining water. I hobbled out of the stall and pulled down a wad of paper towels from the dispenser to dry off my legs, then turned and looked with a combination of dread and defeat at the mangled shoe.

"What am I going to do, Maribel? I can't wear it like this."

Her caramel brow pinched in thought; then suddenly she brightened. "I fix it right up." She scurried over to the hand dryer, turned it on, and put the dripping shoe under the blast of hot air. It took about a good twenty minutes before it was reduced to the level of merely damp. Maribel worked it for another ten and handed it back to me. "It's good now."

I looked at what once was a midnight-blue pump to what was now a midday navy. If you didn't look really close, you might not notice. I figured if I stayed in my office for the balance of the day, everything would be fine.

"Thanks, Maribel," I said, stepping into the shoe. It made a slight squishing noise, but it was bearable.

"A little Vaseline will put the shine right back," she counseled.

I sighed. *Vaseline.* "I'll keep that in mind. Thanks again. I need to get back to work."

"Have a good weekend, Meez Margreet."

"You, too, Maribel." I hurried out and ignored the damp footprints I left on the hallway carpets.

After that fiasco, I felt I deserved a treat. I told Beverly that I was leaving for the day, and she could leave the reports on my desk. I'd review them on Monday. I was going for my very first manicure! If I was going to go clubbing, I wanted to look good.

I decided on the salon that Tiffany and Chantel always talked about: Angelique's. By the time I arrived, you would have thought they were giving out free facials. The place was packed. I actually had to take a number—like in the meat market, and I wondered if it was all worth it. When my turn came, the technician (that's what they're called) offered me an assortment of choices: French manicure, tips, filler, airbrush, acrylic nails, designs, or plain. I chose a combination of a French manicure with tips and the same for my toes. I took a seat at the end of a long row, and my feet were immediately plunged into swirling sudsy warm water, and my fingers dipped into petite pink-and-white bowls filled with some sort of solution. "Soften cuticles," the woman muttered in broken English. I nodded, figuring softened cuticles must be a good thing, from the looks of the number of hands dangling in bowls of solution.

The salon reminded me of a massive assembly line of patients ready to go under the knife. The technicians all wore white smocks, thin latex gloves, white skullcaps, and masks. I concluded the getup was to give a uniformed, sterile look to the place and offer the clients a degree of comfort. But the flip side was, if *they* needed protection, what were *we* being exposed to? No one offered us a mask or a smock.

I didn't want to be exposed to noxious nail remover fumes any more than the next woman. What if I began to feel faint and keeled over right in the whirlpool that lulled my feet and my body into a light doze?

*Sirens blared in the background. The emergency doors burst open as the paramedics rushed me through the ER. Was there a resident George Clooney or Eriq LaSalle technician ready to call a code and jolt life back into my limp body?*

Pink or clear?"

*Clear!* I jumped up, splashing water everywhere. I grabbed my chest, blinked, and shook my head slightly. This wasn't the ER.

"Huh, sorry." I gave her a weak smile. "Bad dream."

Several heads turned in my direction, eyebrows lifted in a perfect arch. I jutted my chin forward. "Pink," I announced, surprising myself.

Pink, the color that had haunted and tormented me since my youth, but not anymore. A moment of triumphant elation flooded through me. I heard music playing in the background. I felt light, powerful—pink!

After clipping, filing, and buffing my nails and my toes, the technician applied three coats of polish and dried them beneath tiny heat lamps. I paid a whopping thirty dollars plus a tip and wondered how women could afford it every week.

Careful not to undo my pedicure masterpiece, I tiptoed back to the Jag and drove back to my apartment barefoot.

When I stepped inside the place I'd called home since college, I was momentarily stunned. It was tiny, cramped, filled with Goodwill furniture and wood floors that needed a serious dose of polish. The dishes from my last meal filled the sink. The lightbulb in the foyer still needed replacing, and the walls remained a dingy off-off white.

I walked around as if it were my first time in the place. This was such a far cry from the way I'd been living lately. My two plants that sat in the windowsill overlooking the building next door were slumped over as if they'd tied on one too many the night before. My favorite chair that held a place of honor near my bookcase of first-edition novels didn't look quite as inviting as it used to.

I felt as if I'd taken a wrong turn somewhere and ended up in a ghost town of castoffs. How could I ever go back to this after the life I'd led?

Depressed, I walked into my six-by-nine bedroom and took some undies from my dresser drawer and an extra pair of shoes from the closet. I took one last look around. I'd seen the promised land, and I had no intention of returning to the land that time forgot.


I made a quick stop at Chantel's—checked her mail, did a speedy inventory of the apartment, watered her plants, scooped up a few outfits for the week—and then headed back to Tiffany's in time to walk Virginia.

234 ★ DONNA HILL

When I arrived, there was a note under Tiffany's door. It was from Willie.

*Margaret, sorry I have not been in touch. Been a little busy this week—some new contributors to the cause.*

I guess that was the code for new victims.

*I'll give you a call in a few days. Willie.*

Well, I certainly hoped that he did. Although he didn't know it yet, Willie was going to be my escort to the soiree. I burned the note on the top of the stove, just in case I was ever brought in for questioning about his misdeeds. I didn't want any physical evidence.

"After I take you for your walk, I want you to help me pick out an outfit from Tiffany's secret closet." I connected Virginia's leash to her collar, and her evening constitutional took a whopping forty minutes. No tree was good enough, and my nagging didn't seem to help. After what seemed like an eternity, Virginia was ready to return to the homestead.

I went straight for the bedroom and to the closet.

The secret door was still wedged open by boxes. I stepped over them and into Tiffany's inner sanctum.

This time I found a light switch that had been hidden behind one of the beheaded mannequins. The room was still a wreck, with detached hands and legs scattered across the floor.

"Oooh, nice." I zeroed in on a hot-pink number in leather. I held it up in front of me. "Now for a top." I poked around the mannequins and found a pink halter top that glittered in the light. I selected a pair of large gold hoop earrings, matching bracelets, and a curly Afro wig to round things out.

"That about does it."

I headed out and deposited my goodies on the bed; then I darted off to the shower, anticipating the evening.

A little less than an hour later, I stood in front of the full-length mirror, and I was stunned by what I saw. My own mother wouldn't have recognized me. The outfit was straight out of the disco '70s, totally retro, totally in. The leather mini cupped my curves like an eager lover, and my Afro wig did amazing things to my face. I looked like a partying Angela Davis.

I figured that between the girdle and the three-inch hot-pink heels, I had about a good three hours before I imploded.

I snatched my bag and slung it over my shoulder. It didn't exactly go with the ensemble, but it was easier to take it than to dig everything out and try to squeeze it all into something smaller.

"All right, Virginia, I'm outta here. Don't wait up."

I set the alarm, stepped out into the night, and smiled. "If I have my way, it's going to be a long evening."


Once behind the wheel of the Jag, I pulled Chantel's diary out of my purse and checked the information about the club's location then headed downtown toward the West Village. The club was located on Houston Street. The parking space I ultimately found after about ten trips around the block was fortunately under a streetlight, a precaution I felt was mandatory in that neck of the woods.

After stepping out of the car and setting the alarm, I took a good look around the neighborhood. Without belaboring the point, let's just say that it bore watching. There was no way I would be doing any lingering, and I truly wondered what was on Tiffany's and Chantel's minds when they came here. This locale was truly waaaay over on the other side of the tracks.

A man about the size of an SUV stood guard at the door. "Never seen you here before," he growled, and three gold teeth flashed at me as his thick lips rose and quivered into a snarl. "Who you wit'?"

I glanced over my shoulder at the line that had begun to form. And the assemblage was an eclectic bunch, to say the least. I felt underdressed.

"Uh, I'm uh . . . a friend of Tiffany's and Chantel's."

The behemoth actually smiled this time. "Hey, any friend of my girls Tiffany and Chantel's is a friend of the house. "Come on in."

He pulled open the black steel door, and music with the force of a sonic boom blasted out the doorway.

The instant I walked inside, I was sucked into a vacuum of wall-to-wall gyrating, sweating bodies, flashing lights, and scantily clad waitresses balancing trays of drinks over our heads.

Bumping and grinding my way across the dance floor, I finally made it to the other side and quickly adjusted my wig, which had nearly been swiped from my head by a wayward arm.

"Wanna dance, hot stuff?" some guy in all black asked. The gold stud in his ear sparkled in the flashing lights.

"Uh, not right now. Thanks."

He grunted something unintelligible and walked away.

"You here alone?" another suspect asked, not more than sixty seconds later.

"No." I looked away.

"What's your name, sugar?"

I looked him up and down and had to admit that he was definitely a cutie pie. He had the body of the Rock and the face of Denzel. His social graces could use some work, but what the hell.

"What's *your* name?" I asked, instead of answered.

The music was so loud, I didn't hear his response, and I guess he never heard me say no. He pulled me out onto the dance floor that was virtually vibrating from the pounding of dancing feet. We were instantly fused together from top to bottom, this Ebony Man and me, our bodies rocking back and forth in time to the ebb and flow of everyone around us.

Mr. Man started whispering in my ear as if I could actually hear him. I did catch something about lifting weights and living at his mother's house—at least that's what I thought I heard. But then the music switched gears to an even faster beat, and the crowd swayed in another direction. My weight-lifting mama's boy disappeared into the crowd as dance partners switched up quick as a group of people playing a game of musical chairs. When I finally got my bearings and looked into the face of my new boogie-down partner, my heart nearly stopped.

"Wayne!"

Fortunately my scream was muffled by the music.

His eyes were closed, and he looked totally transported by the beat. That's when I made a break for it. I pushed and shoved my way to the exit and took in a big lungful of air when I practically fell outside the door.

Wayne of all people! What the hell was he doing there? I supposed he could have asked me the same question had he caught me. Well, with the adrenaline of cold fear racing through my veins, I darted across the street to the car and made a beeline back to Tiffany's place.

As I drove, I kept seeing the image of Wayne on the dance floor: leather pants, fitted red T-shirt, gold chain, and hips that swiveled like those Hawaiian dolls you hang from your rearview mirror. You know the ones I mean.

How long had he been clubbing? I wondered as I took a right turn on two wheels. What would he have done if he'd recognized me? What would I have done? (Okay, I'd have lied.) Did he know about Tiffany? Did she know about him? But, now *I* knew about everyone! I had all the trump cards. All I needed to do was figure out how to play them. And I was pretty certain that I'd find a way really soon.

# Cleaning Day

After a night on the town, although a bit abbreviated, I was beat when the sun rose on Saturday morning with the blare of the alarm clock. My body and my eyes rebelled. But Virginia was having none of that.

When I was finally able to get my eyes fully opened. I was staring right into her beady ones. She was camped out on my chest with her leash clamped between her off-white teeth.

"What the—?" I jerked to a sitting position, successfully knocking Virginia to the floor. "I told you about that! You scared me."

I squinted at the clock. It was 7:15 a.m.

I pulled myself out of bed and stumbled into the bathroom.

After throwing some cold water on my face and tossing on a borrowed jogging outfit, I took Virginia for her walk.

Isn't it always the case that when you look your absolute worst, you invariably run into someone you don't want to see?

I really didn't want to chat. I still had morning breath, and I was pretty sure my hairdo could frighten a flock of crows.

"Morning, Margaret. Hey, Ginnie." He bent down and scooped up Virginia.

"Hi, Wayne." I looked him over. He didn't appear worse for wear, not like a man who'd spent the evening breaking a sweat on the dance floor. He actually looked quite rested. "So . . . what have you been up to?"

He shrugged. "Nothing special. What about you?"

"Working hard."

"On your acting?" He smiled as if he knew something.

"Uh . . . yes, and my job. I did tell you that I've been promoted to executive editor."

He nodded. "I hope that goes well for you." He stroked Virginia behind the ears.

"So . . . ," I tried again. "How was your evening? Do anything . . . special?"

"Nothing out of the ordinary."

So he went there often. "Really?" I hope he caught the note of skepticism in my tone.

"You, on the other hand, look like you've had a rough night. What have you been up to?"

Did he know? Was he trying to trap me? I patted down my hair. "Nothing, nothing at all."

He looked down at Virginia in his arms. "Is that true, Ginnie? Has Margaret been a good girl?"

Virginia barked as if to say, "Hell no."

I cut Virginia a nasty look.

He patted her head and set her down. "How's your grandmother?"

"Last time I checked, she was up to her usual stunts."

He laughed. "She's something else."

"Hmmm. That's an understatement," I murmured. "Anyway, I need to walk Virginia and get back. The cleaning lady is coming, and Tiffany insisted that I be there when she arrives."

His brows rose and then fell. "Ah, yes, Sybil. She's definitely an interesting character."

"What does that mean?"

"Oh, I don't want to spoil it for you. You'll see for yourself."

He waved and strolled off, chuckling to himself all the way down the street.

I didn't have time to really think about his remark, as Virginia was not up for being detained a moment longer. She pulled me in the opposite direction, and we began our walk. But Wayne's parting words still haunted me. The last thing I needed in my life at that moment was another *character*.

When I returned to the town house, we were both famished, so I ordered breakfast from the Spanish restaurant and put it on Tiffany's tab. At some point, I was going to have to clear that all up.

While we waited for the delivery, I took a quick shower and put on some clean clothes. The food arrived in record time, and we wolfed it down. Just as I was throwing away the empty containers, the doorbell rang again.

"Must be Sybil," I said. But you would have thought I'd said "Duck, the sky is falling." Virginia took off like a shot—so fast, all she left in her wake were dust and skid marks. That should have been my cue to do the same. Instead I went to the door and looked out the peephole, but I didn't see anyone.

"Hello? Who is it?"

"Sybil!"

I unlocked the door and hoped it wouldn't be one of those incidents I'd heard so much about on the news: someone pretending to be a utility person (or in this case, a housekeeper) pushes in your door, ties you up and steals all your valuables. Although, I wouldn't be out anything valuable, since it wasn't actually my place, but I'm sure it would still be traumatizing.

Being careful, I grabbed the broom that was by the door. Suddenly this woman (and I use the term with reservation), who couldn't have been any taller than five feet with heels, pushed open the door, hitting me square in the center of my head. She nearly knocked me out cold.

When my head cleared and I could get her in focus, I realized she had to weigh at least two hundred pounds if she weighed an ounce. Her complexion was as pale as a sheet of copy paper, and it was framed by wild jet-black ringlets that weighed at least twenty of the two hundred pounds.

I rubbed the knot that was rapidly re-forming on my forehead and followed her inside.

She looked wildly around at the chaos that had once been Tiffany's pristine palace.

"I can explain," I babbled as she began ranting and windmilling her arms as she went from room to room. Her outrage grew louder and more piercing, and for a moment I wondered if this were all some nasty trick that Tiffany was playing on me.

Sybil wagged her finger within inches of my nose and continued bawling me out.

But when she got to the bedroom and flung open the closet door, I was sure I would have to call EMS. She was one screech away from a heart attack. (Or maybe I was.)

And then, in a blink of an eye, she stopped yelling, whipped out her cleaning supplies from the duffle bag she carried, went to the cupboard in the kitchen, and got a mop and bucket. Sybil went to work.

I watched in amazement as she systematically turned chaos into an oasis, room by room. She tossed, turned, and organized. Dusted, busted, and shined every crack and crevice. She even managed to reconstruct the mangled closet and didn't seem at all disturbed by the contents of the secret room. All the while, she mumbled and cursed.

Through the entire bizarre episode, Virginia was missing in action. Every time Sybil set those eyes on me, she'd hurl a series of comments in a high-pitched squeal that made my teeth vibrate.

By the time she was finished, nearly three hours later, I was in desperate need of a stiff drink.

She gathered up her supplies, walked right up to me, snarled, and then stomped out.

For the next few minutes, all I could do was stand in the middle of the living room. I was too afraid to move, but more terrified that she might come back.

How in the world could Tiffany allow that madwoman in her house? Wayne's cryptic comment made sense. It was at that point that Virginia emerged from her hiding place beneath the love seat. It was lucky for her that she hadn't gotten sucked up by Sybil's frenetic vacuuming.

Virginia eased over to me and rubbed up against my legs. Needing some serious comfort myself, I picked her up, and we both stood rooted in the middle of the floor. It wasn't until the bell rang that we were finally jolted out of our near catatonia.

"Suppose it's her again," I whimpered.

Virginia trembled in my arms.

The bell rang again.

"Go see who it is," I hissed, and tried to put Virginia down.

She dug her claws into my shirt and wouldn't let go.

"Fine, we'll go together."

I tiptoed to the door and looked out the peephole. I was never so glad to see anyone in my life. I pulled open the door.

Willie sniffed the pine-filled air. "I guess you met Sybil," he said, patting my back and Virginia's head.

I looked up at him. "You . . . you know about *Sybil?*" I said her name in a hushed whisper.

"Sure. She's legendary. Cleans everyone's place in the neighborhood."

"She's crazy!" I said.

Willie laughed like he'd just heard the best joke. One of those doubled-over belly laughs. Finally he pulled himself together. "After you get over the first few initial shocks of having her in the house, she really is a sweetheart."

I was hard-pressed to imagine Attila the Hun as a sweetheart. I shivered—then it hit me. "Willie, what are you doing here?" I asked.

He pointed to the FedEx logo on his shirt. "I'm on duty today. I was in the neighborhood and thought I'd drop by and see how you were doing."

I looked him over. He was certainly a far cry from the man I'd seen step out of the bathroom only days ago. In his place was the Willie I remembered: nondescript and ordinary. The one consolation was that I knew he cleaned up good and had the right connections.

I slipped my arm through his and smiled sweetly at him. "Well, don't just stand there. Come on in and sit down for a minute."

He gave me a suspicious look, which was well deserved, of course. It was pretty clear that I was up to something.

"You could at least try to be a little more subtle," Willie stated rather calmly as he strolled into the living room and made himself at home. "Build up to the big question," he said, taking a seat on the couch and crossing his legs. He slipped off his glasses and stretched his arm along the back of the couch. In a wink, that swagger and self-confidence were back. "So what's the deal? And don't con the con man."

I huffed and flopped down in the chair opposite him. "Okay. Let me put it this way: I need your help, and you're not in much of a position to say no. But . . . I do think it will be something we'll both enjoy."

He leaned forward, and a slow smile crept across his wide mouth.

For the next half hour, I explained what I'd been up to, and then I popped the question.

# And the Plot
# Thickens

*W*illie agreed to take me to the soiree, and he didn't
seem at all put off by the fact that I'd managed to
wangle my way into the festivities under less-than-
upfront circumstances. As a matter of fact, he actually applauded
my ingenuity and said I was his "kind of girl." In a burglar's world,
that may not necessarily be a compliment, but I went with it.

With Willie's services secured, I prepared for my date with
James. He'd promised to take me to a place he knew I would love,
where there was plenty of music and an assortment of characters to
keep me entertained all night. He told me to dress casual but with
flair—whatever that meant. I, of course, didn't have anything in
my personal wardrobe that fit the bill, so I opted for one of
Tiffany's party outfits that I'd lifted from her apartment.

I chose a pair of black leather pants, a hot-pink (of course) camisole, and a matching black leather jacket. If we were going partying, there was no way that I intended to have any issues with my feet. So I decided on my standard black pumps from Payless.

I placed my outfit in one of Tiffany's Kenneth Cole suit bags and headed out. I'd told James to pick me up at Chantel's place at nine. That would give me time to take Virginia for her second walk of the day and then get to Chantel's and change clothes.

With a few hours to kill, I decided to pay a quick visit to my mother's house and check on the dynamic duo.

When I arrived, my mother answered the door, looking like a new woman. She'd had her hair done in a sassy auburn that brought out the red undertones of her skin. Her eyes were sparkling as if she'd just taken a toot, and I'd swear she'd lost about ten pounds since the last time I saw her. Mom looked good.

"Margaret! What a pleasant surprise. Come in, sweetheart." She kissed my cheek.

I frowned. *Mom, being gracious?* Where was my real mother? Something was up, and I had no intention of getting stuck with Grandma.

"I'm not staying," I said by way of greeting. I wanted that straight and out of the way, up front. "I just stopped by to see how you and Grandma were doing."

She put her arm around my waist as I walked inside. "You can stay for a few minutes, at least. We haven't had a chance to talk in so long."

I gave her my version of Grandma's evil eye. "Last time I tried to talk to you, you blew me off, said you had everything under control."

She laughed. "But I do, sweetheart."

"Did you find another job?"

She laughed again. "Oh, that. There's no need for me to work.

Let's talk about something more fun. Let's talk about you. What have you been up to lately? How are things going?"

I walked into the living room and sat down on the couch. Mom took a seat opposite me. "Everything is going fine. I got a temporary promotion at work."

"Yes, I know. Congratulations."

Although I didn't recall telling her, I let it go. "Other than that, I've been keeping busy, running back and forth between Tiffany's and Chantel's places . . . checking on things."

She smiled. "You're a good friend. I'm sure it will all pay off in the end."

"In the end of what?"

She shrugged. "In the end," she repeated. "Just a turn of phrase."

*Hmmm.* "Where's Grandma?"

"Upstairs resting. She wore herself out talking about her life as a geisha during World War Two. Why don't you go up and say hello."

"Uh . . . I think I'll just let her rest. Tell her I stopped by." There was no way I was going to go upstairs and have my mother pull a fast one on me again or have Grandma launch into one of her monologues.

"You look really nice," I finally said. "You did something with your hair."

"Yes, I thought it was time for a new look. New life, new look." She grinned like a Cheshire cat.

"There's a lot of that going around." I stood. "I better get going."

My mother walked me to the door. "Sure you don't want to stay for dinner? I'm cooking chicken."

My mother always cooked chicken. For as long as I can remember, my mother cooked chicken. "No thanks. I have a date."

She brightened. "Oh, really? With that wonderful young man that Grandma raves about . . . Wayne?"

"No. Not Wayne." I opened the door.

"Who, then?"

I smiled. "As you and Grandma always say, a woman should have some secrets." I winked, walked out to the Jag, revved her up, and drove off.

After a quick pit stop back to Tiffany's to walk Virginia, I then headed over to Chantel's to get dressed and wait for James. To tell the truth, I was kind of excited. This time it was a real date. I wanted to feel bad about going out with Chantel's boyfriend. But I didn't. All my life I'd lived in their shadows, lurking around in the corners, waiting for the crumbs of their friendship, hoping that they would notice me. Finally I was being noticed. Since they'd gone off to Europe, my life had changed exponentially. My attitude was different. I finally believed that I was worthy. Maybe it was the clothes, the high-priced neighborhood, the car, and the jewelry. I couldn't be sure. The only thing I was certain of was that I was not the Margaret Drew of only a few weeks earlier. I was new and improved, and the only way to go was up. At least that's what I told myself.

At nine o'clock on the dot, the doorbell rang, and my date began.

"You look great, Margaret," James said as he held open the car door for me. "I just can't get over the change in you."

I eased into my seat and placed my freshly manicured hands on my lap. "Change in me?" I said coyly. "What do you mean?"

"Well—" He shrugged and turned the key in the ignition. Luther Vandross filled the air. "—it's just that the few times I saw you . . . before . . . you were . . . I don't know . . . different. You were always kind of in the background, and I could never figure out what you were doing hanging with Chantel."

Should I have been offended? "We've been friends for a very long time. I suppose Chantel is just more outgoing than I am."

"Maybe. In any case, I'm really glad I'm getting to know you. You're smart, funny, you enjoy my music and . . . you're pretty."

I felt my face flush. "Uh, thanks, James."

"It's all true. And I enjoy being with you. You're real. There's nothing fake about you, like some women."

Real? I almost choked. I figured the best course of action was to keep my mouth shut on that topic. "So . . . where *are* we going? Is it still a surprise?" I asked, changing the subject.

He grinned. "You'll see."

We continued the drive across town in a comfortable silence, listening to the music on 98.7 KISS FM and watching the folks on the street get their Saturday night groove on.

About twenty minutes later, we pulled into a parking lot in Midtown Manhattan and walked the rest of the way, finally coming to a stop in front of the famed Roseland dance hall.

The marquee flashed, RHYTHM REVIEW: NOW APPEARING: THE STYLISTICS, THE BLUE NOTES (MINUS TEDDY PENDERGAST), THE DELLS, AND THE FOUR TOPS. I was in heaven.

"James! I don't believe it." Without thinking, I turned and hugged him, and you know what? He hugged me right back. Catching ourselves, we cautiously stepped back, flashing each other awkward smiles.

He took my hand. "Come on—let's party."

It goes without saying that Roseland was filled to the brim with characters. The men mostly in their late forties, early fifties were decked out in the full pimplike attire: bright red, orange, and sky-blue sharkskin suits; wide-brimmed hats; and dark glasses. Straight out of a *Superfly* movie. It took all my home training not to crack up laughing. The women weren't much better, in skin-tight outfits, door knocker earrings, and platform shoes. It was a howl.

The DJ was right out of the disco era. He played all the hits from the late sixties and early to mid-seventies. And the crowd loved it. Me and James stayed on the dance floor until the show began.

"Is it always like this?" I asked when we found a table and sat down.

"Yep!" he shouted over the noise. "At least when they have Rhythm Review."

Chantel and Tiffany didn't know what they were missing. They spent all their time and energy pretending to be above it all, when deep inside, this was the kind of thing they wanted to be a part of.

The groups turned the place out and had everyone singing along to all their classic hits, me and James included. By the time we left, it was nearly two in the morning. I was hoarse, my body was rebelling, but I was oddly energized.

"I had a ball," I said when we pulled to a stop in front of Chantel's place.

"So did I." He turned off the engine and angled his body so that he could face me. "I'm glad you had a good time. Listen, I was wondering—if you're not busy, I'd really like to take you to this exclusive party."

"An exclusive party? Wow. When?"

"Next Saturday. It'll be nothing like tonight. But I'm pretty sure you'd have a great time. I'd love for you to be my date."

"Next Saturday, sure . . . I . . ." *Next Saturday is the soiree.* I couldn't miss that. Not after all the planning I'd been doing. But I would love to go out with James again. "Gee, James, I'm sorry. I already made plans for next Saturday."

All the light in his eyes seemed to dim. "Hey, no problem." He forced a smile. "Maybe we can make it another time."

"I hope so." I didn't know where to look, so I focused on my everyday bag. "I, uh, guess I better let you go."

Then suddenly he leaned forward, cupped my chin in his palm, and kissed me right on the lips. And it was more than just a peck. "Good night, Margaret," he said in a tone I hadn't heard come from him before. It was thick and inviting.

I swallowed hard and reached for the door handle. "Good night." I opened the door and almost jumped out. My heart was pounding. I started to hiccup.

"I'll call you during the week."

All I could do was nod my head and hold my breath. I darted up the stairs to Chantel's building, turned and waved—and he sped off.

By the time I opened the door to Chantel's apartment, I was in the midst of a full-fledged hiccup attack. *He kissed me, actually kissed me,* I thought as I chugged down glasses of water. The line had officially been crossed. Oh, my!

The following morning, I was up at six and headed back across town to Tiffany's in time to walk Virginia. While we were out, I reminisced about my night right up to the impromptu kiss from James.

I'd never expected it. This was all supposed to be fun and games. But I really thought he might like me. And I liked him, too, sort of. *And* I liked Calvin.

*There's definitely nothing between me and Wayne. There never can be. I have to set my goals higher than that. Wayne doesn't fit the mold for a true Diva. I need a man like James or Calvin. And both of them should be fair game. After all, Tiffany and Chantel don't want to be bothered. They said as much.* "So as the old saying goes, All's fair in love and war . . . *and the rise to Divadom.*

I tapped my foot as I waited for Virginia to finish up. "Come on—I need to get back." Calvin was picking me up for brunch, and I wanted to be ready.

There is nothing more endearing than a man who is prompt. I had to give James and Calvin points for that. They always showed up exactly when they said they would. At 11:29, Calvin was at the front door.

"Hi. Right on time. Come on in. I just have to get my bag."

"How are you?" he asked as we walked inside.

"Pretty good. Looking forward to brunch." I started for the bedroom to get my bag and a jacket.

"I hope you're hungry. The food is great."

Virginia heard the word *food,* trotted over to Calvin, and sniffed his leg.

"Hey there, Virginia." He reached down and patted her head. "Have you heard from Tiffany lately?" he called out to me.

I walked back into the foyer. "No, I haven't."

"Neither have I. It's just as well. I guess it's really over."

"Does that bother you?"

He took a breath. "At first it really did. I couldn't believe she would just up and leave like that without a word. And then pack up my stuff in a box marked X. But—" He looked into my eyes. "—being with you has definitely taken the edge off."

"Well, uh, I'm glad I could help."

"You've done more than help. You've shown me what I've been missing. What a true woman really is."

Oh, boy. This was getting sticky. I gave him what I hoped passed as a smile. "I think we should be going."

"Right." He took my arm and guided me out.

We had brunch at the Shark Bar, and just as Calvin said, the food was delicious. When we were about to leave, the owners, Nick Ashford and Valerie Simpson, walked in, looking like the stars they were. And of all things, they knew Calvin by name.

Calvin introduced me to Nick and Val, and I was too starstruck to hold an intelligent conversation.

"I'll see you Saturday," Calvin said as he shook hands with Nick and kissed Val's cheek.

I waved good-bye, not trusting my voice.

"How in the world did you meet them?" I finally asked once we were in the car.

"Oh, we go way back. Seems like I've known them forever. Great couple. By the way, what are you doing Saturday night?"

"Saturday . . . Wow, I have plans for Saturday."

"Oh . . ." He heaved a breath.

*Gee when it rains it pours,* I lamented.

"Date?"

"Uh . . . no, not really. Just plans," I lied, none too smoothly.

"Well, if your plans change, give me a call."

"Sure."


Well, this is your stop," he said when we pulled up in front of Tiffany's town house.

"Thanks for a great afternoon. I still can't get over meeting Nick and Val."

"Hang with me, and I can introduce you to all kinds of people, if that's what you want."

I patted his hand. "I will definitely keep that in mind."

"Call me, okay?" he said as I exited the car. He got out, as well, and met me in front of the Benz.

"I want to keep seeing you, Margaret."

"Uh . . . what about Tiffany? What happens when she comes back? This is all so temporary. We—"

"I'll deal with that when the time comes. In the meantime—"

He pulled me into his arms and kissed me long and slow. I was so stunned, I couldn't respond. I simply stood there like a block of wood in his arms.

Slowly he let me go. "Call me," he said again, and got back into the car then pulled off, leaving me standing on the curb with the scent of his cologne clinging to my clothes.

My body felt hot, my knees weak, my heart pitter-pattering like I was in a romance novel. I shook my head to clear it. First James and then Calvin, both of them wanted more, and I wanted it all. There had to be a way to make it all work.

But question after question plagued me: What would happen when Tiffany and Chantel returned? Would life go back to normal? Would I have to resume my humdrum life, as if this life— the life of my fantasies—had never existed? How could I do that when I'd finally gotten a taste of the pie?

Confused, I turned to go inside when I spotted Wayne entering his building with a stunning woman on his arm who looked as if she couldn't wait to get him inside. They were laughing and smiling as if they'd known each other forever. She kissed his cheek just before he opened the door to let them both in.

For several moments, all I could do was stand there, wishing that my bad eyes were playing tricks on me.

This time my heart really did skip a beat.

# How Could This
# Have Happened?

*N*o sooner had I sat down at my desk to review the reports for the departments than there was a knock on my door. Let's just say I was not in the best of moods. I'd spent most of my night pacing the floor and peeking out the window hoping to see "that woman" finally leave Wayne's apartment. Eventually, about 3 a.m., my eyes and body gave out, and I fell across the bed with Virginia at my feet.

Right up until the alarm went off, I'd had terrifying dreams. I was running through Saks Fifth Avenue, hot on the heels of the mystery woman, but I kept tripping over the clothing racks and knocking everything to the floor. One of sales clerks (who looked suspiciously like Tanisha from the office) called security, and they were none other than James and Calvin. Both of them were out of their dapper attire and garbed in workman-blue shirts with tin badges, narrow-legged navy blue pants, and shiny thick-soled black shoes. Tanisha was yelling and pointing. "Impostor, impostor!"

Beverly was there, too, and she was laughing. "I told you, you'd never make it." She laughed maniacally.

Mr. Savage roared his disappointment. "I knew I should never have given you the job," he boomed.

Everywhere I turned, there was another accusing face. My mother, Grandma, Wayne, even Willie of all people, were shaking their heads with disappointment and shame. They were all jeering and taunting me. Tiffany and Chantel stood to the side, applauding my downfall as I tried to make it to the flashing EXIT sign. The mystery woman and freedom were just on the other side of the door. I somehow believed that if I could unmask the mystery woman, I would be vindicated. Wayne would see her for the fraud that she truly was, sweep me into his arms, and I could put all the misery and humiliation behind me and start life anew.

"Wayne, Wayne! Wait, don't run away," I yelled as I leaped over a fallen mannequin.

"Stop her!" the madding crowd cried.

I ran faster. The exit was drawing closer. I could feel the cool breeze of freedom brush my cheeks. Just as I was about to cross the threshold, alarms sounded, and the guards were mere feet away. Then that damned Virginia grabbed my pant leg, and I tumbled into a heap of cashmere sweaters.

Actually Virginia had been licking my face when the alarm clock went off. Nonetheless, the dream was quite disturbing.

The knock on my door was louder this time. Obviously they knew I was in my office. No point in pretending otherwise.

"Come in."

The door inched open. It was Maribel. "Meez Margreet, I have news. Not so good. But news."

"Come in and close the door, Maribel."

She did as I instructed and walked quickly to my desk. In a very bad stage whisper she said, "Meez Beverly and Mr. Larry are—how you say?—an item."

I sat up straighter in my seat. "Excuse me. What are you saying about Beverly and Larry?"

"She tell the ladies in the coffee room about her date with Larry and what a good time she have." Maribel bobbed her head up and down as if to validate her story.

My throat was suddenly dry. Beverly and Larry? I knew she'd been after him from day one. She hated the fact that Larry and I, well, were friends. But he swore to me that Beverly wasn't his type. How could this be?

"You look funny around the mouth and eyes, Meez Margreet. You feeling okay?"

My gaze drifted up to her pinched expression. "Yes, I'm fine," I mumbled. "Thanks for the information, Maribel. I . . . really appreciate it."

"I no mean to upset you. Just thought you would want to know. *Sí?*"

"Yes, thanks."

"I go do my work now. Be back later to tidy up your office."

I think I must have stared at the wall until my eyes began to glaze over. First it was Wayne and that woman, and now Beverly and Larry. How could this have happened? A better question was, why did I even care? If I wasn't so utterly exhausted, I would have paced the floor. Instead I drummed my two-inch nails on the desk until I gave myself a headache and was forced to stop.

My intercom buzzed, and I actually growled, knowing who was on the other end. I stabbed the flashing light.

"Yes."

"There's an international call for you on line one," said Beverly. She sounded too damned happy, if you asked me.

"Thank you." I pressed line one. "Hello?"

The connection sounded as if it were underwater. "Maggie. It's me, Tiffany."

"And Chantel."

I really groaned that time. "Hi, Tiffie. Hi, Chantie. How is everything?"

"You'll have to speak up," they shouted. "This connection is terrible."

"How is everything?"

"Fine. I was calling to see how things were going. How is Virginia?"

"*Fine.*"

"Have you heard from Calvin?"

My stomach knotted. "You're breaking up," I lied.

"Can you hear me now?"

"*No.*"

"Then, I better talk fast. We're planning on—"

This time I really couldn't hear a thing. Her voice floated in and out. I caught every other word: *plane . . . hotel . . . money . . . home.*

"*Fine!*" I shouted, not knowing what I was saying fine about, but it sounded good. Anything to get her off the phone.

"See you—"

The line went dead, and that was just as well. I had much more pressing thoughts on my mind than talking to Tiffany and Chantel. I hung up the phone and went back to staring at the wall. Who was the woman with Wayne, and why did I give a damn? And what in heaven's name made Larry go out with Beverly?

The answers eluded me. But maybe I wasn't supposed to know.

Perhaps, as in all things in my life, it was just another freaky situation that escaped any plausible explanation.

Perhaps it was best that I didn't dwell on this netherworld where nothing was as it seemed. I had to stay focused even as my life and all the people in it were becoming more and more murky each day.

In the meantime, I had a soiree to plan for. It was the culmination of all my dreams. I had to be prepared. I knew that once I crossed that finish line, the Divas would welcome me with open arms. I would be one of the chosen and live the life that I was destined to live. Nothing was going to stop me!

With my spirits bolstered by positive reinforcement, I tossed aside my worries and decided to sneak a few minutes and watch one of the training videos.

I locked my office door and slipped the tape from my bag and put it in the VCR. (An entertainment system was one of the perks of being in charge.) I tried to focus on the speaker, who was discussing the particulars of selecting the proper associates to enhance one's lifestyle. But Tiffany's voice kept ringing in my ear. And I wished I'd paid more attention to what she'd said.

# No Good Deed
# Goes Unpunished

*W*atching the tape, I felt miraculously renewed. All my doubts and unanswered questions were pushed to the farthest recesses of my mind. And after receiving back-to-back phone calls from James and Calvin about the wonderful time they had and how much they enjoyed my company, I was on cloud nine.

Feeling especially good, I decided to do a walk-by of the staff to see what they were up to. It was important to keep them on their toes and reinforce the notion that the boss (that was me) could show up at any time.

When I exited my office, I was surprised to find my assistant's desk empty of an assistant. I headed down the corridor, peeking in several office and cubicles. No Beverly. My next stop was the employee lounge. Perhaps she'd gone to get us both cups of coffee, like a dutiful assistant.

But when I arrived, the room was empty. Where could she be? The ladies' room! I made a quick left toward my target. As we have discovered, the ladies' room is a hotbed of information. If there was anything to be found out, that's where it would be. This time I had no intention of having another misstep—if you get my drift.

Slowly, I pushed open the door and peeked inside. No one was at the sinks, but I heard voices from the stalls on the end.

Easing inside, I was careful not to let the door squeak on its hinges. I stood in the little alcove out of sight and strained to hear. It was Tanisha and her ever-present sidekick.

". . . that's what she gets," Tanisha was saying. "One day she's just a regular nobody like the rest of us, and the next she's Ms. High and Mighty trying to run things and give orders. She didn't earn the job; she tripped over it. No wonder Larry doesn't want to be bothered."

"Yeah," her sidekick replied. "But I kinda feel bad for her."

"Why would you feel sorry for her?"

"It must be hard to have your life suddenly flip upside down and have your friends turn their backs on you 'cause you get to be in charge."

"Look, you can't have it both ways. Either you're part of the team or you ain't. And she's not part of the team."

"Yeah, I guess you're right. You can't play both sides of the fence."

A toilet flushed and then the other. I heard a rustling of clothing and a shuffling of feet. For a hot minute I wanted to stay there and give them a Brooklyn beat-down. Tell them both they didn't know what they were talking about. That they had no clue what it was like being a shadow all your life and then, finally, through a bizarre twist of circumstances have a new life handed to you on a platter. Who wouldn't take it? Was I wrong?

But I didn't confront them. Instead I slunk away like a coward and returned to my office. I knew Tanisha had it in for me. She totally resented me. So why should her latest comments bother me at all? It was just too bad for her that she couldn't accept the fact that I got what I wanted. She was simply jealous.

Suddenly, I smiled. *Jealous*. I'd never had anyone jealous of me in my entire life. No one had ever been envious. They never wanted what I had, because I didn't have anything they wanted.

Now the tables were finally turned. Ha! All my life I'd wanted to be someone else; now others wanted to be me!

I didn't need Larry. Beverly could have him. I had Calvin and James. Both of them adored me. I had Willie at my beck and call, two fabulous wardrobes at my disposal, a town house, a co-op, a Jaguar, and the handbook.

I was only days away from crossing the threshold into true Divadom. The complaints of mere peons were minuscule in light of my long-term plan. This temporary life I'd taken on was just that—temporary. But I had every intention of making it permanent. With the right connections, a great hairdo, and the perfect wardrobe, anything was possible.

All I had to do was pull it off before Tiffany and Chantel returned, and then, ladies, the world would be mine. I was feeling so good after my internal pep talk, it was like listening to a preacher tell his flock how much he needed their hard-earned money. You become so mesmerized by his passionate plea (and good looks) that you empty your purse and feel good about it.

I returned to my office area with a bit more pep in my step, even though my feet were beginning to bite. But when I arrived, I stopped dead in my tracks.

Larry was leaning on Beverly's desk, chatting away, and Beverly was grinning like he was tickling her under the table.

I loudly cleared my throat. Two sets of eyes focused on me. I adjusted my jacket and walked over to the culprits. "Well, I see you made it back to your desk," I said to Beverly. I turned my steely gaze on Larry. "I'm pretty sure the rest of the department is waiting on their mail delivery."

"As a matter of fact, this was my last stop of the morning," Larry said. "Is there a problem, boss?" he asked in an uncharacteristic Southern drawl.

I jutted out my chin and glanced from one to the other. "There very well could be. People are paid to do a job, not hang around having aimless conversations on company time." I folded my arms and tapped my foot.

The corner of Larry's mouth curved up in a half-grin. "I knew it was just a matter of time." He slowly shook his head and then turned to Beverly. "I'll see you at five. Meet me in the parking lot."

"Sure, Larry."

He cut his eyes in my direction and walked away, pushing his mail cart in front of him.

"In the future, when you plan to be away from your desk, let me know."

"I really didn't think it was a problem. I was only gone for a few minutes."

"A lot can happen in a few minutes. If I can't depend on you, then maybe I need to speak to Mr. Savage and get another assistant. Perhaps you'd be happier back in the editorial pool, back with your old friends and your *old* salary." I smiled smugly.

Her eyes widened in alarm, and for a moment I felt awful for talking to her that way. But it didn't last long when I thought about her meeting Larry after work. Since I'd gotten the promotion and changed my appearance and my attitude, Larry wouldn't give me the time of day. The friendship that we'd shared seemed to no longer matter. Now to add insult to injury, my old nemesis had taken my place in his afterwork life.

"The choice is yours," I added, and then spun away into my office, shutting the door firmly behind me.

I flounced down in my comfy leather seat and brooded over this latest turn of events. What was a Diva-in-training supposed to do? I didn't have any answers. And for some reason, I didn't think the answers were to be found between the pages of a manual or on a videotape. What I needed was someone to talk to, someone to whom I could bare my soul without judgment or recriminations, someone who would listen to my woes as I worked it all out in my head.

As crazy at this may sound, the only person I could think of was Grandma.

I spent the rest of the day squirreled away in my office. I didn't want to inadvertently run into Beverly and Larry or overhear Tanisha and her catty remarks. At 4:45 I announced to Beverly that I was leaving for the day, and I headed to my mother's house in Brooklyn.

When I arrived and let myself in, the air smelled of chicken. I could only conclude that my mother was in the general vicinity. I tossed my everyday bag on the end table in the foyer along with my jacket and walked into the living room. As usual, Grandma was camped out in front of the television watching E! She barely looked up when I walked in the room.

"Hi, Grandma," I murmured, and took a seat beside her on the couch.

"You know this is all propaganda," she began. "Those foolish stars couldn't do half the things the media says they do." She shook her head. "Sometimes folks will do anything for a bit of attention. Then when they get it, they don't know what to do with it. Grass is always greener on the side you're already on!" She tsked-tsked.

"Grandma, I'm really confused."

"The world is a confusing place. That's what makes it interesting."

I realized that the only way to get through what I knew was destined to be a one-sided conversation was to pretty much bypass Grandma's "wisdom" and plow on with my story.

"You see, I thought I had this great opportunity. I had the chance of a lifetime when Tiffany and Chantel left. Everything I ever wanted was at my disposal."

"All that glitters ain't silver," she muttered.

I frowned. "Well, anyway, now everyone who used to be my friend seems to hate me. And folks who wouldn't give me the time of time are begging for my attention."

"Friends are like two left shoes. They sure are," she said.

I truly had no idea what that meant. "Anyway, I'm no longer sure what I want anymore, Grandma. It all seemed so clear in the beginning."

"Can't see the forest for all the damned wild animals in the woods!" She slapped her thigh then slapped mine. She turned toward me, and her eyes actually focused on mine for a moment. "The thing of it is, chile, nothing is ever as it seems." She smiled then turned back to the television. "When I met Shakespeare, he told me personally—and I'm only paraphrasing, now—but he said something like the whole world being a dress rehearsal and everyone was vying for the starring role. Yep, he sure did. And I never forgot those words."

Oh, boy. "Thanks for listening, Grandma. I'll work it out." I stood.

Grandma looked up at me and pointed a slender finger in my direction. A sly smile spread across her mouth. "You know, no good deed goes unpunished." She started cackling and slapping her thigh again. I realized that was my cue.

When I got back behind the wheel of the Jag and headed toward Manhattan, I couldn't say I felt any better by talking with Grandma, but at least I didn't feel any worse, if that was a consolation.

Zipping along the FDR Drive, I kept revisiting her little quips. Bit by bit, they actually began to make sense. That's when I knew I was in serious trouble.

# The Sky Really
# Is Falling

The next few days went by pretty much uneventfully—
miraculous, considering my track record. I'd finally convinced myself after my one-sided chat with Grandma that I
was going to see this thing through to the end, and the hell with
the consequences. So basically, I chose to ignore Larry, Beverly,
Tanisha, and her sidekick unless I needed something. After all, I
was the boss—as Larry felt compelled to remind me.

The office was running smoothly, I'd gotten the whole routine
of running back and forth between Tiffany's, Chantel's, my apartment, and my mother's house down to an art form. I'd conditioned
my mind and body to block out the agony of the too-tight shoes
and the ever-present girdles. My relationships with Calvin and
James were stable. I alternated my dates with them, finding that
two in one night was too much even for me.

The only missing link in the entire scenario was Wayne. He'd been conspicuously scarce, not even dropping by unexpectedly as he generally had. I kind of missed him in an odd sort of way. Ever since the night I'd spotted him at the club and then all hugged up with Ms. America, I'd been . . . well, thinking differently about Wayne Hathaway. Maybe there was an outside chance that Grandma was right. Suppose he really was a nice guy with potential.

I tossed the manual on the floor, and Virginia came scurrying over. You know, that made me smile. Only weeks earlier, I couldn't stand the ball of fur, but now she was like a best friend. I scooped her up, cradled her in my arms, and took a look around at the finery of Tiffany's place: the imported Italian furniture, designer wardrobe, high-paying job, Jaguar, and platinum credit cards. Not to mention Chantel's high-priced co-op, her Victoria Secret lingerie cache, and secret penchant for thugs. And what of my promotion and the great job I was doing? I was a whisper away from it all disappearing as if it had never happened. I thought of my drab apartment, my dull life, uninspired wardrobe, lack of male companionship, and a crappy job as an assistant editor to the worst boss in the history of publishing.

There had to be a way to keep it all. All of it. It was a life to which I'd grown accustomed, and the key to holding on to that life was the soiree. With the slickest man in America on my arm, the right clothes, and attitude, I was bound to be embraced by the Divas. The key was to ingratiate myself to the Grand Diva. She was bound to see my potential and bestow upon me the initiatory rites of passage.

I hopped up from the bed, dropping Virginia unceremoniously on the floor, and walked over to the closet. Sliding open the door, I inspected the line of evening attire, looking for something suitable to wear to the main event. Although Tiffany had every kind of outfit imaginable, I didn't see anything that was just right.

"Come on, Ginnie, let's go for a ride."

When I arrived at the garage with Virginia in tow, my buddy Stanley was still on duty.

"Ah, Ms. Drew." He beamed and came hurrying over as if he was about to hug me.

Suddenly, Virginia leaped up and down and started growling like a pit bull. For a second or two, I was too surprised to react. The only time she ever got remotely excited was when I'd mention food.

"Virginia, it's me Stanley . . . He began backing up, but she wouldn't stop growling. Then she leaped and grabbed his pant leg. Finally, I snapped to my senses and pried Virginia away.

His face was crimson, and the protruding veins in his neck were as thick as ropes. "Take the car and get out! I'm gonna speak to Ms. Lane and tell her about you and her mad dog." He wagged a finger at Virginia.

Virginia tried to bite his finger. His face bunched up in a knot as he snatched his hand away, mere inches from the jaws of death. His breath came in hard and fast gasps, and his eyes looked as if they would pop out of his head; then he whirled around and stomped off.

"What in the world is wrong with you, Virginia?" I hissed. "Now you've gotten us both in trouble." I paced back and forth, waiting for the car to arrive and cutting nasty looks in Virginia's direction. Needless to say, she ignored me.

Finally, Stanley screeched to a halt in front of us and jumped out of the car.

I got in the car, and Virginia walked across my lap and sat in the passenger seat as if nothing had happened.

"You better hope that Stanley forgets all about this by the time Tiffany gets back." I turned on the radio and hummed along with Anita Baker.

About twenty minutes later I pulled up in front of Chantel's apartment, parked, and got out.

"Are you going to behave yourself, or I am going to have to leave you in the car?"

Virginia stuck her stubby tail in the air and trotted past me. And to think that less than an hour earlier I was having warm and fuzzy feelings for her.

When we got inside, I went straight for the closet. Chantel had the perfect dress for the soiree. It was a Vera Wang original. A fitted microsilk gown in soft dove gray with spaghetti straps, a scooped bodice, and a daring split right up the middle. It would go perfectly with Tiffany's diamond studs and matching tennis bracelet.

I took the dress from the closet and put it in a garment bag, then added a pair of pearl-gray pumps to my loot. Of course, I needed the perfect body shaper to contain my voluptuous hips and not-very-flat tummy. I found just what I was looking for and dropped that into the bag, as well.

Satisfied with my take, I turned off the lights, locked up, and headed back to Tiffany's. A good night's sleep was in order. I wanted to be in top form for my big night.

# Countdown
# to Victory

The first thing Saturday morning, I went directly to the hair-dresser and then to the nail salon for a touch-up. I left a note for Broom Hilda to come back on Sunday for her cleanup. The place was a wreck, but one more day wouldn't matter.

Since I had no real experience with makeup, I made a pit stop in Macy's and had a full makeover job done for free for the mere purchase of a few cosmetics. Neat trick, huh?

When the cosmetician was finished and held up the mirror for me to see the results of her work, I was totally transformed. I actually looked pretty, like a star. I was so happy, I actually kissed her cheek.

With my purchases tucked neatly in one of those nifty little shopping bags, I returned to Tiffany's to get ready. Willie promised he'd be there by eight.

While I was squeezing into my borrowed girdle, the doorbell rang. Holding my breath to within an inch of my life, I managed to shove everything in. I grabbed a pink silk robe off the hook on the back of the bathroom door and double-timed it to answer the ring, which had turned insistent.

"Hold your horses!" I shouted on my way down the hall. Virginia was hot on my heels, as usual. I pressed my eye to the peephole.

Wayne! Figures. When I wanted him to show up, he couldn't be found. Now that he was the last person I wanted to see, like a bad penny, there he was. I inched the door open.

"Hi, Wayne. Really can't talk now."

He tried to peer over my shoulder and into the house. "Company?"

"No."

"So why can't I come in?"

"I'm trying to get dressed, Wayne," I said, and knew I sounded impatient because I was.

"You're all dolled up in the face. Another date?"

"What do you care? I'm sure you have plenty to keep you occupied." I hated how that came out. I sounded like a jilted lover.

"I could say the same thing about you. You seem to have been very busy lately."

I swatted at Virginia, who was jumping up and down my leg. "Would you cut it out?" I snapped, then returned my attention to Wayne. "What's that supposed to mean?" I braced my hip against the door and pursed my lips.

"I've seen you darting back and forth, jockeying Calvin and James, getting around town in Tiffany's car."

Heat rose from my toes and settled right in the middle of my forehead. He'd been watching me? The little sneak.

"I guess you actually are an actress. You've been putting on a really great performance. I would have thought better of you, Margaret. Guess I was wrong."

"I don't have to stand here and listen to your insults."

"You're absolutely right. I'm leaving. Enjoy yourself, Margaret." He turned and trotted down the stairs.

I slammed the door behind him. "How dare he? Just who does he think he is, anyway? You're nobody, Wayne Hathaway!" I yelled at the closed door.

I stomped off to the bedroom to finish getting ready, inwardly fuming. He was a mere chiropractor. Not even a real doctor, I thought, slipping—well, not exactly *slipping*—into the gown. I had bigger fish to fry. I'd show him. I'd show them all. Tonight was my night, and nasty remarks from the likes of Wayne were not going to dampen my spirits or my plan.

I opened the pink velvet box that contained the diamond studs and the tennis bracelet, and I put them on. Peering into the mirror, I added a stroke of my recently purchased honeysuckle lipstick to my mouth and then patted my nose with a makeup sponge. I put on my glasses to get a better look. I was stunning, if I had to say so myself. But the glasses, as much as I needed them, totally clashed with my ensemble. They would definitely have to go. I tucked them in my purse, just in case.

The doorbell rang again.

"It better not be Wayne, unless he's here to apologize." I went to the door ready for battle, but found Willie instead.

"You look much too gorgeous to be so pissed off," he said. "I'm only ten minutes late."

"Thanks and sorry," I muttered. "Thought you were someone

else. Come on in. I have to put on my shoes." I stepped around
him and checked outside. "You weren't followed, were you?"

He laughed. "Naw. Lost them on that last turn."

"Not funny, Willie."

He followed me inside.

"Have a seat. I'll be right back."

In the bedroom, I got the purse that matched the shoes. This
was definitely not an outfit that would work well with my everyday bag. Tiffany had a great silver fox stole that went perfectly
with the dress. I draped it casually over my arm.

"Okay, Virginia, this is it. Wish me luck." I sashayed into the
living room for my grand entrance. Willie dropped the magazine
he was reading, and his mouth sagged.

"Did I tell you that you look absolutely edible tonight?"

I tossed my newly installed weave over my right shoulder.
"Thank you. You're looking pretty good yourself." At least I figured he did, since my glasses were in my purse.

He walked over to me and took my arm. "Let's party."

"Let's." I set the alarm, and we left.

When we got outside, I expected to see some form of trans-
portation.

"Where's your car?"

"In the shop. I took a cab, figured we'd take the Jag."

"Oh, you did, did you?" I huffed. "All right, come on. It's
parked across the street." I dug in my purse and handed him the
car keys. "You drive."

He grinned like I'd handed him money. "I wouldn't have it any
other way.

For the first ten minutes or so, we rode in silence, which was
fine by me. My mind was racing to the evening ahead, imagining
all the fun I would have and the contacts I would meet. I was de-

termined that it would not turn out like that horrible dream I'd had. I would be graceful, make witty comments, be well versed and in control. I'd meet all the people who could permanently change my life, and then I'd meet the Grand Diva herself. After that, I knew my future would be secure. The key would be to stay cool and focused and to remember that I belonged.

"Do you know any of these people at this shindig?" Willie asked, interrupting my daydream.

"No, but I will before the night is over."

"Then how are we going to get in? You said it was an exclusive party, invitation only."

"Don't worry about it," I said casually, tossing aside his concerns. "We're friends of Tiffany and Chantel, should anyone ask. That's all you need to know."

"If you say so." He was quiet for a minute. "So you said these folks are the cream of the crop, huh?'

"Yes. Why?"

"No reason. Just asking." He started humming.

I glanced at him but couldn't detect anything out of order in his expression. "No foolishness out of you, Willie," I warned.

"You wound me," he said, patting his heart. "I'm going as your escort, nothing more."

"Exactly. And don't you forget it."

I leaned over and turned on the radio. The Dells classic hit, "Oh, What a Night," was playing. I smiled. Let the games begin!

# Murphy's Law

The house—or rather, the estate—was nestled in a secluded area in Newstead, in South Orange, New Jersey. This was where stars such as Lauryn Hill and Wyclef Jean called home.

My heart began to race as we rode along the winding driveway to the front gate. A uniformed guard walked to the car, with a clipboard in his hand. "Good evening. Name, please."

I cleared my throat. This was the first hurdle. "Margaret Drew," I said, leaning toward Willie to talk out the window.

He scrolled down the first page, flipped to the next and the next. He peered into the car. "What's the name again?"

"Drew. Margaret Drew."

He frowned. "I don't see your name on the guest list, ma'am."

"But it has to be there." Panic rose in waves and bubbled in my stomach. I'd done everything right. I'd found the code, filled out the application, forged Tiffany's information about me. My name had to be there.

"Tiffany Lane is . . . my sponsor," I said.

His entire expression changed. "Oh, Ms. Lane." He searched the list again. "Here it is." He made a little checkmark and then looked Willie over. "And you are?"

"William Thornton. Ms. Drew's escort."

Thornton? It had been so long, I'd forgotten Willie's full name, and I'd never thought to ask.

The guard made a slight bow of his head. "Pull around to the side. Someone will meet you to park your vehicle."

"Thanks, chief," Willie said with a mock two-finger salute.

In the holding area for the cars, it was a veritable who's who of luxury, from Saabs to Lexus, Mercedes and Bentleys, to Escalades.

"I guess you were right," Willie said, pulling the Jag behind a Rolls. He opened the door, got out, and dropped the car keys in his pocket. Then he came around and opened my door.

"I thought the guard said someone would park the car."

The corner of his mouth quirked up in a grin. "A little piece of advice from one who knows . . . Never let a valet park your car. Not only do you have to tip them, you have to wait for them to find your ride. This way, I know where it is and I have the keys."

I shrugged. "If you say so." Not wanting to fall over something I couldn't see in the dark, I took his arm. "Come on, let's go."

Once inside, the splendor outdid itself from one room to the next. Through the haze of my somewhat foggy vision, I could make out the chandeliers that sparkled from the ceilings. There was enough food to feed a third-world country with every kind of delicacy imaginable. An entire wall was glass and overlooked a backyard that resembled Central Park, complete with an Olympic-size pool and tennis court.

Waitresses in tiny outfits balanced trays of hors d'oeuvres and tight-pants butlers refilled drinks without being told.

But it was the guests that took my breath away. Faces that I'd seen only on magazine covers, on television, or in the movies and videos were everywhere. Or at least they looked like familiar faces.

"Wow," Willie murmured as we moved through the main floor.

"Yeah," I replied in awe.

"I thought I traveled with high-maintenance company. I'll have to hang out with you more often." He turned to me, and his eyes lit up like candles. "This is going to be fun."

I was dying to put on my glasses and get a better look, but I didn't want to risk messing up the flow of my ensemble. I found that if I squinted, I could pretty much get everything into focus.

"Okay, let's mingle. But don't stray too far," I said.

"All you have to do is put your lips together and blow. You know how to whistle, don't you?" he quoted. "I see a few familiar faces, my dear. Let's say we meet back here in an hour."

I squinted at my watch. "Sounds good."

He winked and strode off.

Tugging in a deep breath, I went off in the opposite direction and walked up to two women who were engaged in what appeared to be a lively conversation.

". . . when this merger goes through, I know they'll make me VP," one woman said, and took a sip of her champagne.

"You deserve it, Patrice. Ten years is a long time. You've paid your dues."

"It feels like an eternity," Patrice replied. "And what about you, Cynthia, I heard you just made CEO at the foundation. Congratulations."

Cynthia beamed. "Finally broke through that damned glass ceiling. But did you hear about Connie—she got that part in the movie she auditioned for. Got it over Angela B. Can you believe it?"

They both laughed, and so did I. That's when they noticed me.

Patrice set her drink down on the tray of a passing butler. Her right brow arched, and she put on one of those smiles that you fix on your face when you don't really want to. "Do I know you?" she asked.

"Um, I do think we've met before," I said on the fly. "Maybe at the opera?"

"Perhaps." Patrice looked me over. "Is that a Vera Wang you're wearing?" she asked.

I smiled proudly. She'd noticed. "Yes, as a matter of fact it is. An original."

"That's interesting," Patrice said. "I was sure that Chantel Hollis purchased that original. It was the talk of the town this past spring."

"Uh, well, maybe you're mistaken."

She reared back as if I'd slapped her. "Mistaken! I don't make those kinds of mistakes."

"What did you say your name was?" Cynthia demanded.

"Margaret Drew."

"Never heard of you."

"Whom are you here with? Whom do you work for?" Patrice asked, suspicion lacing her inquisition.

I felt a line of perspiration trickle down my back. A hasty escape was in order. "Oh, my," I said, tiptoeing to peek over their shoulders. "There's Kimmie. I must go and say hello. Do excuse me."

I darted off, leaving them with their mouths open. I made a mental note to steer clear of them for the balance of the night.

Easing in and out of the fabulously frocked bodies, I walked up the spiral staircase, grabbing bites of proffered finger food along the way. I spotted Willie in deep conversation with a stunning woman out on the terrace. He didn't waste any time, I thought, and kept going.

I caught a glimpse of someone who looked like Whitney chatting it up with someone who looked like Mary J. What I wouldn't give to be a fly on the wall—or have twenty-twenty vision.

As I wandered about, smiling and nodding, I still had one thing on my mind: meeting the Grand Diva. She had to be around somewhere. And I needed to find her relatively soon. My feet were beginning to hurt. In the meantime, there were people who needed to meet me.

Casting caution to the wind, I insinuated myself into a group of women seated at a table near the terrace.

"Excuse me," I said sweetly, "is anyone sitting here?" I pointed to the vacant chair.

"No. Please sit and join us. If you're like me, I know you want to get off your feet."

The small group laughed as I sat down.

"Margaret Drew," I said, extending my hand to each of them.

"Your name doesn't sound familiar," the one with the red hair said, and looked at the other women for confirmation. "You must be new."

"Actually, I'm a friend of Tiffany Lane's. She invited me."

"Tiffany! Well, that's a different story. Where is she?"

"Uh, she wasn't feeling well and couldn't make it."

"What about Chantel?" another one asked.

Did they all really know each other? "Uh . . . Chantel . . . decided to stay and look after her. You know how thoughtful Chantel is." I forced a smile.

"That's odd," the redhead muttered. "I could have sworn I'd

seen Calvin and James earlier. I just assumed that Tiffany and Chantel were here, as well."

My stomach did a backflip, and I nearly choked on air.

The redhead patted me on the back. "Are you all right? You look positively frightened."

"Yes, fine." I reached for a glass of water on the table and took a long swallow. My attempt at a smile was weak at best. I stood. "Maybe I should go look for them. Say hello. Nice to meet you," I said in a rush and hurried off.

My heart was racing out of control as I peered around in a deep squint, hoping to spot Calvin or James before they saw me. No sign of them or Willie. At least I thought not.

I checked my watch. I still had a half hour before meeting Willie, and I was no closer to meeting the Grand Diva than I was when I arrived.

In the meantime, I needed to keep a low profile. I slipped into the ladies' room that was probably the size of my entire apartment. But no matter how big or small, the ladies' room was always ripe with information. If I was able to hang around long enough, I was bound to overhear something.

Standing in front of the row of mirrors, I made a slow show of removing the shine from my nose and forehead with my makeup sponge while the women filed in and out. And finally, eureka!

"Yes, she's here," a young girl who looked to be no more than twenty-five said to her friend. "She's up on the third floor, receiving all the new inductees."

"I'm so glad I don't have to go through that ordeal again," the other young woman said. "Once was enough for me."

"I know what you mean. When my sponsor took me in to meet her, I just knew I was going to faint."

They both giggled, headed for the stalls, and shut the doors behind them.

Quickly I dumped my makeup back in my bag and ran out the door, smack into Queen Patrice, whose drink splashed all over and down the front of both our dresses.

"Oh!" she screeched. "My dress! I . . . It's you again. Do you see what she did to my dress?" She was drawing the attention of everyone in the corridor.

I froze like a deer trapped in headlights. You would have thought someone had yelled "Fire!" the way folks came rushing over. In a matter of seconds, the hallway was overrun with squawking, gaggling women, all offering stain remedies, from plain tap water to voodoo.

In the midst of the chaos, I was able to slip away as the throng gathered around poor Patrice, giving their condolences as if she'd lost her fortune in the crash of '29.

I made a beeline down the hall, trying to hide the growing stain with my purse and stole. I walked as fast as my slowly swelling feet would allow. I could still hear the raucous echoing behind me. Any minute I expected a frenzied mob to come racing after me, demanding that I be tried for high crimes of fashion.

Finally I made it to the third floor and wound my way in and out of the maze of doorways and corridors and endless streams of people until I saw a line forming in front of an ornate red door.

Judging by the hum of excited voices, this was the place. I checked my watch. Five minutes to meet Willie. I peered toward the head of the line. There were at least ten potentials ahead of me.

I debated running to the meeting spot to find Willie and let him know I'd be a while, but I didn't want to risk running into Ms. Redhead, Patrice, or Cynthia.

The line moved by minuscule increments. The funny thing

was, I saw them go in but not come out. I suddenly had this hysterical image of the room being a huge roach motel.

Nearly thirty minutes later, I was finally at the door. This was my moment. All my preparation, agony, and subterfuge were about to finally pay off.

The red door opened, and a woman dressed in pink from head to toe stood in front of me. The room behind her was dimly lit, like a house in a horror movie. Candlelight flickered in the background, and shadows bounced off the walls.

"Is your sponsor with you?" the lady in pink asked.

"Uh . . ." I tried to look surprised that she wasn't. "She was right here a minute ago. Tiffany!" I called out.

"Tiffany Lane is your sponsor?"

I smiled, showing all my teeth. "Yes, she is."

Pinkie scoped out the line of waiting debutantes behind me and then said in a stage whisper, "This is highly irregular. But since Tiffany is your sponsor, I'll let you in without her."

*Tiffany must really have some clout,* I thought. Her name was like magic. "You're so kind," I murmured.

"Come in." She stepped aside to let me pass.

On the far side of the room, a woman stood with her back to me, staring out the window to the grounds below. She had on the same hat that I remembered from the videos.

I stepped farther inside and squinted really hard to get her in focus. The lighting didn't help. Then all of a sudden, I heard screams coming from downstairs.

The Grand Diva turned toward me just as someone grabbed my arm and pulled me out of the room. It was my escort.

"Willie! What the—?"

"It's time to go," he said in an urgent whisper.

"No!" I tried to snatch my arm away, but he held on tighter, practically dragging me down the hall. "What is going on? Why are people screaming?"

"I'll tell you all about it in the car. Now let's go."

"But wait—the Diva—"

"Come on."

We got to the next floor, and chaos abounded. Men were grabbing their women, and women were grabbing their necks.

Now I was afraid. Obviously something terrible had happened.

We made it all the way to the first floor when I swore I heard sirens off in the distance.

People were shouting and running around. Some stood in clusters, gesturing wildly, others mobbed the coatroom, while the rest headed out en masse. What happened to exiting in an orderly fashion?

"My necklace!" I heard someone wail.

"My bracelet!" said another.

A male voice in the distance was yelling about his wallet.

The sound of sirens drew closer, and that's when it hit me. "Willie, you didn't," I gasped.

He turned to me and grinned. "I couldn't resist."

"But you said you were a cat burglar. Not a pickpocket. Don't you have any ethics?" I hissed as we rushed down the hall.

Just as we neared the exit, I heard my name being called. Oh, Lawd—it was Calvin.

"Step on it!" I shouted to Willie.

And just when you think things can't get any worse, they do. Standing right at our point of escape was James in a heated conversation with another man.

I ducked my head and squeezed between Willie and another departing guest. By some miracle, we made it outside, and now I fully understood why Willie didn't want the valet to park the car.

He disengaged the alarm, hopped in, and would have taken off without me had I not jumped in right behind him. We drove casually by the police car and then took off on the highway back to New York.

When I got my wits about me, I realized the magnitude of what he'd done. "How could you? You ruined everything. I was a hot minute away from meeting the Diva herself." I swatted his arm as hard as I could without breaking my nails.

"I'm sorry, okay. I . . . couldn't help it. It was like being in a candy store without the glass case," he said, as if that were some kind of excuse.

"After all the trouble I've been through to get here," I moaned as a tear of utter frustration rolled down my cheek. "How could I have been so stupid as to bring you? I was a fool to be taken in by appearances."

"I'll make it up to you, I swear."

"You can't! Just shut up and drive, Willie, and pray that I don't decide to turn you in."

"Turn me in! Ha. You brought me there, remember. You'd be an accomplice. And who's perpetrating more of a fraud than you?"

I gritted my teeth to keep from beaning him.

We drove the rest of the way in furious silence.

*So close,* I thought. *So close.* My life was on the threshold of change, and it was snatched away from me by a sticky-fingered thief. How ironic was that? *Grrr.* How could I have been so stupid as to put my future in the hands of a thief?

I closed my eyes, and the preceding weeks played behind my lids. I had been on a roller-coaster ride of mishaps and mayhem, but I'd survived. Until now. There had to be some other way of achieving my ends. But how? Maybe the answers were in the tapes or the training manual or the handbook, something that I missed. If a solution was out there, I was going to find it. No matter what.

Well, I must have worked myself into a stupor, because the next thing I knew, Willie was shaking me awake. "We're here," he said.

I rubbed my eyes and sat up. We were back at Tiffany's place.

"Look, if it helps any, I'll take you back there."

"No thanks. I don't need any more help from you." I clutched my purse. "Just park the car and get out."

"Fine. Have it your way."

"If I had it my way, I'd be pushing you off the Manhattan Bridge right about now."

He shook his head in defeat and eased the car into an available space across the street from the town house. I made a move to get out, but then Willie grabbed me by the wrist.

"Wait," he said in an urgent whisper. "Isn't that Tiffany getting out of that cab?"

A hot flash exploded in my head. I whipped my glasses out of my purse and put them on. And as sure as the sun rises in the morning, that was Tiffany Lane walking up the steps to her apartment door with the driver unloading her suitcases.

"Oh, *dayum*." My pulse was pounding in concert with my feet, which were swelling at a steady pace. I couldn't breathe. I couldn't think. Then I looked down at that stain that decorated the front of Chantel's five-thousand-dollar gown and at Tiffany's diamond bracelet on my wrist, and I sprang into action. "Willie, we gotta get outta here. Now!"

He put the car in gear. "Where to?"

"My place."

# Stick a Pin in Me—
# I'm Done

Me and Willie were making a run for it. We were halfway to my apartment when it hit me. It was only a matter of time before Tiffany and Chantel blew a fuse. I could almost see Tiffany now as she walked through the wreck of her place, discovered that her secret closet had been torn to shambles, and noticed the missing diamonds and the missing handbook. Not to mention Chantel, whose gown had been the talk of Manhattan and now was a ruined mess. And then there were all those missing girdles. A wave of nauseating heat suffused me. My apartment would be the first place they'd look. What I needed was a place where I could lie low and get a chance to put my story together before they came after me.

"Forget my place," I said to my wheel man. "I'm going to Brooklyn."

"Brooklyn? Why?"

"Just drive."

When we pulled up in front of my mother's house, I was surprised to see the lights still on in every window of the house. Curious. My mother was always in bed by ten, and Grandma never stayed up past nine o'clock even on weekends. Said she needed her beauty rest.

"Just pull up over there," I said, pointing out a parking spot across the street from the house.

Willie eased into the spot and cut the lights and the engine. I watched the house for moment and noticed that same black Mercedes parked out front.

"Are we on a stakeout or what?" he asked, and sounded serious.

"No."

"So now what?"

"I'm going inside."

"You need some backup?" He reached in his breast pocket like he was going for a weapon.

"Whatever you're getting ready to take out, I don't want to know about it," I said, and squeezed my eyes shut. If I didn't see it, the prosecutor couldn't convince a jury that I knew anything about it.

"Relax, it's just a cell phone." He pulled it out and showed it to me. "In case you want to call someone. Why are you so jumpy?"

That was it, the last straw. I reached over and grabbed him by the throat. His eyes bulged. His mouth opened, but he couldn't speak.

"Why am I so jumpy? I'll tell you why I'm so jumpy!" I shook him back and forth like a rag doll. "I'm jumpy because my entire world is beginning to unravel, Willie! I was at the threshold of a new beginning, and the rug was pulled out from under me. I put my future in the hands of a burglar, and any minute, two women whom I've known since childhood are going to discover what I've done simply because they came back too early, and they are probably going to try to murder me. I'm on the run. I have nowhere to go but my mother's house, a woman who is suspect at best, and to an eccentric grandmother who believes that she was once Cleopatra."

Willie started gasping, and even in the dimness of the street-lights, he looked like he was turning blue. Another wave of panic set in, and I let him go, knowing that if he passed out, I was not performing mouth to mouth. That prospect was enough to sober me. I cleared my throat and straightened my clothes.

Willie coughed a few more times before he spoke. "You didn't have to do that." He coughed again. "You could have killed me."

I cut him a look. "If only," I muttered. "Look, I think you better leave. Forget you ever knew me, and I'll do the same."

He took a handkerchief from his pocket and wiped his face. "Fine." He coughed again and adjusted his jacket. "I'm really sorry it had to end like this." He reached for the door handle then stopped and turned back to me. "All things considered, it was good running into you again."

I couldn't believe he'd said that.

He opened the door and got out, then leaned down to the window. "Take care of yourself, Margaret. I hope everything works out for you. And, uh if you ever need me, give me a call."

I rolled my eyes. "Good-bye, Willie."

I sat in the car for a few minutes and watched him saunter down the street as if nothing had happened. I shook my head, took my purse and fox stole, and got out. After setting the alarm, I walked across the street and rang the bell.

It took a few minutes before my mother answered the door.

"Margaret, what on earth are you doing here?" She looked positively traumatized and stood in the doorway as if she had no intention of letting me in. "Why are you dressed like that?" she asked, still blocking the door.

"It's a long story."

"Well, maybe you can tell me about it another time."

"What?" Was my own mother telling me to get lost?

"I'm . . . uh, busy at the moment. Why don't you come back tomorrow?"

"Tomorrow?" I whined, sounding like Dorothy from *The Wizard of Oz* when she was told that the wizard said to "come back tomorrow." Maybe if I broke out in tears as Dorothy had, my mother would cut me some slack. And breaking out in tears at that point would not have been a stretch.

My mom looked over her shoulder and then sighed in resignation. She reached for my hand and squeezed it like doctor ready to deliver bad news. She led me inside. "There's someone I want you to meet. Well, not actually meet, since you two already know each other."

My thoughts were too jumbled and my nerves too frayed to make sense of whatever she was talking about. After the horrific events of the evening and the girls getting back early, there was no way I had the mental agility or the inclination to figure her out.

Numbly I followed her inside into the living room, and I nearly passed out when I saw whom she wanted me to meet.

Obviously it must have been some sort of parlor trick or something weird and freaky that magicians do with smoke and mirrors. There was no way that the man standing in front of me was Mr. Fields.

"I guess I should have told you, sweetheart," my mother was saying. But it sounded as if her voice were coming from very far away or from underwater. She slid her arm around his waist.

The image was too much for me to handle in my weakened condition.

Everything began to blur, and the next thing I knew, I was stretched out on the couch and my mother was putting cold compresses on my forehead.

The room slowly came into focus. My mother was hovering over me with Mr. Fields in the background.

"Wh-what happened? Where am I? Is this hell?" I asked, and attempted to sit up.

"Sssh. Just relax, sweetheart," my mother said, being very motherly. "You fainted."

I blinked and looked around. "Mom . . . you and . . . uggh." My head started spinning again.

"We've been seeing each other for quite a while."

"But . . . quite a while. How—?"

He turned loving eyes on my mother. "I met her at the post office. She looked so wonderful in her uniform, and when she asked me if I needed a confirmation for a package, I just knew she was the one." He focused his attention back to me. "I didn't think it would be good company policy if anyone ever found out that I was dating my employee's mother. We tried to keep it just between us." He leaned over and kissed my mother's cheek.

"But . . . but you're supposed to be in the hospital with a heart attack."

He shrugged. "Very mild. I was out in a week."

I turned to my mother. "So that's where you were running off to in the Mercedes—to see Mr. Fields?"

She nodded. "He's so thoughtful to send a car for me."

I pushed myself to a sitting position. "So you two are—?" I couldn't get the words out.

"Yes," they said in unison.

I stood and began to pace. I couldn't seem to get my mouth to work right, so I had to speak from between clenched teeth. "Let me get this straight. My mother, you—" I pointed an accusing finger in her direction. "—is having an affair with you—" I stuck another finger at Mr. Fields. "—my boss." I swung back and forth between the two culprits. "And the both of you have kept this—this—this—thing a secret." My head began to pound. I pressed my palms to my temples.

"If you're worried about your job and your promotion, please don't be." Mr. Fields said. He leaned closer to my mother and kissed the top of her head. "I have no intention of coming back. You worked hard. You deserve the spot. Besides, your mother and I want to build a life together."

My mother beamed and actually looked happy. *Mr. Fields—my stepfather?* My stomach balled up in a knot, and the room began to sway again.

I inhaled deeply, hoping the added oxygen would clear my head. Looking at their smiling faces, I secretly prayed that it was all a terrible dream. But when I blinked, I realized that it wasn't. Truly these were the last days, as Grandma always said.

Grandma. She would listen to my woes, and maybe by some miracle she could help me make sense of them with one of her stories. Probably not, but there was always hope.

"Where's Grandma?" I asked, feeling beaten and weary.

"She's up in her room."

I walked past them toward the stairs, stopped, and turned around. "Congratulations, Mom . . . Mr. Fields."

"Thank you, dear," they chorused.

Climbing the stairs felt like scaling Mount Everest. I made myself believe that at the end of my journey, the answers to life's most mysterious question would be revealed: Why had the heavens forsaken me?

I tapped on Grandma's door and was surprised to hear her sound so wide awake.

"Come in," she sang out.

When I stepped inside and closed the door, the first thing that caught my attention was Grandma's face. It was fully made up as if she were ready for her close-up. Her gray hair, which she pretty much kept hidden beneath a scarf on an everyday basis, was now a lustrous black, and it framed her face in waves like those pictures of starlets of the 1940s. She had on a full-length black slip that outlined a pretty nice figure. If I didn't know better, I'd think she had a body shaper on under it.

"Grandma?" I widened my eyes, the better to see her with.

"That's a lovely dress," she said, and walked to the mirror, keeping her back to me.

I sat on the side of the bed. "Grandma, my whole life has come tumbling down."

"Tell Grandma all about it," she cooed, and patted my back.

Through tears and tirades, I told my story—from the pilfering of the clothing to finding the handbook to dating Calvin and James, right up to almost meeting the Grand Diva and then hiding out from Tiffany and Chantel.

By the time I'd finished, I was sobbing uncontrollably. "All I've ever wanted was to be noticed, to be important, to have people respect me, to wear great clothes, have men run after me, and have the kind of life that I've been dreaming of since I was an infant. Tiffany and Chantel had it all. They had everything. And I was always on the sidelines. Then I had my chance. And I took it. And now—" I covered my face and cried some more.

"The grass usually needs mowing on the other side," Grandma

said. "You think you want what someone else has until you actually have it. Then you realize it's not all that you thought it was."

I looked up at her from between my fingers. That was probably the most coherent thing I'd ever heard her say. She sashayed across the room with a dip to her hip that made my mouth drop open.

"To get anywhere in life, granddaughter, you need to work to get there. All that energy, ingenuity, and effort you used to make this night happen were all unnecessary. You had what it took to get what you wanted all along. You were just too blinded by the glitter of Tiffany and Chantel to see it." She turned to me and smiled. "It's all in the genes."

That's when she stopped making sense.

"I was rooting for you, even though you went about it the wrong way. You think I'm just a crazy old coot, but I'm crazy like a fox." She winked and then chuckled. "I wouldn't be where I am today if I wasn't."

My heart started to beat a little faster. "Grandma, what are you saying?"

She walked over to her closet and opened it, reached up on the top shelf and pulled something out. Then she turned to me.

"Look familiar?"

In her hand was the hat that I'd seen in the videos, the hat that I'd seen earlier that night. The hat that the Grand Diva wore! She put it on her head and posed.

"A *true* Diva gets what she wants by working for it. Using what she has to get to the top of her game, whatever that may be."

"Grandma!"

"They're going to come looking for you, and rightly so. And you're going to have to deal with them and everything you've done. Maybe it will work out and maybe it won't. That part is up to you. You already have all you need. Like I said, it's in your genes. Now, dear, if you will excuse me, I need to get my beauty rest. It's way past my bedtime. And yours, too." She ushered me to the door and opened it, practically pushing me across the threshold. "Good night, dear. Are you coming for dinner tomorrow?"

I couldn't speak. I couldn't think. It was all some bizarre aftereffect from the trauma of my evening. That was the only explanation.

I turned to say something, and she shut the door in my face. Dazed, I somehow made my way downstairs. It was all too much to process. Obviously, this was yet another of Grandma's delusions. I passed the living room on my way out and heard the giggling and cooing of my mother and Mr. Fields.

Yes, I had somehow been transported into *The Twilight Zone.*

I stumbled out into the night and made it to the car. By pure instinct, I found my way home and awaited my fate, which I knew wouldn't be pretty.

# And the Fat Lady
# Belted Out a
# Good One

So here I am in my borrowed and ruined Vera Wang gown, huddled in my apartment in the dark, tripping over furniture, trying to make sense of everything that had happened and to figure a way out of the mess I'd gotten myself into. Adding to my confusion and turmoil was the discovery of my mother and Mr. Fields and the impossibility of my grandmother actually believing that she was the Grand Diva. That notion was simply too far-fetched.

The whole evening had had a stamp of disaster on it from the very beginning. But I could have pulled it off if it hadn't been for that insane Willie and his sticky fingers. I had a good mind to call the cops or at least the *Daily News*. But then again, I was the last one who should point fingers.

To be truthful, I felt like the spy who'd been kicked out into the cold. My cover was blown, and all the operatives were on my trail, determined to hunt me down. But if I was captured, I would reveal only my name and shoe size. They wouldn't break me.

Chewing on my manicure, I contemplated my alternatives. I had about forty dollars in my bank account, certainly not enough for a plane ticket out of town. For forty bucks, even Greyhound wouldn't get me much farther than Philly.

But I still had the Jag and a tank full of gas. I could always return the car after I was settled on the other side of the planet. Then it dawned on me. Why was I running, hiding like an escaped con? What had I done that was so terribly wrong? Borrowed some clothes, a few wigs and jewelry, run up a few credit bills, hacked into someone's computer? All that could be explained. Couldn't it?

I felt ill. And then the doorbell rang.

My first thought was to pretend I wasn't home. After all, the lights were out. No one could prove I was there . . . other than the fact that Tiffany's Jag was parked in front of my apartment. But that was a minor detail. There were plenty of midnight blue Jaguars in the Big Apple. Well, not necessarily in my particular neighborhood, but they were around.

All I had to do was play it cool and wait it out. Eventually they would get the hint and beat it. It was probably the neighbor's bell, anyway.

But what were the chances of it being the wrong door, too? I thought when the visitor started pounding.

"Margaret! Open the damned door." It was Tiffany. *Bam, bam, bam!* "I know you're in there."

"Come out, Margaret. You have some explaining to do," Chantel yelled with a sharp edge to her voice I'd never heard before.

"Margaret!"

Outside, Virginia barked.

Fortifying myself, I switched on the lights and crossed the short space to open the door.

Pure, unadulterated fury flashed in Tiffany's eyes as she held up her mangled blue shoe. Then her eyes widened like saucers. "My earrings! My bracelet!" She suddenly turned pale.

Chantel screamed once. "My dress!"

"I—I can explain everything," I said as calmly as my racing heart and throbbing head would allow. I heard several doors open on my floor. The last thing I needed was a scene in my hallway. "Come in if you want to talk."

Tiffany pushed me out of the way, and Virginia stepped on my foot on her way in, followed by Chantel who gave me a death stare. I eyed the open door and thought of making a run for it—when Calvin and James appeared in the doorway. The room spun. I held on to the doorframe, and the only thing that kept me from going down in a heap was the high pitch of Tiffany's tirade.

"Talk! What I need to do is snatch that weave off your head."

*Ouch.* I closed the door and slowly turned to face my accusers. Each face looked more menacing than the next. I took two baby steps into the room, and they let me have it.

"You lied."

"You cheated."

"You stole."

"You two-timed."

"You drove the Jag!"

And then they started talking and yelling at once, firing at me, belittling me, telling me what a terrible, insignificant person I was, that I needed to feel like somebody by being them. That I would never amount to anything, that I didn't deserve anything. I was a liar and a fraud.

The words and accusations came flying so fast and furious, I couldn't digest them all. I started to feel smaller and smaller, started to believe that what they were saying was true. I was a nobody.

But then like an apparition, I saw Grandma in all her finery standing in the center of the room, and her words, crazy as they may have sounded, came back to me. *I always had what it took, but I was too dazzled by Tiffany and Chantel to see it.* And you know something? For the first time in my life, I realized how true that was.

"Hold it! Hold it just one doggone minute," I yelled, and everyone stopped shouting in midsentence. I braced my hands on my hips. I had nothing to lose at this point except the rest of my dignity.

"You two left me in charge, didn't you? You didn't think enough of me to ask me to even go along. Did you? Noooo, not boring, old plain-Jane Margaret Drew. I wouldn't have fit in with your fancy friends. But I was good enough to house-sit your apartments, look after your dog, pick up your mail, water your plants, and deal with your insane cleaning woman. And even put up with Wayne."

I turned on Calvin and James. "You two never even realized I existed until I put on their clothes. You never thought I could hold a conversation or was interested in music or art or the opera or understood world affairs. None of you did."

At least they all had the decency to hang their heads, including Virginia.

"But I did it. And you know why? Because I was tired of being invisible, and I had this stupid notion that your lives were so much better than mine. And for so long, I thought that I was exactly what you all thought I was—invisible and insignificant. But

I'm not. I found that out the hard way. And I realized that if I want the finer things in life, then I have to get them on my own and not get taken in by appearances. I admit, I've done some unscrupulous things these past few weeks, and I may have made a mess of it all, but you know what? It was worth it. It was worth it because I finally discovered that who I have been searching for all these years was inside me all along. And I realized that I will never allow myself to be used or mistreated ever again. I have each of you to thank for that. My friends."

"Margaret—," they all said at once.

"Don't." I held up my hand. "I will pay for any damage. And I apologize for making a mess of your places. But I won't apologize for being Margaret Drew ever again."

I walked across the room, took Tiffany's car keys from my purse, and handed them to her; then I walked to the door and opened it. "Good night everyone. I must get my beauty rest." I tossed my very expensive weave over my shoulder and watched them as they filed out.

I'm not sure how long I stood there after they were gone, but finally I looked around at my tiny apartment on the wrong side of town, my wall of books, and my favorite chair. I thought about the forty dollars in my account and the discount wardrobe in my closet. But then I thought about all I'd done, how I'd managed to almost pull it all off. And for the first time in longer than I could remember, I realized that my life really wasn't so bad at all. For the first time in hours, I smiled. I really smiled.

# To Make a
# Long Story Short

*T*hose six weeks—bizarre, disorienting, and crazy—actually changed my life. I learned a lot about myself. And I made some serious decisions, too.

Even though Mr. Fields said that the job was mine, I decided to quit. It was time for me to move on. I heard that Beverly finally got the promotion, and I was actually happy for her. Rumor has it that Beverly and Larry are an ongoing item and that wedding bells may be in their future.

My mother and Mr. Fields are still dating, and I guess I can get used to it. Mom has never been happier, and who doesn't deserve some happiness in their lives.

As for Tiffany and Chantel . . . Well, they are still Tiffany and Chantel. I worked nights as a waitress to pay off the damage that I'd caused, and you know what, when it was time for me to pay up, they both said to forget it, that they owed me much more than whatever I could pay them. Hey, go figure. Maybe they aren't so bad after all.

I ran into Wayne a few weeks back, and he said he'd love to get together for dinner sometime. Hmmm. Maybe.

And Willie—well, he turned up on the front page of the *Daily News* the other day, with APPREHENDED stamped across his face. I wonder how much time he will get.

As for me, well I finally wrote that book I'd been planning to write since I was a teenager, got a great contract and can live off of my advance for a few years without any major worries. I still shop in discount stores for my clothes but I've decided to skip Pay Less for my shoes.

And Grandma, to this day I still don't know if half the things she told me over the years was true, and it really doesn't matter. What does matter is that she passed along her crazy wisdom and it was the turning point in my life. Oh, by the way, her real name is Tess—at least that's what she finally told. That doesn't really matter either. To me she will always be Grandma.

Well, I've held you long enough. I have so much to do. There's a big party tonight, all the who's who will be there and Grandma is waiting for me. She says all the new recruits are dying to meet me. I have plenty to tell them.

Now, if I could just get this hat to sit right on my head!

# The Divas, Inc. Quiz

## *"Are You Divalicious?"*

**When you walk into a room do the people there:**

  a. whisper about your fabulous outfit

  b. run over to meet you

  c. turn to look at you

  d. ignore you

**If you and your best friend were up for the same job and the boss invited you to lunch to discuss the possible promotion, would you:**

  a. talk about your goals at the job

  b. highlight your best friend's qualifications

  c. talk about how wonderful the boss is

  d. not discuss work at all

**If there was a sale at your favorite boutique and the dress you were dying for had been sold, would you:**

  a. buy something similar even if it cost more

  b. look for the dress in another store

  c. set your sights on something else

  d. wait for the next sale because you couldn't really afford the regular price

**If there was a man you knew who was perfect for you but you had not been introduced to him, would you:**

  a. arrange for a coincidental meeting

  b. let a mutual friend make the introductions

  c. invite him to lunch

  d. find out his pet passion and fulfill it

**If you were at a dinner party with a group of people outside of your usual circle, would you:**

  a. introduce yourself to a friendly face

  b. join in on an ongoing conversation

  c. sit at the bar and wait for someone to speak to you

  d. go home

If your best friend left you in charge of her apartment while she went on a trip, would you:
- a. behave accordingly
- b. check her medicine cabinet
- c. wear her clothes
- d. see if you could find out any dirt about her

If you had to make a major presentation at work and you really needed help to get it done, would you:
- a. do the work without help
- b. give credit to those who helped you
- c. take all the credit yourself
- d. throw in the towel

If you went to your high school reunion and you wanted to make a good impression, would you:
- a. lease a Lexus
- b. hire a handsome escort
- c. rent a designer gown
- d. go as yourself

If you were on a first date would you:
- a. order whatever you wanted
- b. offer to split the bill
- c. wait for him to order
- d. get a salad

If you had a choice of exotic places to go, all expenses paid, would you:
- a. take the trip
- b. offer the ticket to a friend who has never had a vacation
- c. cash in the ticket and spend the money
- d. pay the cost of taking a friend with you

## Your Score:

A. 10
B. 8
C. 5
D. 2

**Add up your score.**

100-85:  A True Diva
75-84:  A Diva in Training
65-74:  You Have Potential
50-64:  In Need of Work